KAVEENA

Global African Voices

DOMINIC THOMAS, EDITOR

KAVEENA

BOUBACAR BORIS DIOP

Translated by
Bhakti Shringarpure & Sara C. Hanaburgh

Foreword by Ayo A. Coly

Indiana University Press
BLOOMINGTON & INDIANAPOLIS

This book is a publication of

Indiana University Press
Office of Scholarly Publishing
Herman B Wells Library 350
1320 East 10th Street
Bloomington, Indiana 47405 USA

iupress.indiana.edu

Original publication in French
© 2006 Editions Philippe Rey
English translation

© 2016 by Indiana University Press
All rights reserved

The paper used in this publication meets the minimum requirements of the American National Standard for Information Sciences—Permanence of Paper for Printed Library Materials, ANSI Z39.48–1992.

Manufactured in the United States of America

Library of Congress Cataloging-in-Publication Data

Names: Diop, Boubacar Boris, 1946– | Shringarpure, Bhakti, translator. | Hanaburgh, Sara, translator.
Title: Kaveena / Boubacar Boris Diop ; translated by Bhakti Shringarpure
    and Sara C. Hanaburgh ; foreword by Ayo A. Coly.
Description: Bloomington : Indiana University Press, 2016. | Series: Global African voices
Identifiers: LCCN 2015033962| ISBN 9780253020437 (cloth : alk. paper) | ISBN
    9780253020482 (pbk. : alk. paper) | ISBN 9780253020567 (ebook)
Subjects: LCSH: Africa, West—Fiction.
Classification: LCC PQ3989.2.D553 K3813 2016 | DDC 843/.914—dc23
LC record available at http://lccn.loc.gov/2015033962

1 2 3 4 5   21 20 19 18 17 16

To Koulsy Lamko, the Obstinate Hopeful
For Adja Bâ and Bintou Ndiaye

CONTENTS

FOREWORD

*T*he Cameroonian writer Mongo Beti (1932–2001), one of the foremost African writers of the twentieth century and a virulent, often caustically opinionated, critic of African literatures, wrote the preface to Boubacar Boris Diop's first novel. Beti lauded *Le temps de Tamango* (1981) for its audacious aesthetic experimentations and political savvy about postindependence governance in Africa. The acclaimed novel set the tone for Diop's rich plays, short stories, and dynamic corpus; he is a prolific author whose output includes novels, screenplays, and collections of essays on writing and the role of literature, neoliberalism and globalization. His sought-out opinion pieces on current events have secured his standing as a noted public intellectual and one of the most incisive commentators on African affairs and global geopolitics. In his works of both fiction and nonfiction, Diop exerts a dexterous intellectual vigilance that has roots in a sociocultural and political background that spans colonial and postindependence Senegal.

Boubacar Boris Diop was born in 1946 in Dakar, the capital of Senegal, a country that gained its independence from France fourteen years after Diop's birth. Diop first taught literature and philosophy, and later contributed in significant ways to the development of an independent press in Senegal through his activities as a journalist. He launched his literary career with *Le temps de Tamango* and went on to publish several award-winning novels, including the highly acclaimed *Murambi: Le livre des ossements* (2000; *Murambi, The Book of Bones*, IUP 2006), about the 1994 Rwandan genocide, and *Doomi Golo* (2003), a novel written in his native Wolof as a political act. Diop's writing is unflinchingly political in its relentless critique of African totalitarian regimes, its meticulous unraveling of official history, and its minute attention to the politics of cultural and collective memory. His novels may intimidate the more pedestrian reader because of their intricate narrative composition characterized by an incessant deferment of meaning and a stubborn inconclusiveness and refusal of narrative closure. Indeed, Diop tasks readers with seeking out meaning for themselves. Compelling them to assume responsibility in this way, never letting them off the hook, and holding them accountable for their elucidation of the problematic posed by the novel are functions of Diop's appropriation of the oral tradition of storytelling. In that tradition, the storyteller and audience collaborate in the process of producing meaning.

It is therefore fitting that Diop selected the genre of the detective novel as the narrative framework for *Kaveena* (2006), a political fable which lays the postcolonial situation in the form of an intricate and aberrant puzzle for the reader to figure out. The novel clearly exposes the travesty of political independence and denounces postcolonial African dictatorial regimes. The candid admission, in the very first sentence of the novel, that the narrator has missed out on crucial information, appropriates the oral storytelling technique of seeking complicity with the audience. In fact, the narrator is relying on letters left behind by a deceased African president. And, simultaneously with the reader, the narrator is trying to make sense of the letters. The narrator often engages in suppositions and speculations as he combs his way through the archival maze of documents. Diop's choice to incorporate at full length and reproduce in italics some of the letters for the eyes of his readers is clearly an invitation to the latter to formulate their own independent interpretations and possibly reach different conclusions than the more tentative narrator. The choice of the non-omniscient narrator thus mobilizes competent readers of the novel and entrusts them to fill in the narrative gaps and sort out the complex lay of the postcolonial situation. Furthermore, the implication of the narrator in the political matters he is recounting renders him unreliable. Diop deliberately leaves readers on their own, inciting them to seek a self-transformative reading of the novel. This plotted reading experience clearly underpins a pedagogy of critical thinking conducive to the creation of an aware reader-citizen of the postcolonial nation.

Kaveena is set in an unnamed African nation. By all indications, this nation is a former French colony. That it could be any former French colony in Africa speaks to the particular form of French neocolonialism known as *Françafrique*, which has been a constant target of Diop's novels, essays, and journalistic writings. *Françafrique* is an economic and political structure that France engineered in 1960, in the immediate aftermath of the independence of France's former African colonies. This setup was the brainchild of Jacques Foccart, an established businessman and influential advisor to French presidents Charles de Gaulle, George Pompidou, and Jacques Chirac. Foccart, whose identity is barely disguised in *Kaveena*, was the architect of gangster-style French policies in Africa between 1960 and 1995 that resulted in the overthrow of recalcitrant presidents and the rescue of embattled presidents, as well as numerous rigged elections aimed at installing friendly dictators. This hands-on approach allowed France to continue funneling resources out of its former colonies.

Discussions of France's neocolonial interventionism in Africa are still very much alive today under the presidency of François Hollande. In 2013, France launched military interventions in Mali to liberate the country from Al Qaeda–linked Islamists. France also intervened in the Central African Republic to stop sectarian conflict. Two years earlier, in 2011, France helped oust Ivory Coast's Laurent Gbagbo when he refused to surrender the presidency to his democratically elected rival. France still maintains important military bases in Senegal, Gabon, and Djibouti, and in January 2014 announced plans to increase its military presence in order to more effectively fight terrorism. Perhaps the most damning evidence of neocolonial practices exposed by *Kaveena* concerns the fact that former French colonies in Africa have yet to achieve monetary sovereignty. The Franc CFA currency used by Francophone African countries is no more than a derivative currency controlled by the French treasury. *Kaveena* is thus a timely and crucial novel exploring the unfolding neocolonial present in Africa in the broader context of globalization and shifting geopolitical alignments.

Ayo A. Coly, Dartmouth College

KAVEENA

I DON'T KNOW WHAT HIS LAST WORDS WERE.

He twitched his lips when he saw me come in. The movement was very brief, almost imperceptible. Maybe he was just asking me to shut the door or get him a drink. I'm sure it must have been something very banal. The man, whom I knew well, was not the type to come up with famous sayings that would resonate from generation to generation. He didn't care about that sort of thing. I also don't think he recognized me. He had most likely lost consciousness several weeks earlier. Later I learned that by then he didn't remember anything anymore. Not even the fact that he had been a powerful man, and that the mere mention of his name would make hearts stop with fear.

I wanted to close his eyes, but my natural reflex as a policeman held me back. A woven loincloth covered the lower section of his body, and a short *faso danfani* tunic in pale yellow with wide gray vertical stripes left his skinny, wrinkly flank exposed. His arms lay scattered on the bed. They looked useless, as if they'd been separated from his torso. A black metal square stuck out from under the pillow. It was an automatic pistol. A 7.65. I used a handkerchief to pick it up. As I'd suspected, it was loaded but hadn't been discharged.

I backed up a little to get a look at the entire corpse. The man was spread out lengthwise on the living room couch, his feet slightly parted and pointed toward the street. I say street, but it's really the end of a small path wedged between acacia and mango trees, so narrow it first looks like a cul-de-sac. It is a small, discreet bit of Jinkoré, a fairly calm neighborhood. During the civil war, which ended less than four months ago, the district had been fiercely disputed territory. The leaders of armed factions—there were so many—were convinced that seizing control of Jinkoré was enough to take over the capital, and thus the rest of the country. This is the reason why fighting here was particularly violent and so many atrocities occurred.

At first it might seem unfathomable that N'Zo Nikiema would decide to take refuge in this place. If his enemies knew, they would say he didn't have a choice. I suppose he didn't have the time to think it over when Pierre Castaneda's militias seized the presidency. But I doubt the rumors are true that he disguised himself as a Red Cross aid worker in order to slip through the destruction as mortar shells rained over the palace. That would mean that he had not prepared himself for the situation. Nothing could be more false: Nikiema never found himself taken by surprise. The truth is that many of our fellow citizens still hate him. So much so that they need to believe that Nikiema, overcome with panic at the last minute, lost his arrogance and hightailed it like a rabbit, yelling in terror and calling out to his mother for help. I was a witness, thanks to my role as chief of the secret police during the final hours of Nikiema's rule, and I can attest to the fact that that was not how things went down. Nikiema fooled us all by coming to stay in this small house in Jinkoré. At the same exact time we were securing the borders to impede him from joining his family in exile. He must have had a good laugh at that.

The door at the back opened into a second room. On the wall to the right, a *bogolan* curtain, blackened with a mix of dust and smoke, caught my eye. The wide, dark opening between the two curtain panels revealed a very poorly lit place. I went toward it, and standing in the doorway I turned my head in every direction. The darkness was almost total. After a few seconds, I could almost make out the outline of a table stretched out lengthwise in the middle of the room. I thought maybe an armed man was lurking in the shadows, ready to discharge his weapon into my chest. Actually I was not afraid. The idea came to me by force of habit: the war is not completely over in our minds.

I parted the *bogolan* and looked for the light switch. It made a click but the room remained dark. I remembered it would soon be ten days that the city had been without electricity. Luckily, I always have a flashlight with me. In its yellow light, I discovered a sort of storage room converted into a painting studio. Two of its walls were covered in paintings. One was still on an easel. On the long rough wooden table—or rather, the irregularly assembled planks—were several cans of colored paint, rolls of canvas, and a small toolbox.

This quick inspection was sufficient for me. I promised myself I'd go over the house and its surroundings with a fine-tooth comb the next day. The dining room and the eat-in kitchen would perhaps reveal the secret of President Nikiema's death. It wouldn't be easy since I planned on doing everything myself. Under normal circumstances, I'd have called my men and joked, "This little bird is food for the worms." Well, maybe I wouldn't have said exactly that, but something of the sort. That's our undercover cop humor. The work we do is very hard. Tracking people down and killing them—sometimes knowing they are innocent—is not an easy job. We need our jokes to convince ourselves that life is not such a serious thing and, in the end, to kill or be killed are one and the same. In any case, my guys would have turned up in Jinkoré without delay. Then our bosses would have joined the dance. For such a huge catch, Pierre Castaneda would have been the only one to have a say in the matter. I'm not supposed to concern myself with his emotional state, but I think he would be unhappy not to have gotten N'Zo Nikiema alive.

He'll be spared the upset since I want to play solo for a bit. Time to wait and see what happens. I fear Pierre Castaneda more and more. He has become very suspicious and might find it odd that I found the fugitive all by myself. It looks bad for me. And if one day Pierre Castaneda, looking straight into my eyes, says to me, "Between us, Colonel Kroma, do you think it's possible to just chance upon the

3

hiding place of a fleeing head of state? You know very well that's absurd," if one day he does ask me, I'll leave the factual evidence aside and say this: "No, Mr. Minister of State, it is not possible. It makes no sense."

I can just see him raising his hands toward the sky, apparently sorry. "So then tell me what happened, my dear Asante."

From that moment on, there will be only one way out for me: to admit to crimes I did not commit—a strategy to carry out a coup d'état, or whatever else—in order to have the right to die in peace. I mean to die without being tortured. These are the rules of the game and I know them well.

Across from the bed on which N'Zo Nikiema lies, there is a wicker chair. I sit down on it, my arms crossed at my chest, my head slightly tilted to the left. My legs knock together lightly in spite of me, from my knees to my ankles. Those who know me well would easily guess how tense I am. Of course, to see this man so dreaded not long ago reduced to a small mass of inert flesh makes me think about the vanity of human passions. I don't dwell on this, though. I am particularly concerned with what I am really going to be able to do with Nikiema's body. I have no idea. I decide to proceed secretly with the investigation, for whatever purpose it will serve. I still want to know more about N'Zo Nikiema's last months inside these four walls.

That is most definitely a story worth telling. For the living? I suppose, but perhaps especially for the future. Fate has burdened me with this task. I'll carry it out as best as I can. I am going to share this tale of young hooligans, *femmes fatales*, and those wounded by life with whoever wants to hear it. It's funny. For once, I am going to tell stories instead of keeping them to myself. It's a little intimidating for me too, I have to say.

As I leave, I make sure that no one could have seen me. Once outside, I realize something that had escaped me at first: The door to the living room can be made invisible by an ingenious system that transforms the doorknob into a simple decoration. I disappear into the high grass, and when I believe I'm far enough away, I look back.

The small house in Jinkoré is nothing more than a block of gray cement with metal spikes jutting out of its roof.

—⁓—

Through the window, I can see clouds gathering in the sky over the Bastos II district. A bird with a red beak that's too long for its tiny little body comes crashing into the window. It lets out a cry and then disappears. I turn to Ndumbe, whom I had called in a few minutes before. "Where have you been?"

Ndumbe stares at me. Before answering, he wants to know if I woke up on the right side of the bed. Of course, he's going to lie, but he doesn't want to tell the wrong lie. That's his forte. He has been getting to work later and later, almost always at the end of the morning. Soon he'll start missing entire days. He starts to explain, and I just motion him to be quiet. As he returns to his office, I reproach myself for letting my bad mood get the better of me. When it comes to the small everyday things, my state of mind can shift rather quickly. I am not so sensitive when I interrogate the detainees. That goes without saying. But in normal life, I hate to humiliate people. What I just did with Ndumbe is not good. I must say, too, that Inspector Ndumbe, the others, and I make a real team. In our line of work, we don't much like the bosses who play boss. We let them carry on and they have little to show for it.

I call him back in. "Come in, Ndumbe, sit down," I say.

My voice has clearly softened, though it does not seem to have the effect I'd intended. Ndumbe sits down on the chair facing me, sullen, his expression somber. "There's a new development," he says.

Ndumbe is what we call an elite element. I had put him on the Nikiema case from the beginning. "Listen, Ndumbe, I want to tell you one thing first: you are the best guy here, but you're starting to feed me bullshit."

"I'm tired, man."

I stare at him silently for a while, to make him believe I am just as shocked as I am enraged and infuriated that things could get ugly, and that even if I had superhuman abilities, I would not be able to control myself. Then, apparently overcome with rage, I throw this at him: "You mean you're poorly paid? You want to be decorated and get promoted, is that it? Is that it, Ndumbe?"

He just looks back at me. I sense he is a little confused. He stammers, "It's so tough in this country."

Ndumbe's problem is simple: he's recently fallen for a young lady from high society and he's got to provide for her. He spends lavish weekends on the coast and he needs more and more cash. But I'm supposed to ignore all that. So I spin it differently: "I know, my man, you're worried about your wife and kids. That's fine, Ndumbe. But you think *I'm* well paid? And all the other guys here? We don't believe in money here. We are in the service of the state. Imagine if we arrest former president Nikiema. This guy's going to shudder at the sight of you, and you're going to yell at him. Is that nothing to you? And that's not even the biggest thing. More than anything you're going to keep this country from engaging in another civil war. Do you think there is enough money in the state's coffers to pay for that?"

Glumly, he says, "OK, boss, I got it."

"Good. So, speaking of the N'Zo Nikiema case, what's new?"

"We've located him."

For a moment, things are muddled in my mind. Does Ndumbe know that I went to the small house that he himself had pointed out and that I have already seen Nikiema's corpse? Very naturally, I say, "Located? So, where?"

"In Ewum. A small village on the border."

I am so utterly relieved that I start making fun of him. "Are you kidding me, Ndumbe? The border? Which border?"

"He is among the refugees coming from Tendi," Ndumbe continues. "He was disguised as a nurse, but one of my men recognized him."

"Why didn't you say anything earlier?"

He replies dryly, in the tone of someone who is taking his revenge: "I come in and you reprimand me, boss. You didn't let me get a word in."

"OK. Tell me, man. I want all the details."

I suddenly sense him swelling with self-importance.

There's a reason behind it. Since Nikiema fled, the state—that's to say Pierre Castaneda—has no clue anymore where its head is.

Before going any further, I would like to give some advice to the reader: he will encounter from time to time in this narrative the name of the new president, Mwanke. He should pay no attention to it. We also know almost nothing about him. He was Pierre Castaneda's private secretary during the colonial period, and now for four months he hasn't stopped trying on the head of state's new clothes. He learns fast, though. His words are less bungled, his bovine gaze diminished, and as for the way he carries himself—for a true charismatic leader must display his arrogance—there too he has made noticeable progress. If we stick to the facts that I am reporting here, Mwanke is a secondary character with a grand-sounding title. The military gives him honors, delirious crowds cheer for him, and courtiers pander to him. In short, he is the president. I will therefore call him President Mwanke. That's the way it's got to be. Aside from that, he's a loser and he can go to hell or drop dead with his mouth gaping open. That wouldn't change anything in our history.

Coming back to Ndumbe's alleged discovery, it's important for one simple reason: the fugitive held this country for nearly thirty years. He is thus capable of blackmailing a lot of people. My guys and I have been known to take out judges and journalists. Nikiema risks taking the easy way out with those he trusts. That's how it is for any ordinary guy: the man has nothing more to lose and he could really sully many reputations if he publishes photos or documents. Names can be leaked to the press. But, believe it or not, there's no chance it's really going to get the new authority's attention. Everyone knows how we've managed to maintain certain agitators.

On the other hand, the images of little Kaveena's murder could cause some serious political damage. People are apt to be cynical and won't be able to handle watching the reel of this ritual killing. Kaveena, the little six-year-old girl. I saw the video back then. The man who holds the real power today, Secretary of State Pierre Castaneda, appears in every scene. In one shot, he has a bloodstain—little Kaveena's blood—on his lips and he wipes it off with his fingertips as he laughs like the devil. Don't ask me what made Castaneda behave like that that day. I have no idea. I'll merely venture a simple explanation that's only worth—well—what it's worth! I've met a lot of people like Pierre Castaneda throughout my life. The more these men want to be powerful, the more they secretly want to destroy themselves. It's an infernal coupling: the desire for power and self-destruction. When you're around guys like Castaneda or N'Zo Nikiema for a while, you manage to not even be able to hate them anymore. Even when they are cruel and ready to bury anyone alive who happens to pass through their midst, there is always a moment, a brief moment of truth when they pity you. You see very clearly that they are just like little lost children, sucked into the power vacuum just as others are fascinated by death.

I think of all this while Ndumbe is giving me his report. I listen to him distractedly. I notice certain tics he has—in particular a light twitching of the eyebrows—playing off my inexpressiveness. He has seen me work day and night on this investigation. And now that we've got the old man, he can sense how utterly unexcited I am.

As Ndumbe speaks, I see N'Zo Nikiema's corpse again in the small house in Jinkoré. Ndumbe's self-assurance stupefies me. How can it be that he doesn't have the slightest doubt? All of a sudden, a strange feeling comes over me. I ask myself, could it be that Ndumbe has been assigned to keep me under surveillance?

Anyway, I was wrong to demand all the details from him. He tries his best not to leave any out. Doing so nonetheless proves distressing to him, and he gets so muddled up that he has to stop himself twice and beg—agitatedly—for my permission to continue his narrative.

For no apparent reason, he insists on talking to me about his informant. "A very clever fellow," he insists. "I've never had one like that."

"Oh really?" I say, amused.

I notice Ndumbe's body suddenly stiffen; my ironic tone has given him a jolt. I didn't mean any harm, though. Could it be that he is feeling guilty about something?

I ask him nicely, "And where did you dig up your ultra-efficient informer?"

"On the street," he says, his face suddenly lighting up with a wide smile. "He's a huckster..."

"Oh?"

"Yes, one day, around midday, he was peddling bananas at the intersection between the Petit Lycée and the port, and he asked me if I wanted some. I didn't, so he leaned over my door and said to me, 'Mistah, these are bananas from France!' And then I burst out laughing. So did he. And there you have it; from that day on we were friends, and now..."

I think to myself, "Bananas from France.... What the fuck. What-the-fuck..." I'm having difficulty recognizing Ndumbe. What if he is going mad? The war had left us with our share of cripples and mentally ill. You see them wandering about completely naked through the streets of Maren, filthy and covered with fleas. But this one's the result of another devastating force, of greater consequence and nearly invisible to the naked eye. Ndumbe, although used to making himself comfortable in my office, now barely lets half of his ass rest on the chair. He stammers a little and avoids my gaze, he clenches his jaw every now and again, and I can see by the way he moves his shoulders that he is wringing his hands nervously.

All of a sudden, I get up, determined to risk all I've got. Nobody knows the workings of this house better than I. Standing near Ndumbe, hands in my pockets, I say to him, "Everything you're telling me is false, isn't it?"

Instead of responding, he throws his head back and stares up at the ceiling, immobile. His eyes seem lost deep inside of him and I can sense how miserable he is. But I need to know. "We don't have much time. You have to tell me the truth."

9

"No one knows where N'Zo Nikiema is."

"And this business about Ewum?"

"Not true, boss. You've got to leave."

I watch him silently for a moment, then say to him, "You were supposed to eliminate me. You didn't. You know the price! Get yourself out of here."

"Oh, I . . ." he says casually.

"You're afraid of losing that beautiful chick, huh? The love of your life. . . . Yeah, right! I know her well. She works it at our place, too, the slut. She's gonna waste you! And believe me, her finger won't even tremble when she pulls the trigger! What's wrong with you, Ndumbe?"

That really wakes him up. He shakes his head slowly, like someone who has just come to understand—at last—a whole slew of things.

"You saved my life, man," I remind him. "Here's a little dough. Split tonight, take your family. In the meantime, don't panic. We stay at the office and we work. It's just business as usual."

Ndumbe, almost affectionately, blurts out, "We're first-rate at that: business as usual."

"But some do waver on occasion. . . . Right?"

He smiles. I pat his left shoulder, and he does the same to my right shoulder. That means we won't see each other again.

A ceremony of brief and ambiguous goodbyes—as is required in our line of work.

—⁓—

In the middle of the night, I slip past the tall grass around the house. I hear some noises and assume they are snakes sneaking through the red and black rocks since all the land around Jinkoré is infested with them. I see some shadows under the faint light of the moon. Some stray dogs. They are used to rotting corpses because of the war. They must have been prowling for hours around this block of concrete. One of them growls at me with obvious hostility.

I look around me one last time before turning the key in the lock. There is not a soul within a mile or two of the house. The door creaks a little as I open it. And as soon as it's ajar, a fetid odor hits my nose. During the two days of my absence, N'Zo Nikiema's body has begun to decompose. I hesitate to go in. I am afraid it will make me sick. I feel my tongue stuck to my mouth and a little taste of quinine at my throat. The small house is quiet and plunged into total darkness. It would be dangerous to switch on my flashlight. I grope around in the darkness, trusting my vague memory of the previous time I was here. I know that N'Zo Nikiema's corpse is on the couch to the right. I try to avoid it and after about twenty steps find myself in the center of the room. I make it there somehow. I manage to hold my breath for a few seconds to find the door to the little studio, where the stench is slightly less virulent. I pull the door shut and stretch out on an old mat.

The solitude does not scare me. I feel that it's safer here than anywhere else in the city. In a way, it's like a new life awaits me.

On waking up the next morning, I am surprised to realize that I had a pretty peaceful sleep. I had brought a small radio and some food. It didn't take long to discover that N'Zo Nikiema had thought of everything. I want to press the button on the radio. For years, this has been the first thing I've done when I wake up. I don't listen to the radio to find out what's happened. I listen to it to find out how the happenings have been distorted. But this morning, I want to remain outside of the world and indulge my sense of solitude, the way you'd scratch an old itch. The idea that I'm just floating in empty space is pleasant. I am nobody and am aware of nothing. I'm lying here in the studio of an unknown artist. I only know that her name is Mumbi Awele. Maybe she will come here one of these days? That would surprise me. I am intrigued by her relationship with Nikiema. I may need to eliminate her. If I realize that she is a danger to me, I will have no choice.

Even though you breathe a little better in the studio, the smell of the paint is still mixed in with that of the cadaver. I refuse to look at my watch but it must be almost noon. In spite of this, the daylight hardly enters the room. I suppose I am a little afraid to get up and confront some hideous spectacle. I imagine pink repulsive maggots squirming all around N'Zo Nikiema. They must be all over his body. In his ears and along his eyelids. In his mouth. Everywhere.

I straighten up a little. Unable to get off my mat quickly, I sit still for a few minutes, my head on my knees and my arms around my legs.

—m—

Ultimately, I must say it is not as hard as I thought it would be. I mean, I thought life in this small place with a decaying body would be unbearable. And the first five days were not easy. Actually, they were awful. Within the house itself, I could not venture too far from the studio. I felt that I was trapped in the false bottom of a huge box. I thought of leaving on several occasions. But I had to find a way to make it to the border to take refuge with our neighbors to the south. It was doable. But I had to wait until things calmed down.

First I got some bad news: Ndumbe's sudden death. He was shot down by unknown aggressors while exiting a swanky nightclub. The police are calling it a crime of passion. Absolute lies. I can guess what happened. Ndumbe had gotten careless about this woman. I had warned him. May he rest in peace.

The news of my disappearance has increased tension in the country. Even Pierre Castaneda is flipping out. All day long the radio plays military music and songs of resistance against colonial intrusion. People are talking about an attack by mercenaries who had been driven back from I don't know which front. The opposition has just issued a call for unity around President Mwanke. This isn't surprising. Almost all his top men are eating out of Castaneda's hand. His Lil Boys—that's how Castaneda refers to his child soldiers, who were the reason he won the war—have been marching for two days to their base to shout out their bloody oaths. In short, they're mobilizing for battle. Probably a little too much excitement for one person. I could have felt flattered but there is nothing amusing about this. Fortunately, some young radio presenters come on and deflate the tension a little bit with their biting humor. And I am one of their favorite targets. They were asked to broadcast a description of me on the airwaves but they are using this opportunity to drive me up the wall. I didn't know I had protruding ears and a triangular face. "Small. Clear skin. Forget about his famous striped hat; he's probably thrown that in the trash. But if you see a kind of dwarf with shifty eyes and an incredible skull marked by long pink and black features, don't be stupid, guys. Don't get all like, 'Is it you sir, Colonel Asante Kroma, I wanna surrender you to the police to win the million at stake.' For God's sake, don't be stupid, just bring him down then and there without warning and get rich! Millionaire rich, I'm tellin' you!" They also say that there are photos of me and of N'Zo Nikiema posted at every street corner and in all public spaces.

This is the most vulgar piece of news. Pierre Castaneda has always taken good care of his image. I've known him a long time. Even his small everyday gestures show that he comes from another world, and in that world of conquerors, he deserves fear and respect. How can I explain this impression he gives of always putting on a show? To be at the same time himself and someone else, amongst us and elsewhere? A few years ago I saw a documentary about the small town of Clermont-Ferrand under German occupation. Well, they had these Nazi officers who showed exquisite courtesy, they gave up their places for women and elders in the trams, and unlike the French, who were under their boot, they were eager to present themselves as punctual to work, not too talkative, methodical and efficient. I think that Castaneda has, like the colonial administrators before him, the typical mentality of an occupier, conscious of showing a superiority of race and nation to the people he subjugates.

I must also say that this man, more than anyone else, really needs a moral alibi.

One can judge by the facts here.

At once the owner of a mining company—Cogemin—and a minister without portfolio, Pierre Castaneda covertly runs this supposedly independent country. It is really quite embarrassing. In the embassies of Western countries and abroad, they think that he's preventing an outbreak of blind and routine tribal cruelty in the land of the Negroes. But actually, he is the lesser of two evils. These people would be shocked to discover the true Pierre Castaneda, the one I've worked for over the years. . . . Or do they just pretend not to know?

Moreover, this image of a man with goodwill, firm but fair and rational, impresses the lower classes. I've often received reports of what is said about Castaneda in the poor neighborhoods of Maren and in the hinterlands: "Fine, he's a white guy, a foreigner, but with him at least there's no corruption. The Whites don't know about that and everybody follows the rules, they only know their work, no one dares to arrive at whatever hour they please with stories of my wife's given birth, my grandfather died last night and I gotta go to the village chief. No, it's not like that at all. I believe that with this white guy we can really achieve sustainable development that will last. We just have to wait a little, that's all."

The civil war definitely ruined our friend Pierre's image. Let's just say his Lil Boys were not exactly angelic. But hey, it was war. And now my disappearance is making him crazy. Silent terror. Rage. The former head of the Secret Services, he could do a lot of damage, especially if he's feeling chatty.

On Friday morning, the tenth day of my arrival in this small house, I go to see N'Zo Nikiema's remains. I hope the body dries up quickly. I prefer to live with a cleaned-out skeleton, dry and tidy. I know it's shocking to talk like this. But try putting yourself in my position before you judge me. I have treated N'Zo Nikiema's body in an appropriate manner. I took off his clothes and dressed him in a beautiful red and blue *pagne*. I propped him up in a decent position. And you'll soon learn that the deceased was from the royal family of Nimba and I have prayed for him to Fomba, who has been declared the Ancestor of the Ancestors. All in all, I've done everything to pay respects to the dead even in these difficult circumstances. But I won't lie: the sticky black liquid flowing out of N'Zo Nikiema's body makes me sick. It smells awful. I do have the right to say I don't like it.

14

After this inspection, I gather all the pages from the school note-books scattered on the floor. They come from several different note-books. The ones covered with dust had obviously been piled up for months in the drawers and on the shelves. I can deduce from this that the place has remained unoccupied for months. Everywhere else, in the musty rooms and even in Mumbi's studio, I get an unpleasant suffocating sensation; the spiders have woven their webs in the darkest corners of the ceiling and behind the furniture. In the little corner that serves as the kitchen, I found two half-loaves of moldy bread hanging over the edge of the sink.

To stretch my legs, I walk around as I scan through N'Zo Nikiema's notes. The same question about the same person always comes up: Mumbi Awele. She is apparently young and I also believe I know whom these notes are about. I promise myself that I will check out some of the details later when I am more relaxed. I already have one theory, the kind that comes from intuition, from weak and disparate signs and a certain *atmosphere*: President Nikiema lived here in some way—but how? With this artist? During the last four months of his life, which he spent in this house like a trapped animal, he wrote letters that often seemed desperate and which she will most likely never even read.

During my little stroll around the house, I feel something under my feet. A discreet bulge under the zebu-skin rug. Almost nothing, in fact. If I weren't gripped by this nervous tension, I'd probably not have realized anything. I also believe that having been a good cop has helped me in this particular situation. Most normal people— those who haven't been involved in investigations or interrogating suspects or haven't spent their entire lives looking for clues—would not have paid attention to this bump on the floor. But me, I stopped to examine it, and I can boast that it's exactly what needed to be done.

I didn't immediately discover the entry to the underground passage. But less than a week later, I find it. N'Zo Nikiema had installed a secret shelter in the small house. To get there, one has to go up the terrace by a staircase that is carefully hidden behind a wardrobe and then again down two floors. To get to the heart of the shelter, one has to cross many intertwining galleries. Nothing, though, leads me to believe that Nikiema hid down there permanently. I believe he was safe enough in the living room, the back room, and the studio. But at the slightest suspicious noise, he could get out of danger in a few seconds.

How many years had it taken N'Zo Nikiema to get this bunker constructed in the depths of this small house? He had managed to do it without anyone's knowledge, including Castaneda and myself. He had already hoodwinked us by building an allegedly secret passage beneath the palace. Castaneda and I were not supposed to be aware of that either. We were secretly amused about that. Each of us used to say, poor Nikiema, the moment will come when he'll have a nasty surprise. The tunnel opened up at the ocean and helicopters waited permanently on a beach that was obviously forbidden to the public. To keep themselves from getting bored, the pilots—originally from Ukraine, though there were also two giant Greeks among them who were actually twins—padded around on the beach with an air of importance. They wore big dark glasses, had dreadful tattoos on their forearms, and chewed gum all the time. Yes, you've seen them—or their type—in American action films. And of course, during the final assault on Nikiema's palace, Pierre Castaneda waited for him on the beach. The president was supposed to flee his residence like a rat smoked out of his hole and he was going to be picked up stealthily on the beach. But good old N'Zo Nikiema! He was no fool, and Castaneda made the mistake of underestimating him.

I doubt the construction of the bunker took much time. These things are done pretty quickly, to limit any security leaks. After it's done, you have to kill the architects, workers, carpenters, to eliminate all potential leaks. Nikiema must have slaughtered all those people with his own hands. I come from this profession and I know the term "methods adapted for the situation." This one's called major force number one. I'm kidding but that's the idea. To tell you the whole truth, these secret presidential shelters are often sweet little graveyards. The bodies of the unfortunate ones are probably down there somewhere.

Pieces of broken bottles litter the ground. I bend down to pick them up one by one. After wrapping them up in a piece of cloth, I throw them into the blue plastic bucket that I am using as a trash can and I give the floor of the living room a quick sweep. The dust starts to fill up my nostrils and I manage to block my sneezes so that I don't make any noise.

While sweeping the living room, I pass N'ko Nikiema's body several times but it hardly even catches my eye. This is a good sign and proof that I am gradually becoming the master of this place. After putting away the cleaning supplies, I come back and lift the cover. Nikiema's skin, always clear when he was alive, has become waxy and black like coal. It seems to stick more and more violently to his bones.

—⁓—

In order to better understand how it feels for me to be face to face with N'Zo Nikiema's corpse, you have to remember: this man was my boss. Of course, I dropped him when it became obvious that Castaneda was going to win the war. But I could never forget our refined collusion. Beyond our working relationship, we had true mutual respect for one another. Nikiema didn't expect me to lick his boots, and that I rather appreciated. He used to like to cruise around alone at night through the streets of Maren behind the wheel of an inconspicuous Toyota. At times, he would ring my doorbell in Lamsaar-Pilote, order a coffee, and head into the children's room to help them do their math homework. He would talk to them for hours about Mansare, the old man who was responsible for his education since he was, at the time, the crown prince of the Kingdom of Nimba. He would come back and find my wife, Mberi, and I in the sitting room. And dreamily, in a drawling voice, he would say things like,

"We are all so good when we are small children! It's only afterwards that we start to rot."

In public, we managed to communicate through discreet signals. That way, I could keep watch over him without anyone noticing. But it wasn't always possible to shoo away the pests. That brings to mind a memorable reception at the Tunisian embassy that I must tell you about. Nikiema had to make a personal appearance at the commemoration of that country's Independence Day. He was chatting with his host and, I believe, our minister of foreign affairs. These types of conversations with the bigwigs of the world are difficult: one must never remain silent for a single minute and yet, at the same time, one must really say nothing. People would avoid, for that matter, being in the presence of the president on these occasions, out of respect, but also so as not to open themselves up to the risk of saying something foolish. And on that particular day, an individual wearing a black tuxedo decided without the slightest awkwardness to join the group. I was, as always, about six feet away from N'Zo Nikiema. I saw him give a questioning look to the two people he was talking to. And the intruder, wearing the bow tie and glasses of an armchair intellectual, was completely at ease. Each time the Tunisian ambassador or his two hosts would try to say something, he would cut them off and talk complete rubbish in a pompous tone. On top of that, he was talking so fast that no one managed to make him shut up. Nikiema was very irritated. Only here's the thing: there is no law that forbids a citizen to speak to his president. Apparently, in a democracy it's even recommended. Had Nikiema snapped at the guy, the newspapers would have made a big fuss about it the following day. The guy was putting on airs the whole time and each time someone would try to get a word in, he would hasten to say, forcefully, as he waved his glass of grapefruit juice, "Ah, yes! That is the fundamental problem, Your Excellency!" I do believe he repeated that sentence a dozen times. Then, without warning, he went into a rant about the construction of a hotel where the old Wandimbe market used to be: "Do you realize, Mr. President, what they have done? A ton of cement was used there to suffocate the joyous cries of the stallholders. Have you heard our sellers? 'Come here, little madam, with my chicken meat your husband will never go seeking a co-wife, you'll be all alone at home, madam, forever the queen. That said, madam, your headscarf is so elegant.... And this perfume!' Hmm! Mind your own business! There they are, Your Excellency, our brave street peddlers in front of their fruit stands, teasing the young women—neither young nor beauties, mind you—who smile and proceed nonchalantly on their way, and, well, all that sure is charming. Surely, you weren't aware of this scandal, Your Excellency. 'Yet another scandal,' the gossipmongers will say, but I don't meddle in politics, Your Excellency. And that's not all.... The cement, that horrible greenish lump, locked away the smells of mango and papaya in its nocturnal greenhouses. And the peppermint! And the jasmine, the laurel leaves! Yes, jasmine, Mr. Ambassador, allow me a little playful wink, for I know your lovely country well. Some mornings I've haunted every nook and cranny of the Ariana Market, a lively place, full of color, spices, and delicious fruits if there ever were any! It all filled the air with fragrance, I say! Replaced with what? With a five-star. Again, one must look closer, Your Excellency, because those stars, without intending to denigrate anyone, are more often about the company and its schemes. And what happens is, they replace those noble and ample fragrances with the mediocre smells of rancid oil, marinated meat, and imported chocolate. Imported chocolate! And they will tell me that it's all beneficial for the nation! Your Excellency, my respect!"

As he said those last words, he bowed with profound reverence, bending completely in half, and headed toward two stunningly beautiful women standing in the background. I have never seen an individual squawk like that and at such speed. What's more, he didn't even have the excuse of being drunk. Naturally, no one dared to come gather around the president. But everyone was waiting for his reaction without making it obvious. He wore a forced smile on his face, though I'm pretty sure that at one point he burst out laughing without meaning to. When the guy left, Nikiema looked over at me with a gesture I knew well. Message received loud and clear.

Three days later, my guys and I went to grab the fellow at dawn. I said to him, "We are aware of your activities, sir."

He began with an air of detachment: "That's why you come to my home at five in the morning?" he sniggered. He was the leader of a phony environmentalist party and he began to threaten us, saying he would call his network of foreign lawyers to go after us, and other things of that sort.

I said to him, "Sir, your accomplices have given you up. We've found the plans and your arms caches. If I were in your position, I would not play dumb about it. You are the leader of a conspiracy against the state—have the courage to assume responsibility for it."

He had no idea what I was talking about. We warmed him up with some electric shocks, crushed his fingers, and then went for his ears as if we were about to cut them off. He admitted to one elaborate terrorist plot after another with no end, but we didn't give a damn. Then I told him to go back home and keep quiet.

On the evening of the same day, I gave my report to the president. I think he'd had some drinks, because he launched right into a completely wacky impression of the little freak from the Tunisian embassy. It was pretty well done and we laughed a lot.

That's how the deceased N'Zo Nikiema and I got along. You must never believe, though, that it was always simple. At times, I also had to deal with his presidential moods, which I did not understand at all. Like the night when a call came in on my special line. It was Nikiema's aide-de-camp. I hurriedly got dressed. N'Zo Nikiema was in front of his big-screen television, flipping through hundreds of channels. The palace's technical services had installed a rather sophisticated setup and I'm quite sure the president had access to any program on the planet. Nothing interested him. "Except," he said to me one day, "totally moronic movies. Those are relaxing."

I entered the sitting room just as he was trying to use the television remote. It jammed and he went into a wild fit of rage. He pressed a button. His assistant dashed in. As soon as he saw the president, he began shaking all over. His rage sustained and ferocious, N'Zo Nikiema asked him where the second remote had gone. The assistant immediately got down on his knees and started searching around for the clicker on the carpet and under the armchairs. I did not like that at all. Humiliating a meager employee like that, treating him like a dog, it was heinous. The more the guy crawled around the floor, the more I hated N'Zo Nikiema. When he retrieved the remote for him, still wracked with fear, the president dismissed him without even a glance in his direction.

I didn't wait for his permission to sit down facing him. He had called me in at three in the morning and pretended not to even notice my presence. Every minute, he would change the channel. We saw rap groups, several bits of soccer and American basketball games, commercials, etc. He stopped at a documentary. A leopard set off in pursuit of a gazelle. The image fascinated Nikiema. It was really something. Instead of hurling himself on his prey as we would expect, the big cat had chosen to exhaust it. It seemed like the chase would be endless. Every now and again, he would leap onto the gazelle, and each time he did he would sink his fangs into a different part of its body. When its blood had drained, it began to falter and, in a sudden fit of despair, tried to make itself seem threatening, rearing its horns in a forward motion. The leopard stood still for a few seconds, then started circling around it carefully, not taking his eyes off his prey for even a moment. In the next segment, it was the feast.

If it had been a good day for him, Nikiema would have told a little joke about the big cat's tactical genius. Maybe he also would have taken the opportunity to denigrate General Mobutu—"that phony leopard with his ridiculous cap, a real disgrace to Africa"—who only showed bravery when up against defenseless beings. The president hated his Zairian colleague with all his might. I heard him say once

21

or twice, "With Lumumba, the Belgians got their hands dirty, that's for sure. They could not let a Negro publicly insult a white king and get away with it like that. But for Mulele and the others, their dear friend Sese Seko got along just fine on his own!" The both of them having died the sad way we know that they did, I prefer not to get into the reasons—rather inglorious, I might add—for the enmity between N'Zo Nikiema and Mobutu Sese Seko.

Nikiema clicked off the TV and turned toward me. "I am sorry to have made you come so late, Colonel Kroma."

I was not happy, and I barely responded to him. His distracted, mechanical apology offended me even more.

He proceeded to tell me why he was feeling so miserable that night. When I noticed that he was about to break into tears, I wondered, annoyed, what he expected of me. That I pity him? There was no question about that. A man of his rank couldn't let himself go like that. It put too many people in danger. He perceived a look of disdain on my face and little by little pulled himself together. I promised him, without actually having to say anything, that our discussion would remain between us.

We concocted numerous other dirty tricks. I remember one of our schemes, sort of a classic, which is worth sharing.

When friends would come from far-off places to see him, N'Zo Nikiema would often invite them to dinner. Most of them readily claimed to be anarchists, but they were proud to come break bread at the palace with the president. Sometimes he would say to them, "Let's take a tour. I am going to show you Maren, my great city."

Accordingly, they would pile into two or three cars. He himself would get behind the wheel of one. Actually, those drives were always a little sad. Nikiema would wonder what his guests were thinking as they saw the broken red dusty roads and breathed in the smoky exhaust around the city. Were they, too, saying that it was all his fault—the open canals, the dilapidated houses, the bad odors wafting through the air, the women frying their fritters seated next to piles of trash overrun with scruffy dogs? The dim lights beneath the giant cashew trees, the little beggars who would hold out their blood-streaked stumps at red lights, all of those pathetic things, were they his fault? The dust had always been there; no one could do anything about that. It seeped into living beings, eating away at their organs and destroying their bodies from the inside out with neither haste nor respite.

These foreign visitors came from rich countries where the streets were so wide and clean that one never even saw them. They were shocked by so much misery and imagined perfectly well the embarrassment Nikiema felt.

In order to break a potentially very heavy silence, one of them asked whatever came to mind: "What is that building?"

The president looked around him. "The little yellow building there on your left?"

"Yes."

"Asante, what is that building?" (He never called me Colonel Kroma during those drives.)

"That's the Satellite, Mr. President."

He slowed down to get a better look at the leprous facade of the building and the dull lighting around it before saying more precisely to his guests, in a detached tone, "That belongs to a large insurance company."

"Funny name," one of them said.

And he explained, "No one knows why it's called that. There are also apartments and some private offices inside."

A brief silence ensued inside the car. I was imagining the president's guests laughing silently to themselves. Did any among them know what the Satellite was really used for? Those people knew everything. You could always tell them whatever bullshit and they'd shake their heads as if to say, go on, keep talking, little one, I'm interested. Of course, they were not going to make a big story of it, about what went on in the basement of the Satellite. That's where the tough

23

ones were interrogated. They were buried on-site. Nobody could get out alive. It wasn't even conceivable.

It is important to know, by the way, that in those days N'Zo Nikiema and Pierre Castaneda were the best of friends. Most of those who visited Nikiema were otherwise more or less connected to Cogemin. All they had to do was plug their noses, and this reassured them that the country was led by a man with an iron fist. Those people were adults, not some young idealists. They had no need to involve themselves in the internal politics of a sovereign state.

Sometimes, to show how popular he was, Nikiema would make a stop with his little nocturnal procession. We would enter any old bar to drink some beer. At first intimidated, after a few minutes the customers would summon the courage to come gather around us. Some little wise guys would ask to meet with him; others would shout about how devoted they were to his regime; some made critical remarks since, after all, we were in a democracy; and there was always a half-blind old lady who would pull him aside to say affectionately, while feigning sternness, "Do you remember me, my child?"

He would respond with an awkward smile. "No, mama."

And she would cry out, her hands in the air, "Would you look at that! What an ingrate! Eight days after his birth in Nimba, it was I who organized his *ngénte*, and he no longer remembers me! Don't forget your past, my son—you mustn't let the power make you go mad." She went on speaking in proverbs and ended on a moralizing tone, all choked up: "As God is my witness, you are too good, my child! We all pray for you. The day you were born, when I cradled you in my arms, I knew you were destined for great things! And not only because your father was the king of Nimba! *Wallaay!*"

Everyone acquiesced warmly and it caused some excitement in the bar, leaving them feeling nice and relaxed. N'Zo Nikiema held the old woman in his arms and they stayed there without saying a word to one another, almost stifled by the emotion of it, and he seemed to remember his childhood years. Then he bought a round for everyone and still managed to make a path through the middle of an increasingly dense and active crowd. His guests were fascinated to see that Nikiema's popularity was the only thing that could cause riots in the country. I personally could see in their eyes that they were mostly impressed by the president's mastery. If for a moment they realized that it was all an orchestrated act, they would still be unaware of the extent to which the people were ridiculing them. Not for a moment did one of them suspect that the little old lady, the bar manager, the passersby, the *akara* fritter vendor at the bar entrance, the musicians who were playing whatever they fancied on the little poorly lit stage in the back—in short, all of them there were *my* guys. I especially loved the old woman. An all-time pro. A filthy old lady, besides. She had invented all kinds of refined torture techniques to use against N'Zo Nikiema's and Pierre Castaneda's adversaries. When she'd finished with one of them, he would drag himself to her feet begging her to give him sweets. She killed me, that old woman: to be such a bitch at that age, it was really something.

Those are the kinds of things I did with the deceased N'Zo Nikiema. Were he to wake up in that small house there, we would not be bored. We could muster up so many shared memories . . .

—∞—

The first explosion was followed by a couple more, brief and a little muted. Within a few minutes, the sounds of ambulance sirens from near and far could be heard across the entire city. Nikiema instinctively cocked his head toward the window and stayed alert, listening anxiously. He heard the firefighters' trucks from within the ruins of Jinkoré, but a moment later it seemed like the screams were coming from the other side of Maren. It seemed like several fires were flaring up, one after the other in different parts of the capital.

I had seen him again a few hours earlier in the presidential palace. The country's highest officials were seated with stoic faces around a long oval table. The president had never seen them so tense. Everyone stared intensely at him. They knew it was the end of the war and there was only one question running through their minds: who would be the final victor, N'Zo Nikiema or Pierre Castaneda? They didn't want to end up in the wrong camp.

I was there, and like everyone else I thought, I have very little time to negotiate this turn of events. At the same exact moment, N'Zo Nikiema was thinking about one of his counterparts—some dictator in Asia or Latin America—who had summoned everybody under the pretext of wanting to thank all who had served him, some of them for several years. After a moving speech on loyalty, he had slaughtered them all before they could flee.

Yet, in a voice that was calm and strong, the voice he used every day, the president turned to me and said, "I put Colonel Kroma in charge of reviewing the situation. We all appreciate the rigor and precision of our colleague. Colonel?"

I opened my folder and promised to keep the presentation brief. As I spoke, I saw the same nagging question in everybody's eyes: Who is this guy, anyway? They had never been able to get a read on me and they hated that. Of course, my position certainly made them anxious. The boss of information services was generally supposed to know whatever they concealed from the world. Despite this, they really didn't care. They could embezzle huge sums of money, tamper with currencies by the tens of millions, or lead lives of debauchery. As long as they seemed clean, they didn't have to worry. No, I was not the man in the shadows who could shake up these masters of the hour. These bastards, much like young people with their whole lives ahead of them, had a truly carefree attitude and a real gift for happiness. They had faith in their good fortune. Nothing scared them and they thought they could fool fate with some decoy moves if it managed to piss them off.

More than anything else, they were wondering what I was doing among them. They felt that a senior official should wear a ceremonial costume with brightly colored medals and ribbons. They imagined someone prosperous and pot-bellied, maybe somewhat depraved and a little bit of a scoundrel who gesticulated a lot and had a booming voice. In short, someone who fit into their world. I was far too dowdy for their taste. Even for special occasions, I wore gray or dark blue suits—very sober. I'd never worn a tie in my life and some of them hated me just for that. And why exactly? Well, they wondered, who does he think he is? He thinks we like to choke under these ties? It made these people sick when you didn't behave like everybody else. With my goatee and the messy stubble on my hollow cheeks, I didn't quite fit the profile of the dignitary, as they would want. They also knew I led a disciplined life and I wasn't rich at all. Not that this stopped me from liquidating a lot of people in the name of the stability of the state and from getting involved in all kinds of dirty stuff. They were all completely corrupt but were unable to hurt a fly. How did they get this way?

Usually my briefings were models of clarity and I was happy to just report the facts. This allowed N'Zo Nikiema to make the right decisions pretty quickly. But that day, everything was messy in my head and I obviously lacked confidence. The cunning bunch in front of me never listened to words; they only read signs. And my entire attitude said to them that N'Zo Nikiema's fall was imminent. Besides, none of them had failed to notice one specific detail: I was not wearing my famous striped cap, which is part of my legend. President Nikiema had granted me permission to always keep it on, even in his presence. So the mere fact that they didn't see it on me wreaked havoc in the ranks. A few days later, alone in his Jinkoré refuge, N'Zo Nikiema must have made the following observation: "Well then, it was Colonel Kroma's bald head with its badly healed wounds and grotesque pink coloring that signaled the end. Fortunately, I was able to decipher God's message just in time."

That is probably what saved him. The day before, I'd promised Pierre Castaneda that I would neutralize Nikiema.

"What does that mean, to neutralize?" he had asked, squinting at me as he smoothed his mustache.

"To eliminate. We have a meeting in the palace tomorrow in the late afternoon. I'll shoot him in his office."

"No, I want him alive."

Castaneda wanted Nikiema to suffer and probably hoped to kill him with his own bare hands. And this is what allowed Nikiema to slip through our fingers. He had definitely played this game very well.

I look back today—a little late, I admit—to certain details that should have betrayed him. First, the firmness of his voice during that final meeting. After taking suggestions from everyone present, he had given precise orders. He would not stop arranging the portrait of the Mother of the Nation—his wife—above the row of Chinese vases in front of him. And perhaps I should have suspected something given the way he was crossing and uncrossing his fingers nonstop. I thought it was quite normal for everyone to be a little nervous on such a day. I was wrong.

Everything he said to us boiled down to one word: resistance.

After describing Pierre Castaneda as an adventurer leading his Lil Boys, a desperate young bunch drunk on blood, he added, "We will not leave him this country." All of us around the table watched him as he paused and then whispered in a voice that was meant to be deep and definitive, "This is the land of our ancestors."

Which meant exactly, "This is the land of our ancestors, after all." He hadn't spoken those last two words but each of us understood them clearly. And then we thought, it's his royal blood talking. N'Zo Nikiema, heir to the throne of Nimba, will die here rather than flee or surrender himself.

The moment was almost magical.

This is the land of our ancestors, after all.

But I had not understood that for this too—the surge in dignity, the panache, the final stand, or anything along those lines—it was too late. For thirty years, each day we had had the opportunity to pull ourselves together and we didn't do that. The moment had come for each of us to follow his own path. Toward an uncertain future or toward a horrible death. N'Zo Nikiema, smarter than all of us, was only looking to save his skin. He had performed his little act as the resolute patriot, and without any fanfare he had risen against the face of a foreigner who was coming to take over the country. I had really believed—and the others did too—that Nikiema refused to be, in the eyes of future generations, someone who would tolerate such disgrace. How could our memory be so short! How could we have allowed ourselves to be fooled by these antics when we had seen him walking hand in hand with Pierre Castaneda for so many years?

Less than two hours later, he was staggering like an old drunk through the streets of Maren. It was night and it was impossible to recognize him. The hardest part had been getting to the small house in Jinkoré. Pierre Castaneda's militia had seized the city and was preparing to launch a second assault against the presidential palace. The militiamen were stationed near the columns of public buildings and at all the intersections. It was pretty tight for him. He could neither be too careful nor decide too early to take shelter in the deserted streets of Maren. In order to save his life, he had to imagine that the militiamen were looking at him every second. He had decided that if he was stopped he would burst into laughter, lift his eyes up to the sky, and say whatever nonsense came to mind. Despite his situation, he had the strength to wonder, in jest, whether it would be better to recite some poetry. Of course, his voice could betray him. It was between calling it quits or being captured. The militiaman could kill him off on a whim or shake his head, smirking in amusement.

Luck was on his side, because he was able to find his way to the small house without any trouble. As soon as the door was closed, Nikiema sat down on the divan in the living room. It was not very common for this bed to be in the front room of the small house. He loved this spot. It was the only place where, from time to time, he experienced true happiness.

The second he got out of his disguise, three explosions went off. As the firefighters roamed the flaming streets of Maren, we were waiting for him on the beach at the end of the secret tunnel. Castaneda was not in position yet. I myself was excited by the idea of witnessing this exceptional moment in our history: the encounter between N'Zo Nikiema and Pierre Castaneda on Nawom Beach on the last day of the war. In this case, all that mattered was the very first second. They would look into each other's eyes and would experience something they had never felt before. In spite of knowing each other for years, they would feel like true strangers. N'Zo Nikiema and Castaneda would each say to himself, it's true, I never imagined he was so different from me, before the conflict between us and the civil war that ensued. We believed we knew each other all too well and yet now here we stand on Nawom Beach under the intense watch of the Ukrainian mercenaries in their dark glasses and heavy faces. In this single second, which I know will escape into eternity, I will never grasp why we became enemies and why there lie between us thousands of corpses and ruins, ruins, and more ruins.

Then Pierre Castaneda would feel a small pang in his heart despite himself. What a mess, my man, what a mess, we made a good team, why did you suddenly imagine that you could become a real president of some fucked-up African country? Just like that? Both of them would remember the time when they were like brothers, killing off their enemies in unison—Abel Murigande, Prieto da Souza, and others who were executed in a joyful collaboration. N'Zo Nikiema wasn't all that tough during those days. He had nightmares about the children whose throats he had slit open or strangled. Instead of crying, those kids skipped happily around him, laughing like celestial angels, and he didn't understand their jubilation, and it broke his heart. It turned his stomach and he vomited sometimes, and Castaneda, the hardest of them all, would mock him and tell him to dream of the stars above, of all those planets gliding side by side through space, and of this immense world with its virgin forests and unending rivers and of people on a July evening seated on restaurant terraces in Washington Square. You think these brats crying over their asshole fathers in this hellhole are more important

30

than the profound and mysterious brothel of life? Think about the movement of stars, my man, and drink to our friendship. Hey there, Ta'Mim, another small Premium Club. This was often the routine at the Blue Lizard, Ta'Mim's backyard bar under the mango tree. They downed their bottles of beer and soon it was no longer necessary to talk to Nikiema about Jupiter and Pluto to make him forget his crimes. He came to like the blood and he didn't have nightmares anymore.

There, facing the sea, all these images would flash before their eyes. And then, to shield himself from this moment of sheer honesty, Castaneda would make one of his enigmatic little comments whose meaning only he knew. Maybe he would have said to Nikiema disparagingly. "You already look less proud than in your official photos!"

He didn't really have the pleasure. The reality was, at the end of the day we had to face the facts: while we waited by the sea, President Nikiema was either already en route to the border or safe in a neighboring country.

Never was victory more bitter for Pierre Castaneda.

He had no one to blame but himself. I could have settled this matter in a tidy way but he had been determined to get N'Zo Nikiema alive. That's what happens when you get too greedy.

—m—

He could not sleep that night. But he didn't feel worried. He had gone from the living room to the bedroom several times, and then into Mumbi's studio. Each time he would light a match to admire her work, which she had apparently not had time to finish. There were all kinds of black-and-white geometric shapes—circles, diamonds, triangles, and squares—painted on a calabash. N'Zo Nikiema remembered the day she had started to work on this. She admitted that she didn't know what she wanted to do but was letting her instinct guide her.

He also thought he would never see her again. Maybe he didn't really want to. What name could you possibly give to all his years of involvement with Mumbi? This was the best-kept secret of his life and that's how it would remain. Anyway, whom could he discuss it with now?

N'Zo Nikiema was aware that he had little chance of ever living outside of this house again. But in my opinion, this would not have dissuaded him from negotiating his survival once the storm had passed. In this bunker, right under his feet, were all the state secrets that I had not been able to gather during the course of my entire career in the Secret Services. Recorded conversations. Handwritten documents from Pierre Castaneda. And most importantly, the video of the murder of Kaveena, Mumbi's daughter. N'Zo Nikiema knew: this was the one thing that mattered to Pierre Castaneda. Of all the crimes he had committed, strangely, this was the only one he was ashamed of. He was willing to do anything to be exonerated. Yet, perplexed, N'Zo Nikiema asked himself: desperate enough to let me leave the country? Nothing was less certain. It was just a possibility. But it didn't interest him at the time. He, too, wanted to be acquitted of the murder of this little girl. I'm not here for nothing, he told himself in exaltation mingled with anger and a vague sense of relief. True, he thought, he was only innocent of this crime by chance. He had committed so many others but there was no reason to assume he was responsible for what had happened to Mumbi's child.

And Mumbi, where had she gone? He had no idea. A few weeks before his fall, he had come to see her and she had said goodbye with these words: "It's time to leave." By this she meant, it's now or never. This was a country where you had to know when to leave. All of a sudden, you could be trapped, and in a single moment people could be reduced to powerlessly facilitating their own destruction.

Mumbi avoided his eyes as she gave him a set of keys. "I have a copy," she said. He wanted to ask her why she did that, but he stopped himself. Both had understood from the very beginning, without discussing it, that at times they would be forced to talk through allusions. Given the position he was in, he had no choice, and on top of that, if Pierre Castaneda were to discover the relationship, the less she knew, the better it would be for her.

He glanced at his watch. Almost three in the morning. The Maren slums were completely ablaze. The rescuers were somehow trying to do their work. The fugitive imagined big red fire trucks arriving at a dead end. The driver braking to death in the middle of the street and then swearing loudly as he reversed. All the while the terrified cries of kids turned into live torches rose up into the sky. Most definitely too, the zealous, young state employees would make an anxious attempt to be the first on the scene of disaster. And there, in the middle of the flames that danced before their eyes, they would start to bark orders they had learned at Maren's College of Administration. None of them had the faintest chance of escaping death. They were all condemned to burn alive.

He stood up and walked over to the fridge without knowing what he was looking for. Not really hungry, he took a few sips of lemonade and returned to lie on the couch. After his agitated night, and since it was so early in the morning, he wanted a strong cup of coffee. But it took him a few seconds to remember that he had to make it for himself.

—◈—

In spite of the late hour, I continue my inspection of the underground bunker. I haven't done anything else since I arrived here. I pick up the tiniest piece of paper from the ground, scrutinize it for a long while, and put it in one of the five binders I have opened. One must overlook nothing, even these little crumpled bits of paper covered in grease stains. I had learned, in my life up to that point, how useful they can be. All one needs is a little time to solve their secrets. And time I do have. It won't weigh on my days, because I'm not lacking things to read. All the things I am discovering are astonishing to me. I didn't know how poorly informed I was. Sometimes it's a little vexing, I must admit. One can also see the good side of it: coming to terms with one's ignorance makes you modest.

33

No one ever knew anything about Nikiema's relationship with this young artist named Mumbi Awele. Only yesterday I became certain that she is the mother of Kaveena. Remember that this little girl's murder triggered quite a storm. The newspapers held back their opinions about the case for several months. And that was only the beginning of the harassment, since we have continuously come back to it over the last fifteen years. At the time, journalists had called upon experts of all types, friends and neighbors of the family in the working-class district of Kisito, and a few distant relatives as well. My men and I were following all of it very closely. One thing had intrigued us: the father and mother of little Kaveena had never made a statement to the press. It seemed that one knew nothing of the father and that the mother was described as either a painter or a ballet dancer. At the time, I noticed there were a few nasty remarks regarding her corrupt sense of morals. According to some of our dailies, she was a young, heartless woman wholly indifferent to the death of her only daughter. What can you expect, one reputed columnist nearly came right out and said; the ordinary people of Kisito had seen so much of this, and in their merciless struggle to survive, "crying for the dead is practically a luxury." That phrase then had, if one can say so, its hour of glory in the public debates. Other analysts, in contrast, maintained that Mumbi's pain was so great that she had lost her voice and perhaps even a little of her sanity.

All this seemed quite muddled to me. In our line of work, we don't like vagueness. I put one of my guys, Mike, in charge of a small investigation. A little while afterward, Mike came back to me. "Nothing to report, boss."

I looked at him. "What does she do for a living?"

"She's a whore."

"Oh?"

"I did her."

"For how much?" It's kind of a bizarre question, I know. But I've always been successful working this way. These little factual details interest me the most.

Mike's mouth curled up in disdain, which meant, almost nothing. He added, "She's a horny broad, boss."

When I think back to these sorts of discussions with Mike—that's not his real name, by the way; he got it from an American TV show—I realize that of all of my agents, he was the most enigmatic. No one knew much about him. He didn't get along well with his colleagues and he was the only one who felt pure pleasure when he was torturing. I always put him on the most difficult interrogations. The majority of the guys we grilled knew that after a few days we would either pity them or become disgusted at what we were doing. Generally, our customers weren't your ordinary run-of-the-mill types. As they suffered, they were watching out for the first signs of our weakness. Well, with Mike that was always in vain. He didn't stop crunching his roasted peanuts, one after the other and not the least bit hurriedly, all the while trying to get their confessions out of them. The sound of his jaws horrified them; they saw Mike take delight in their agony and sensed that the ordeal could last an eternity. It was too much all at once for them: in the end, they cracked.

"In the papers they say, though, that she's an artist," I noted.

"True. For about a year, she was in a dance troupe. She paints things, too, but in the art world hardly anyone knows her."

"And what about her daughter?"

"Little Kaveena? She doesn't care. Her grandfather, a man who goes by the name of N'Fumbang, was the one who took care of her." Mike also told me about Kaveena's father; he was killed in a brawl coming out of a bar in Kisito. "It seems Mumbi was there. Some say she fought like a lioness."

"That sounds right to you?"

"No, frankly. I'm not saying in bed . . ."

"Fine."

We continued to talk and in the end I felt relieved. There's nothing more foul than the murder of a little girl. If the mother—especially the mother, her face apparently ravaged by silent suffering, her clenched lips and her melancholic eyes—decides to put pressure on you, you're lost. I've seen governments spend enormous amounts in order to calm weeping widows and then one day they say, "OK, enough is enough, that's it, we don't have billions to hand out to you every month. Cry for your dearly departed and shut up!" Don't talk to me about the grief suffered by the families. For us, the widow and the orphan are really pains in the neck.

I insisted anyway: "Are you sure she doesn't care, Mike?"

"I got her to talk," he said, with a look that said there was a subtext. Mike was convinced that once a woman was in bed with him, she could no longer hide anything from him. Funny guy. There were only two things in his life: refined torture and sexual tricks. And those two things served the same ends: to get information. But Mumbi proved him wrong—beautifully. I try to imagine the scene. In the shabby room of a pay-by-the hour hotel, the clever inspector tries to worm something out of the young woman. After all, she's only a prostitute, who doesn't have the "luxury" of mourning her little girl. Conceited Mike just didn't know that he was facing such a challenge. Mumbi Awele treated him as if he were nothing, like an imbecile, which he deserved. It must have been child's play for her. Naturally, little did I know at the time that she would be so present in my life now.

I don't know how she did it, but she managed to get Nikiema to eat out of her hands. Right up till the end, he wrote very moving letters to her, though at times they were a bit bizarre and incoherent. Every day, I find traces of them in the small house. They're handwritten and often seem unfinished. For a short while, I believed that he had ripped them up when he sensed his end was near. But in the end, that didn't seem plausible: N'Zo Nikiema liked talking to Mumbi Awele. He even liked talking to her about the afterlife.

Which makes me think that they aren't love letters, even if at times some emotion shows through discreetly. In reality, N'Zo Nikiema's only concern was to convince Mumbi of his innocence. All those letters can be summarized in one sentence: "Mumbi Awele, I did not kill your child." I had the opportunity to read, for that matter, that very sentence in his hand.

I'm starting to think that my being present in this solitary place is a gift from God. I relish every discovery before it even happens.

I go back up to the living room. A little light shining through the window tells me that it's dawn. And inside the house, the air is less dense. Soon I will no longer have to spend my nights in the studio. The smell of N'Zo Nikiema's body is a lot less putrid. The maggots have disappeared after sucking the last drops of blood and pus. I delayed approaching it again for a long time. It didn't scare me, but still, a corpse is repulsive. Now I am ready. In a few days, I'm going to be able to lift the pieces of *faso danfani* that are still stuck to his chest and legs. I'm going to disinfect the divan and transfer the body to Mumbi's studio. He'll no doubt feel his best in there. Perhaps I'll do nothing with it. I don't want to get involved in something that has nothing to do with me, after all.

Before going to bed, I take a nice shower and I brush my teeth for a long time. Banal gestures that give me the feeling I've finally settled into a place where nothing can ever happen to me.

—⁊⁊⁊—

N'Zo Nikiema had been lying down in the darkness for the last twenty minutes. He had no idea what time it was. All he knew was that it was night. The faint rays of light that flitted through all the cracks during the day had vanished discreetly. A few minutes earlier, he had watched them disappear one after the other, like so many stars losing their brilliance little by little.

He murmured, "So that's how it all began. Or maybe that's how everything ended. I'm really not sure."

Ambiguous, uncertain words, little blows dealt by life, but so relentless, swirling around in the emptiness, then finding their place, one next to the other. Even if he'd had the strength to get up, he wouldn't have been able to finally begin writing his letter to Mumbi. During these final days of the civil war, Jinkoré was, like most of

Maren's neighborhoods, without electricity. All he could do each night was to wait to feel tired. Luckily, it never took long. Anyway, he didn't remember when he had ever slept so much in his entire life. In truth, it was impossible for him to do anything else but sleep and, as soon as it was dawn, jump out of bed, secretly exalted. Why he had this ephemeral happiness in the morning remained a mystery to him right up till the end. It didn't mean that he was ready to fight. He didn't say to himself, another good day, Castaneda will end up getting me, but I'll demand a good price for my skin. No, he didn't say that to himself. The game was lost and he knew it. All he had left to do was to let himself die. Maybe he was simply happy to be able to savor every second of his last moments of life on earth.

Once, he got the idea to light a candle and place it at the end of the room, next to Mumbi's studio. He didn't dare. The little flickering light would be enough to attract those groups of pillagers who were scouring Maren. For several days, the battles had been even more violent than usual around Jinkoré. At sunset, there was a vague ceasefire: it was then that each side gathered up its dead.

With a smile of amusement, tenderness, and contempt all at once, he thought, my army continues fighting out of habit. Out of pride, too, no doubt. These are well-trained soldiers and they cannot comprehend that militias have definitively defeated them. He knew, too, that some of his officers were refusing to disarm so that Castaneda would have to negotiate with them. But that wasn't what he wanted to talk to Mumbi about. He imagined her next to him, like before, in the small house. Perhaps she would accept what he said and believe him, now that he was nothing. He was nothing anymore, he had nothing more to lose, nothing more to hide. N'Zo Nikiema was certain, however, that she would not come back. It just wasn't possible anymore. "There are dozens of roadblocks in the city, maybe even hundreds, and heavily armed youth are patrolling as they throw back cans of beer. They continue to kill whomever they want." He said this half out loud, and these words, resonating in the still of the night, seemed to have a surreal tone to him. The words bounced around the room before getting lost in the nearby street.

There was another truth, but he was afraid to face up to it. Mumbi could very well be dead, like so many other people in the country. After all, that's what a war is for; it's for people to die. Meanwhile, he found a way to reassure himself: I refuse to believe that you are dead. You are very strong. You are the kind who survives a war. Just like that. Because it's you.

More out of boredom than out of necessity, he began mentally preparing the letter he intended to leave for her. Suddenly it seemed unexpectedly easier to write. The sentences took shape in his head with surprising ease. He could even repeat them, to hear the sound of his own voice, the way a musician plays his scales: "It wasn't so simple, and I found out about that incident in the newspapers, like you did. Don't forget the role fate plays. I was a powerful man at the time, that's true. But do you believe I could hold the life of each citizen of this country in my hands for so long? No, only God . . ."

But as soon as he uttered the word "God," he stopped. Reading this letter, Mumbi was going to foam at the mouth and her delicate facial features were going to tense up: How dare a man such as he mingle God's name in his dirty business? You killed my daughter and then you come play the big game of betrayed innocence, she would say. It's not me, he'd answer; it's one of my overzealous supporters. Or it's Castaneda. Castaneda, the white man who crossed the seas just to come kill all the Negroes around here! Castaneda, the bastard, right? A bit too easy.

When Mumbi was angry, she would say anything. She had entered his life not out of love but to know the truth about her daughter's death. Each time she would ask him questions, he would force himself to answer patiently and honestly. In vain. It would always end badly. When they would make love, she would sometimes stand in front of him, gigantic, heinous, completely crazy, with a horsewhip in her hands, and whip him until he bled, calling him a murderer and

39

a coward. Then he would cry. Balled up in a corner of the room with his hands on his head, he would sob with perverse joy.

—⁓—

I must pause to reflect a little more on Kaveena's murder. This is the event that eventually came to exist at the core of N'Zo Ni-kiema's life. It clarified the entire puzzle. I surprised myself when I discovered—through my random excavations around the small house—that the only thing that tormented this man, at once wealthy and complex, deceitful and violent, was a crime he did not commit. I almost wrote: the only crime he did not commit.

A few words on the Kaveena case.

This is what we remember without any uncertainties: *Tomorrow's Times* was the first newspaper to report the story of a six-year-old girl who was raped and then brutally murdered. Despite its name, *Tomorrow's Times* is a weekly newspaper. According to the article, the murderer had been taken by surprise in the Gindal Forest while cutting up the victim's body and spreading it out in seven piles on an old mat. As he recounted later in an interview, he only had two more piles to make when the villagers emerged from the bushes and pounced on him, closing in on him from behind. His accomplices managed to escape. At the police station, the man had no difficulty making a confession. He only regretted having been captured at the last minute. The investigators noted that the murderer felt no remorse. His somewhat incoherent comments could be summed up like this: "It's pretty stupid, huh? A few more seconds and everything would have been OK. I am really unlucky." At no point did he seem aware of the gravity of what he had done. It was as if he had missed scoring the winning goal at the last second in what had been a close game. Furthermore, though this was clearly a heinous crime, *Tomorrow's Times* had reported the details more or less vaguely. The reporter was more focused on being witty than on actually relaying the facts about little Kaveena. In short, all the facts that surrounded this story were quickly forgotten. After all, in our world today, the murder of a young girl of humble origins can move sensitive souls for

40

only a few days at best. Once this brief moment of compassion that preserves the value of an undeniable human tragedy has passed— even if she was from a poor family, a child like Kaveena is not an animal—the story of her death comes out in the press, and the press gradually strips away any sense of reality. A small body has disappeared from the face of the earth but everything is kind of the same. It's unfortunate but true.

And if, in the end, this was not how it played out this time, it was because the *Tomorrow's Times* reporter was a very smart fellow. Two observations had put him on the right track. First, there was the evidence that it was a ritual killing. He saw the proof of this in some of the gruesome details, and he logically deduced that a powerful person was behind this crime. Those who know our country well are aware that the services of witch doctors are quite costly. You want to get an important job? They will take you into a small dark room and without even deigning to look at you, they will tell you, here's what you need to do and this is how much it costs. And what you've got to do is: at cockcrow you must kill an albino or a light-skinned six-year-old girl or a stray madman or any other person of your choice. They tell you how to proceed and you must listen carefully—these things are very complicated and these witch doctors, as you know, do not like to repeat themselves; if, for example, the victim's right eye is gouged out before her left eye, everything will be screwed up and that's too bad for you. That will cost you more. In short, only the strongmen, determined to make something of their lives, have the means to carry out such operations, which can be indefinitely renewed for whatever reason.

A second fact troubled the young journalist: the murderer seemed sure he would be released rather quickly. When the investigating judge asked him certain questions, he gave cryptic answers that sometimes sounded like threats. And after several days, he had become more and more impatient. Then, overnight, he changed his attitude, to the surprise of his jailers and the judge. After he had successfully made the case that he was mentally unfit, he appeared to have all the traits of a normal person and even a sort of formidable intelligence. Besides, if so many years later the case still has some gray areas, it is because he seemed to be a gifted manipulator.

We insist upon seeing Kaveena's murder as the great enigma in our political history. That's a bit of an exaggeration, in my opinion: with so many confessions and all kinds of evidence, the case is closed, as they say. The merit of the journalist lies in his perseverance. That is not all: sensing the coup of the century, he had managed to get an interview with the prisoner awaiting trial.

All this happened, if I remember correctly, about fifteen years ago. Well, our country has not yet recovered from this banal interview. The prisoner made veiled references to being the main henchman of an influential politician of foreign origin. He claimed to be overwhelmed by remorse and ready to confess everything to ease his conscience. He spoke of having nightmares wherein a little girl asked him every night why he was such a wicked uncle. With admirable perspicacity, the journalist suggested that the girl in question could be Kaveena. The murderer's repentant words made headlines very quickly. There were the usual pompous and hypocritical editorials about the dangers of impunity. At first the government tried to lie low; it tried to suggest that it was too busy working on the country's development and had no time to devote to nonsense. Unfortunately for the authorities, the man was diabolical and had secretly filmed the murder. I remember that, at the time, there was no bad blood between N'Zo Nikiema and Castaneda. But they fought a ferocious battle behind the scenes to get their hands on that tape. Luck was on N'Zo Nikiema's side. I also believe that I was quite helpful with this issue.

It is not an exaggeration to say that this tape completely changed the recent history of our country. It continues, too, to weigh on its evolution, as you will come to realize later.

I was one of the half dozen or so people to whom Nikiema showed the film. As you know, I am not the emotive type. But I was really very shocked. However, I didn't show any of this during the secret screening. I limited myself to offering the president purely technical advice.

"There is a fourth character, Mr. President," I said.

Everyone stared at me in amazement. "What do you mean, Colonel Kroma?" asked Nikiema.

"We almost always see the murderer from the back. Little Kaveena and the one who ordered the kill are constantly seen facing us. This means that an accomplice was holding the camera, not the murderer himself."

It was just like the end of a detective novel. The investigator who is always smarter than everyone else pulls on his pipe a couple of times and then reveals the key to the mystery. There was a small commotion. Suddenly there was a blinding clarity to the situation.

Let's note that I never uttered Castaneda's name. He was shown from all angles, with his mouth covered in blood and hurling the vilest profanities. I was content to have called him the mastermind behind the murder. I didn't know for what political reasons N'Zo Nikiema had not yet decided whether it was good that Castaneda appeared in the video. It was ridiculous but it also showed that politics had nothing to do in a world governed by the five senses of ordinary people. For now, the real question was, who had made this film? Each of us knew that this was the type of person who could blow up the country. There was no question of letting him live. There were episodes like this in a country's history that one might find peculiar: a girl is killed and it leads to a series of assassinations planned in high places with a kind of relentless logic that make it absolutely necessary. The question that plagues us during this time is not about respect for human life. It is whether everyone agrees that the following day the sun will be rising in the east again, as always.

Within our small gathering, nobody really liked the invisible cameraman. I was responsible for finding him and killing him off. That was quick. As for the overly talkative prisoner, we encouraged him to escape. He was made to believe it was an order from his chief. He rushed toward the center of Maren driving a car that he stole in

43

front of the prison. He got onto a one-way street, honking like crazy, causing a spate of accidents and agitating the peaceful citizens. Our elite snipers were dispatched and they shot him right down. It all happened at the peak of broad daylight. Nobody could suspect that we had mounted this operation. It was clean work.

But we had seen nothing yet.

The Kaveena affair was the start of the first serious rupture between N'Zo Nikiema and Pierre Castaneda. They had fought over small things without any real consequence. With this crime, the distrust had been sown for good. If we look at everything that came after, it can be argued that Kaveena's death cost us a bloody civil war. Also, when it erupted, neither of the two friends was caught unawares: the troops had been deployed to war for nearly two years. Two years during which Pierre Castaneda felt very lonely. Every morning, the newspapers reminded him of his foreign origins. Owner of the largest mining company in the country and Nikiema's mentor, he was described as a lingering colonial, racist and paternalistic. A private radio station managed by this somewhat crazy guy had organized a quiz about who plotted Kaveena's murder. The correct answer was one of the following three: someone who's been very active in the French mining industry since the colonial period; a myopic shoemaker from Minsk, Belarus; or finally, a bus driver from Yokohama.

There were also articles just about Kaveena. An only child, she was described as an intelligent girl who was full of life. Her father, a young gang leader in Kisito, didn't make much time for her and she had been raised by her grandfather, a modest taxi driver. Completely broken, the man relied on divine justice. Newspapers claimed that she had the best grades in her class. She had never set foot in a school but no one was bold enough—or mean enough—to recall that. It was important for N'Zo Nikiema's enemies to show that Kaveena was gifted. It was a simple idea: as long as the president remained under the negative influence of a foreigner, little girls with beautiful futures ahead of them would be murdered.

Pamphlets from mysterious organizations discussed the video. According to them, you could see Castaneda slitting Kaveena's throat. Castaneda suspected Nikiema of spreading these rumors. Sensing that they would be caught between Nikiema and his mentor, the opponents of the regime decided to turn the knife in the wound. They taunted Nikiema's ego. Would the noble heir to Nimba's throne, not to mention a democratically elected president, always remain an errand boy for Pierre Castaneda? To illustrate this, Castaneda would snap his fingers and President Nikiema would come right away to stand in front of him, nose in the air, tail wagging like a little spaniel. From then on caricatures showed him at the end of a leash held by his master.

Presumably these contrived caricatures were too coarse to be effective. It was also not the first time N'Zo Nikiema had been criticized for being a puppet. But it was only then that the assertion started to exasperate him. If you ask me why, it won't take me too many words to explain: the video of Kaveena's murder. I also found this famous tape stashed away in the basement of the small house. Thanks to this, Nikiema finally believed he could get Castaneda. He didn't want to have him arrested; he wanted to force him into fleeing the country. The government could then nationalize Cogemin, the famous mining company. This was an old dream of Nikiema's and he had never felt so close to its realization.

No one will ever know why N'Zo Nikiema chose to spare Castaneda. Opinions on this issue were mixed. Some said, "Nikiema was misled by the nobility of his soul. He could not shed the blood of a man who had helped him a lot over the years, and who had become a true brother to him." Pan-African humanism, essentially. Others argued the exact opposite. For them, Nikiema believed that humiliating Castaneda would allow him to spare his life but enable Castaneda to escape. What was the truth? I was better informed than most of these discerning analysts. But I confess I didn't have the answer. In fact, the situation seemed to speak for itself. Nikiema had the opportunity to eliminate Castaneda and he did not. He was the leopard propelled in pursuit of a frightened gazelle. But instead of pouncing on his prey, he left it to die slowly from exhaustion.

This is a hypothesis. I am not sure of anything.

Anyway, everyone knows what happened next. What followed were the crowds, which, within only a few months, poured into the streets of Maren and our other major cities chanting, "Casta-ne-da president! Casta-ne-da president!" It was up to the former head of Cogemin to take power or stay put, the elders announced over our heads. He was wise enough not to push his advantage beyond what was reasonable. I saw the winner of the civil war hesitate for weeks in deciding among the many candidates who might succeed Nikiema. Ultimately he zeroed in on Mwanke, who didn't seem like a bad choice to me—from a purely technical point of view. It's hard to see the new president trying to be under Castaneda's thumb. Mwanke doesn't like these stories, and having an official photo taken with the president-general is enough to keep him happy. It must also be said that except for the short time that he was the improvised captain of the ghost army for national liberation, Mwanke remained throughout his life in the service of Castaneda. He had even been his night watchman and then was promoted, with dedication but not without difficulty, to the position of his private secretary. Well isn't that convenient, a puppet used to long night vigils. While President Mwanke snored like a fool all day, Castaneda took the country. At night, Mwanke, obviously an insomniac, brought girls to his palace and watched porn with them all night, emptying bottles of whiskey, beer, and gin. Mwanke was kind of a clumsy giant—each of his legs could carry two or three of his drinking companions, and the ones he chose were always weak and full of endless crap.

During these years in the small house, N'Zo Nikiema found a thousand and one ways to tell her one thing: Mumbi, I am innocent. Appearances were not in his favor. Nor were the rumors. Nor were his other crimes, real as they were. It's true: he had never intended

46

to build his career on the nobility of sentiment and things like that. No one rises to the top just by reciting God's Ten Commandments by heart. It has never been the case anywhere on man's earth.

But the words . . . the words formed in his head and swirled around ad infinitum. The words, like the palace goldfish in their bowl. He sometimes looked at them and thought: an imitation ocean. An ocean with glass walls. Little rocks made of rubber in ghastly colors. You give me a good laugh, you. But even though trapped in his throat, these words sometimes escaped from him in the middle of the night. Mumbi just could not hear them. No doubt he was afraid of her. She looked at him with contempt and his heart froze with shame. Often, there in his palace, Mumbi's image loomed over him. This could happen at any time of the day, during a meeting with the unshaven and arrogant emissaries of the World Bank or on some other occasion. He believed he saw her nod gently with a contemptuous smile on her lips: So this is why you killed my little Kaveena, to shit in your pants in front of these foreigners, just for this, to sell off this country, and now that Kaveena is dead, there is death everywhere, on the roads and at the foot of the mountains.

He had a strong urge to tell her the truth then. He finally felt he had the strength to do so. But not a word left his mouth.

—m—

You can do whatever you want with these letters. Maybe tear them up. Maybe not even read them. It doesn't matter. I don't feel any shame in telling you what everyone knows.

Yes, I have blood on my hands. And now? The people I killed will not torment me. Frankly, I don't even remember them anymore. It was almost a game—all about winning or losing. But wait, don't get me wrong here: in this world, even to lose one round is to die like a dog, with your mouth open. I did what I could to stay alive. Often while reading the newspapers I felt that I was responsible for all suffering not only in my country but of our entire time. Maybe I don't deserve so much credit. But I do have staunch enemies: when they capture their prey, they don't hand it over.

I know that you know. Our future has already been determined very far from here and in our absence.

I imagine them sitting around a table one morning. In an office of one of their government departments, don't know which one. Whatever. It's cold, the street is gray and humid, and their faces are dead. Nearby, the old folks play pool. Pierre Castaneda is there, no doubt. He is among those whose names are hardly remembered in History. They are not very talkative. However, you find them at the core of all the big decisions. For some years I was his friend and the only black employee at Cogemin—the powerful mining company. On returning from one of his trips, Pierre Castaneda seemed very happy to announce some good news. It wasn't everybody who returned from a trip and told a friend, almost in a joking tone, "My brave fellow, the time of independence is here for your country and, shhh . . . don't tell anyone, hmm, hmm." Muttering, winking, little confidential bits.

I knew enough to realize what I should do. Colonialism had decided to let itself die. So I created a fiercely anticolonialist party. Good old Pierre Castaneda did not spare me his support. Everything went pretty well. There were so many who wanted this, this job as the Enlightened Guide of the nation. And Pierre and his friends rooted for me. As simple as that. Only morons imagine it happens otherwise. I certainly didn't miss the support of some of my rivals in this, either. We tried, on the basis of my speeches, which were often truly incendiary, to pass ourselves off as anti-white. But this country is Cogemin before it's anything else. Pierre calmed everyone down by offering good explanations. And after a few bloody fights against Communist guerrillas, I became president of the republic.

Maybe you're too young to know how it happened in all the countries formerly occupied by France. I wouldn't say this has been hidden from your generation, but nobody tells you about it, which is the same thing. A shame. There was a ceremony on July 14, 1959, at the Place de la Concorde. Cheikh Anta Diop is indignant about it in one of his books. General de Gaulle shook hands with each of us, gave us a little flag, and said something like this: "My dear men, I hand over your land to you in good condition. Take good care of it. Farewell and see you soon." Do the servile ones merely grumble distractedly about the end of centuries of cruelty? We were not stupid enough to take this seriously. In fact, in our hearts, it was such a sham. The less cynical ones believed there was perhaps a small opportunity. But they were naive. Everyone knows how these things happen. They open the door for you, screw your ass on the soft armchair of a black president, and then immediately close the door behind you. You're clearly a puppet. You are now not aware of anything. If you're lucky enough to love whiskey, cola nuts, porn films, and all that goes with it, like that idiot Mwanke, then your days are fulfilled and you don't feel the passage of time.

At that time, we didn't pay much attention to appearances: Castaneda was both my advisor and the ambassador to France who was feared elsewhere. He also kept an office at Cogemin, where, to tell you the truth, he went less and less. Alleged patriots treated me like a collaborator, a henchman of Jacques Foccart, and there had been kidnappings and bombings, young people went underground, and believe me, Pierre took security into his own hands. I think this is also where, incidentally, he learned to wage war. He had a heavy hand, so to speak. You've heard of the Warela and Mirindu massacres. Thousands dead in three days. A colossal devastation! I am not one with a tender heart but I was really horrified. Cogemin brought mercenaries from everywhere, especially from South Africa, Rhodesia, and Central Europe. They had a peculiar title: "operating instructors"! In fact, they commanded the troops on the ground. Pierre Castaneda and his military subordinates saw my emotional state. They did not like wimps. They told me, "This is a fucking war, my friend, what do you think, you gotta do what you gotta do." I understood them. They meant, if you keep whining we'll fuck you in the ass pretty fast with a coup.

Pierre Castaneda wrote me a good speech and I read it. I remember this colorful phrase that he had been so proud to put into my mouth: "In the Warela and Mirindu neighborhoods, we have managed to crush the serpent's head with a glowing stone. The evil beast will not be rising anytime soon." I remember this phrase because Castaneda had had a hard time giving it shape. First he'd tried "burning stone," and then after reading it aloud, he decided, "No, it's too emphatic—it will be more powerful if it's said simply: 'We have crushed the serpent's head.' You have to take a deep breath and then let it out forcefully." And then at the last minute, he changed his mind once again and came back to, "We have crushed the serpent's head with a glowing stone." That day he said to me, "Words are what drive the world. Don't ever forget that, boy. People want words, and the less they understand them, the more effective they are." Castaneda had a protective side, in a boxing-coach kind of way, where he was rude and paternal in order to push his disciple to give it his very best. These vanities of Castaneda's could also be surprising since he mainly had the reputation of a fighter. In reality, it was a complex from not having had a real education. But that's another story and I'll get back to it when it's time.

Today, I really want to tell you about my first big fight with Pierre Castaneda. It was in March 1963, shortly after the carnage in Warela.

—◊◊◊—

N'Zo Nikiema stopped writing and gazed into an empty void. I guess he was seeing yours truly, a few years earlier, in his office. I wasn't yet Colonel Kroma. I was training as a young sergeant in our army and I had just pointed out the elite army unit in Warela to my boss.

That Monday morning around eleven o'clock, a man asked me to let him see President Nikiema urgently. He didn't want to speak to anyone but the president. The guy was tough and not easy to intimidate. He kept repeating, "Get me a meeting with the president or I'm out of here." He was confident and I believed he had an important message for the head of state. When I informed the latter about it, he asked me, "What does he look like?"

I might have been a novice in my duties as assistant to Security but I wasn't stupid. In the presidential palace, everyone spoke through allusions. The true meaning of the question had not escaped me. "We searched him, Mr. President," I replied.

He received the man, who told him some sensational news. The leader of the rebellion, Abel Murigande, better known as Com-

mander Nestor, had decided to disarm. Murigande was a tough opponent, the kind you were obliged to respect while dreaming every
night of cutting him into little pieces.

Soon after the emissary had left, Nikiema went to find Pierre Castaneda. Commander Nestor's police file was there, right in front
of his eyes. Let's be clear: I'm not trying to make you believe that
Castaneda thought of Abel Murigande night and day. It so happened
that the day he was looking at the picture of the guerrilla leader in
silence, Nikiema tiptoed into his office as if he were trying to trick
him. When Castaneda saw him, he quickly closed the brown work-
book. Nikiema smiled to ease his friend's embarrassment. Neither
needed to open his mouth to understand the other. He had long
been aware of Castaneda's fascination with Abel Murigande, a.k.a.
Commander Nestor.

"I was looking at the photo of public enemy number one," he offered sheepishly.

"A fault confessed is half forgiven," replied N'Zo Nikiema, dropping onto the couch in the parlor office.

"A coffee, Your Excellency?" Castaneda said in his usual tone of
derision.

"Thank you. I'll make one myself."

Nikiema took the coffee machine off the shelf. He liked the name
of this machine, Fonzetta, and it had been given to Castaneda by
his ambassador to Italy. Using it required a series of complex and
almost absurd maneuvers. Nikiema, for example, found it amusing
to have to hold it upside down for at least three minutes while it filled
up with boiling water. When ready, the drink was delicious. As he
cleaned the filter, he felt Pierre Castaneda's gaze burrow deeply into
his neck. He turned to him and said with studied closeness, "Hey, I
have some news, bro."

"I guessed that as soon as you came in."

"Yes," offered Nikiema in a tone of mockery and complicity. Centuries of dirty tricks there. . . . At the end of the day, they knew each
other at the deepest level.

"Come on, let it out or I'll shoot it out of you."

"Our Commander Nestor is ending it all."

"All . . . what, all? Who?" Pierre Castaneda stroked his chin and stared intensely as he asked this question.

N'Zo Nikiema said again, taking his time, "He's stopping the fighting. No more guerrilla attacks."

Pierre Castaneda remained pensive and N'Zo Nikiema saw his face darken. No doubt dozens of images were flashing through Castaneda's mind for those few seconds, and N'Zo Nikiema wasn't sure why, but they avoided looking at each other. It was one of those fleeting moments where each of them felt the nakedness of his soul, one of those moments where you cannot lie to yourself. It's true that they had no reason to be proud of their long struggle against the guerrilla leader. Nothing could bend Abel Murigande. This showed them the futility of their power.

Commander Nestor's decision to disarm completely changed the political situation in the country. Pierre Castaneda could not help but ask N'Zo Nikiema all kinds of questions. Despite the occasional mocking tone of his friend, the latter was aware of Castaneda's tension and bafflement. Evidently, he found it hard to believe that a stranger had come to N'Zo Nikiema, just like that, to declare, "Commander Nestor sends me to tell you that the guerrilla stuff is over."

Maybe there had been secret negotiations that no one had known of. None of this boded well.

—⁂—

Do you remember the night I told you about Abel Murigande, a.k.a. Commander Nestor? We were sitting in the living room where I now find myself alone. I believe I told you everything. I wanted to, anyway. That night, I was haunted by the ghost of Abel Murigande. Maybe because I was completely drunk?

Abel was a childhood friend. He meant more to me than his armed rebellion against the state. He was, first of all, a very tough trade unionist. But, for example, when he came to the palace with his comrades to negotiate the end of the strike, we kept our distance for several long minutes. People had become accustomed to seeing us laughing, stirring up memories of our youth in Nimba. Nobody dared to approach us. The truth is, we didn't need to isolate ourselves. We had too many things that bound us which excluded everyone else. If we wanted, we could speak in public without being understood by anyone. It never occurred to me that this man could be bought. He was truly incorruptible. Such villainy would have surely erased our childhood. When I first got the information about the liberation army that he was trying to put together, I told my wife Salima, "This is it, our Abel is about to get involved in some real bullshit." Salima remained silent. Abel had seen her grow up and she had a lot of respect for him. By then, the Mother of the Nation had allowed her mind to be completely taken over by God, so to speak. At least, that's what she claimed, because finally . . . anyway, forget it. I thought I heard the hypocritical woman mutter something about the coming of the Lord of the Worlds.

In truth, Abel Murigande's surrender was proof of his lucidity. He couldn't win and he knew it. Castaneda had managed to infiltrate his headquarters in the bush and turn several of Murigande's lieutenants against him. With our mercenaries, known as "operating instructors," who were actually the real war junkies, we had caused a lot of damage. Three hundred thousand were dead since our arrival. Your generation tends to forget this: the first decade after independence in Africa was terrible. All these independences were like clockwork—every time people like Um Nyobé, Lumumba, or others like them tried to disturb the symphony, there were large-scale massacres like here, in Bamileke country, and elsewhere. I don't need to tell you about Algeria. Don't ever forget: the colonizer has killed far more people while exiting Africa than while conquering it. It has to be said that leading the country during this time must not have been too difficult. Times have changed.

Today, they have these tribunals for trying former presidents, with slimy little lawyers putting their noses in photos of mass graves and mockingly asking, "And this one, sir, do you remember it or not?" It's all one big circus. In the sixties, Castaneda and I were quieter in our small operations. And by the way, Mumbi, let me confess: whenever I try to understand the causes of my defeat, it occurs to me that I was not perceptive of the mutations in time. I stayed in power too long and I did not take into account that everyone had become a little more conniving. Ultimately, this is what got me. I didn't see it coming that there would be a time when police interviewing a journalist would be an alleged crime against human rights. Such beautiful hypocrisy, right?

Commander Nestor didn't have the opportunity to be heard in Europe and America. A nasty Communist—you'd think that no one wanted to listen to him. Basically, he saw that we were the strongest. Go, surrender, it was the only way for him to save whatever he still could. In the days following the announcement, I saw Peter Castaneda at the height of his excitement. Commander Nestor was a myth. His death had been announced and denied several times. I know it's not good to simplify but I'd still like to tell you: Commander Nestor was the spirit of our people's resistance. He was someone who had gone head to head with a regime that was completely at the beck and call of the special services of a foreign country, people like Foccart and Co. For Pierre Castaneda, his surrender was a personal triumph.

In response to Commander Nestor's message, I announced a call for national reconciliation. I personally went to welcome Murigande and his small group on the right bank of the Saasun. As soon as he got out of his dugout and walked toward me, it all became clear: Abel was dying. He was dying and wanted to be buried in his homeland when the time came. His eyes were filled with a fierce pride! Even Pierre Castaneda, who found our friendship annoying and who had no restraint in such situations, did not dare to join us. I glanced at him from afar and he seemed to have a furtive manner, like a jealous, sulking woman.

Taking Murigande in my arms, I promised to take care of him. I was amazed at how sad I felt. It was impossible for anyone, even Pierre Castaneda, to despise Abel; he would never have surrendered out of cowardice. I felt that it was almost unfortunate that he had not been killed in battle with weapons in his hands. Due to our shared memories, I owed him an end that was not too bitter. There was no question about letting him suffer. I also thought about taking a little trip to Nimba with him.

I wanted to hand him over to his parents and cheerfully declare, "Abel wanted all this bullshit, but now it's a done deal." The African way! We would have all laughed and drunk beer.

But the next day, one of my French advisors said to me, "The poor bastard!" I don't know why but I was immediately sure he meant Murigande. I could sense from a certain expression in his eyes that he was only speaking of Murigande. The Whites had decided to make him pay for ten years' worth of their fears, during which from his underground hold in the Haut-Danande, he had defied them as they intended to make our independence their only business. They had no reason to kill Murigande. Yet there was something that remained within them, and it was a good deal stronger than their political considerations: hatred against the Negro who dared to stand up to them.

I asked my advisor, "What's happening, my dear Jean-Sebastien? You look really happy this morning!" This is how I spoke to these people, without any airs. I didn't play the president with them. They would have had a good laugh at that!

"Oh, nothing important," said Jean-Sebastien. "I'm just thinking of a naughty little bird. He's warming up for his turn, heh heh!"

I said, "Commander Nestor, you mean?" Jean-Sebastien then launched into a spiteful diatribe, the kind of thing where he asked what kind of world was this where even the Africans are involved in guerrilla warfare—they have to be pretty organized, even to make a fucking mess! He kept guffawing and alluded to Che Guevara, who had taken a lot of risks, like Tintin, in the jungles of Congo. But even he had quickly taken to his heels because the Congolese are all about multiplying their brothels and it's a matter of national pride. A bearded Argentine was not going to be teaching them to fornicate and drink and belch and fart the whole goddamn day.

I couldn't listen to the young Jean-Sebastien any longer. I already regretted having accepted Murigande's surrender. Basically, I'd created this bullshit. Abel. They were going to kill Abel. It was very clear. And when they did, with a refined cruelty that appalled the world—foreign newspapers have reported everything in detail—I was supposed to take the blame. Don't believe me if you don't want to, Mumbi Awele, but I really thought about rebelling that time. I barricaded myself in my office and started to drink like I never have in my life. The phone rang every minute. It was them. "Mr. President," "Your Excellency." . . . They spoke in smooth, round words in voices suddenly filled with respect, you know, the lousy little show they put on to make you feel like you're an important Negro, and each time I would scream, "Shit and some more shit!" before hanging up. I said this to everyone, even Castaneda. They could make me jump through hoops, and the country with me, but I didn't care. They let the storm pass, the crafty little bastards.

Then Pierre Castaneda entered with a serious and resolute air. He barely opened his mouth. When he entered and sat in front of me, the shadows from the past rose up before us. Especially that of Prieto da Souza—I'll tell you about him one day. Prieto da Souza was our first real crime. My rebellion was not only ridiculous; it was almost comical. At no point did Pierre Castaneda say to me, "The affairs of the state are serious, and not because you ate attiéké with this guy thirty years ago, but because the country will sink, body and soul." He didn't have to say anything but I understood perfectly. The next day, Pierre wrote my best "Address to the Nation." Commander Nestor, I said in a loud, serene voice, had wanted to make us let our guard down with his fake surrender. I talked about the weapons we found in secret places and about the small groups of supporters with experience in guerrilla warfare who had already infiltrated the population. Everyone was invited to report on suspicious activity to defend the freedom that had been snatched away as the price of the suffering meted out by yesterday's settlers.

I won't try to make you believe that my lies made me feel shame or remorse. No, Mumbi, I felt good about myself. Maybe there were a couple of seconds, because of the peculiar effect of autosuggestion, that I thought Murigande had the kind of plan that could only emerge from the sick mind of Pierre Castaneda, where, seizing the palace with his gangsters, he would then exhibit my remains on the crazed city streets. It was strange. The more I lied, the more I felt my hatred for Abel Murigande grow. He wanted to fool us. During my speech when I used the expression "two can play at this game" with a knowing smile, I wasn't joking at all. Basically, I didn't care about Abel Murigande. After all, he had chosen to take sides with the eternal losers in his politics. If he had managed to bring me down, he would have probably felt some sadness, like me, but his comrades would not have allowed him to go further than that. They would have said, "OK, you have cried for your childhood friend, your little squirrel stew in Nimba was good, but the revolution, my friend, is not about personal feelings." That is how things happen in the real political world; it's just terrible.

But I do owe you a confession: my only problem was Miranda, Murigande's widow. As I insulted the memory of her husband, her image appeared before my eyes. Continuing to speak in a firm voice, the voice of the merciless man of the state, I was saying to myself, "But what does Miranda think of all this?" Like me, did she think about the time when, barely out of adolescence, Murigande and I came to court her? She was not much older than a kid at that time. Miranda. The typical wife of a hero of the people, the kind who is dedicated to martyrdom. We had obviously stopped seeing each other but I sometimes thought about her, and I told myself that funnily, she had been caught in the trap of History. When Abel was trying to hit on her, we would often visit her parents. She would serve us banana beer before making us maafe or squirrel stew. Then the years passed. Abel went underground and it became too hard for Miranda, monitored day and night by my police. She eventually took refuge in Tanzania. There, Nyerere took care of her and made sure she was left in peace. He was a remarkable man, Mwalimu Nyerere, and I want you to know how much I admire him. But agitators from all the countries wanted to turn Miranda into a pasionaria, a kind of Winnie Mandela before the type existed, marching at the front of a crowd, fist in the sky. It was all in vain. This simply could not work. She did not know what to say to these bearded, hysterical people. In the newspapers, photos showed a humble woman, overwhelmed by events.

I also want to tell you this: Commander Nestor's execution earned me Castaneda's final trust. I was a little angry, but in hindsight he found this moment of madness rather sympathetic and reassuring. I must say that Pierre Castaneda had taken this matter to heart. For him, it was a kind of singular struggle. Commander Nestor was already in agony. Castaneda had beaten him, punctured his eyes, and after tying him up in a jute sack, thrown him to the sharks from a helicopter. I had heard about the rest of it. It seemed that while the plane was flying over the ocean, Castaneda had continued to insult Commander Nestor and kept describing the torture that awaited him. Abel was still conscious and talked back to him defiantly. Blood flowed from the bag, and I was proud to learn that Murigande had enough strength not to moan or beg for Pierre Castaneda's pity.

The thing that seems a little crazy to me in all this is that at one point, I was pretty sure I had killed Abel with my own hands. And I was convinced that Pierre Castaneda believed, in all honesty, that he had never been involved one way or another in Murigande's atrocious end. Maybe he had even written a letter to his relatives in Haute-Savoie lamenting all the unnecessary bloodshed: "My African friends, they are always bickering among each other. We keep trying but it's all in vain. . . . Even I, Pierre Castaneda, cannot stop this sea of blood on my own." What a nice little shithead! In any case, from then on I was ripe for the dirtiest jobs. Commander Nestor was dead and it was time to profit from the spoils. Pierre and I didn't always have the same enemies. We left each other alone by tacit agreement. Those were the good years: all we had to do was accuse someone of being secretly affiliated with Murigande and he would be liquidated without the chatter of the young lawyers who we now have here for the trial. When I was drunk, which was often the case, I pretended to punish my own people to let Pierre Castaneda go free—the foreigner, the torturer and murderer of Murigande, my childhood friend.

I rarely killed for pleasure. But Castaneda and I were sometimes given to the vertigo of omnipotence. We worked out our personal business along the way. It was petty but inevitable.

Every newspaper in the world started to call me a psychopath. A bad reputation, no matter what.

—⁓—

N'Zo Nikiema saw the crowd gathered along July 21 Boulevard. Some people led the procession shouting, "Ni-kie-ma, murderer! Ni-kie-ma, murderer!" Others shouted, "Casta-ne-da president! Casta-ne-da president!" But overall, tens of thousands of people from unions and political parties marched peacefully. When they arrived in front of the gates of the palace, one of the leaders, with a white bandanna around his head, walked up to the balcony with a megaphone: "N'Zo Nikiema, come out of your palace if you're a man! Murderer, get out!" He shouted these words mockingly and— at least in the leader's memory—without any wickedness, and they were met with laughter and cheers of joy.

The serenity and smiling congeniality of these family men contrasted with the tension in the country. In spite of these appearances, we headed straight for civil war. When it came to my services, there was no longer any doubt: my work was merely to inform President Nikiema, and I did. As far as I could judge, the opposing camp, that of Castaneda, was better prepared. Castaneda felt he was ready for the clash, and with all sorts of instigations he laid the groundwork for lighting the house on fire.

On the eve of the march, someone on the radio promised to plant Nikiema's skull on "the pointed and flamboyant bayonets of freedom." Nikiema immediately recognized the voice of one of his most zealous admirers, a young poet now eager to dedicate his verses to the service of Castaneda. Although he was far from believing that he had been defeated, Nikiema could not banish the images from his mind, the images he had often seen on television during the last three years. Classic scenario: After more or less spontaneous riots, protesters force open the palace gates. The bloody tyrant flees by helicopter and his giant bronze statue in the center of the city is toppled amid the pandemonium. The actual *historical* sequence only lasts a few seconds. It begins the moment the statue wavers under the hammer and ends when the dictator's bronze nose touches the very ground that has been bloodied by his unspeakable crimes. If the cameras unfortunately miss this sequence, then everything has to start up again: strikes, marches, popular uprising, the poet's hymns to the rebellion, flowers thrown at intimidated and radiant soldiers, and the demolition of the statue—on horseback or not, marble or bronze—of the dictator. This is the only moment of interest—a counterpoint to lavish swearing-in ceremonies—and no TV in the world wants to miss that. Nor do parents. They go to the show with their children and later they declare proudly, "I was there too—I was six years old when N'Zo Nikiema the Tyrant was overthrown, and that day, sitting on my dad's shoulders, I truly understood the meaning of the word 'freedom.'" And in some tarnished town in Kisito, a fanatic will beat his breast and boast at one time or another, "Yes, young man, you have before you one of the real heroes who defeated N'Zo Nikiema! I was the one who took that first shot at Freedom Square that morning!"

"History repeats itself, every time," Nikiema declared in a low voice, almost in a bad mood. He remembered the end of Almamy Samory Touré. Shortly before being deported to the Missanga Forest in Gabon, Samory was led by the poor Whites of the colony at the end of a rope through the streets of Saint-Louis in Senegal. The crowd on the sidewalks laughed as he passed them and flung banana peels at him. They treated him like a monkey and a warrior Negro, and the women of the city came out in large numbers to jeer at him and mock him to his face. "Well, here he is, the savage who wanted to shake our empire, don't you doubt it," they spat in French, and also, it won't surprise anyone, in Wolof too, because the Negroes there, those from Senegal, were already "children of the Fatherland" and company. What struck Nikiema the most, and what he found difficult to cope with, was the joy of the populace. Almamy Samory Touré was not even worth their hatred—no one cursed him angrily. They just found his many battles against foreign forces amusing. His victories in Bouna against Monteil, and in Bouré against Combes, and with Henderson and the English in Dokita, weren't worth anything. All that remained of this great epic was a Negro tied to a rope in an old French city in Africa. Nikiema tried to get inside Almamy's head: what wouldn't he have given, Fama, to hear at that moment at least one cry of hatred before going into exile in Missanga the next day? N'Zo Nikiema also wondered if Almamy had gone to Gabon aboard the *Bou El Mogdad* or some other boat. For some peculiar reason, this suddenly seemed of great importance to him and he promised to consult the history books in the basement.

He had already circled the room several times, ruminating on these dark thoughts. Throughout the house, there were portraits of little Kaveena drawn by Mumbi. He stopped at a sketch but hardly saw the smiling face of the girl. His mind was elsewhere. And what if his hiding place was unfortunately discovered? He would never agree to get out alive from the small house. He would never fall into the hands of his enemies. He would not walk, tied to the end of a rope, through the streets of Maren. He had shaken up that bastard. He had killed; he should not be afraid of dying.

—∞—

As for Kaveena, it wasn't me. I did not kill your daughter. You reprimanded me one day for not letting the investigators do their work. How furious you were that night! For a few moments, I toyed with the idea that you were going to stab me in the heart with a kitchen knife. Yes, I covered up the Kaveena case. It doesn't cost me anything to admit it to you now. What I've learned in politics is that, in the end, only your worst enemies can really understand you. Anyway, they are often the only ones with whom there are common memories and shared emotions, being men of the same world, far from the clamor of militants. Ordinary people like you, you imagine naively that there are good people and bad people. You go to bed at night and you wake up in the morning with the idea that such-and-such regime kills and tortures and that seeing this, others want to put an end to those horrors. Well, know this: the others who see it, they want to put an end to the regime, yes, but not to the fact that one kills people and all that. They stand by their noble positions, and they themselves end up believing that they are troubled by I don't know which grave human rights violations, and if you ever get hung up on it, you're ruined. We are all villains and we know it.

61

Their Independent Investigation Commission, for example, was a bad farce. If I had left those experts to do their work properly, they would have no doubt discovered the truth. There is so much damning proof. That imbecile Pierre Castaneda behaved like an amateur. I have the video. In it, he talks about the place where the little girl's skull must be buried and about the other place, under a kapok tree to be exact, where the left leg had to be put, etc. "And the heart, where'd you put it, man? The heart of a little girl is the symbol of eternal innocence. My enemies will have to come face to face with my purity. Their blows will never reach me again." Pierre Castaneda had gone mad. All those stories about having to bury the victim at the four cardinal points make me vomit. The guy admits to Castaneda that he raped the little girl before killing her and he laughs as he says, "Well, yes, in any case, she was going to die, so why get upset, eh, my good man?" And you know what? He adds, "I hope you liked it, at least!" Bawdy jokes between the guys, you know.

You are shocked, Mumbi, you think that I shouldn't tell you that? Well, yes, I should: I don't have any other choice than to tell you all that. And if we see each other again, I will show you this cassette. And you will see this: after a moment of reflection when you believe he's going to succumb to remorse, Castaneda pulls himself together, shakes his head, and declares, "Yeah, it's not pretty, but what's done is done and anyway you've got to consider that she didn't even have time to realize what was happening, the poor thing." It's a totally vile document. It's right here, the film! I have it with me here! Pierre Castaneda, son of the Age of Reason, champion of the democratic freedoms in its great works . . . Pierre Castaneda knows that I ran off with the cassette. That's why he did everything he could to rally Colonel Kroma's support. As long as I live, that man will not be left in peace. But at the time, did you see me bringing Pierre Castaneda to justice? This country would have been ransacked and pillaged. Is that what we wanted? It's true the country did not escape ransacking and pillaging. That was no reason, though, to have to put up with the chaos sooner than was expected.

—∞—

I try to imagine N'Zo Nikiema's first days in the small house. It's not hard: the fugitive left clues, and all it takes is a little patience to transmute them into words. And besides, when you really think about it, that's all I've ever done my whole life. True, I'm missing a good part of my usual material: the tips from our informants and the confessions yelled out by the tortured victims in the Satellite basement. But I'm managing very well with what I've got on hand.

Here's, roughly, what must have happened. N'Zo Nikiema had just escaped from the palace. His partisans were hunted down. I had drawn up the list of them myself. Castaneda added some names and crossed off others. Then he told me, "OK, Asante, you can go right ahead." At this terrible hour when Nikiema's regime was crumbling to pieces, Castaneda addressed me in a familiar tone and was on a first-name basis with me. These signs were not misleading. I knew that I had to act quickly: soon it was going to be peacetime and it would be more difficult to finish off all those men under Nikiema.

As for the latter, we were looking for him everywhere. His head had a price on it. In addition to being furious about having been taken in like a real greenhorn, Pierre Castaneda feared seeing his good white name sullied forever. I could read the anguish in his eyes. It was true; the video of Kaveena's murder was a bomb that N'Zo Nikiema held in his hands. Pierre Castaneda was behaving like a real jackal.

During this time, the war didn't manage to end completely. Some soldiers pretended that they were still fighting. There weren't very many and the pockets of resistance were cleaned up one after the other. In spite of everything, it was a mess. What's more, Castaneda was beginning to wonder whether it wouldn't be safer to give these killjoys a little piece of the national cake.

All of that seemed to be happening in a time and a world that did not concern the fugitive.

As was the case every morning at dawn, he was content to stand at the window, contemplating the deserted boulevard. His mind was empty, and a minute earlier, passing in front of one of the small house's windows, he saw an absent look on his reflected face. The sky above Jinkoré slowly cleared. Kids set out on their old mopeds putt-putting through the streets of Maren; they sped straight ahead, crouching down over their handlebars at the turns, as they'd seen in the movies, and let shots ring out through the air. What did these young soldiers do with their nights? He thought, Castaneda likes to boast about their bravery and he proudly calls them "my Lil Boys." They are said to be disciplined enough in combat. They're also very cruel.

Across from him, three-quarters of the houses were nothing but a mass of stones and rubble. Some rats fled from a truck transporting troops. The truck was part of the convoy stopped dead several days ago by shooters lying in ambush in the ruins. The soldiers of its army—the "loyalists," as they were called—hadn't had the time to counterattack. Cleared out by Castaneda's Lil Boys' bursts of machine gun fire. N'Zo Nikiema had seen his soldiers peel themselves off the ground, whirl between the trees like dead leaves, then come back and crash to the ground, and he'd had the impression that this was a game and that he was sitting in the front row at the Theatre Doura Mané, Maren's largest hall. The gunfire ceased abruptly and after several minutes N'Zo Nikiema saw an officer come out of his hiding place, looking worried and waving a white flag. He was looking all around him, terrorized. He wanted to give himself up and seemed to be wondering if it was really a good idea. The Lil Boys quickly put an end to his doubts. It was as if the kids had sprung out from everywhere, and Nikiema's heart began pounding very hard. At such moments, we all want—without daring to admit it—for something to happen, and sometimes the more bloody it is, the happier we are. The Lil Boys could see very well how afraid the guy was. And all they had done was to circle around him grimacing and crying out like Cherokees on the battlefield. One of them had stuck a dagger in the guy's abdomen and he had fallen forward, saying things that N'Zo Nikiema couldn't hear. Anyway, it had to have been very funny, because the kids were laughing nonstop. They laughed, stamping the ground with their feet and holding their stomachs.

Once the guy's body had stopped wriggling, the Lil Boys started rifling through his pockets. One of them, young but hefty, had put on his uniform. One of his comrades gave him a manly thumbs-up, meaning, it's a little broad in the shoulders but fine, it'll do, my man.

Seeing this officer, N'Zo Nikiema had shaken his head resentfully. The uncommissioned officer had waited for all his men to be killed before coming out of hiding. There was nothing surprising about his army's retreat. N'Zo Nikiema felt a deafening rage rise up in him.

———

He was potbellied like a character in a comic book, grotesque, with frightful eyes. A coward. He was definitely one of those guys they made me name an officer. They all wanted to be generals or colonels, well decorated with yellow or red epaulettes, long shiny ribbons, and black mustaches, and well built, as if all of this were distributed to them in their army stores. "Colonel." "General." Two magical words which, when there was a dearth of enemies, served the purpose of breaking the hearts of little bitches and middle-aged broads burned by their last affair. I resisted as long as I could. But you know, Mumbi, in the end, you've had enough. Everyone joins in, the Mother of the Nation as they call her, your childhood friends, everyone, they don't give you a minute of respite and you say to yourself, OK, the days are short and I need a little rest too. If I don't make this guy a superior officer, the sky's going to fall on our heads. I'll never be able to live in peace, and plus, it doesn't cost me anything. Mistake. Because when the war arrives, like now, those guys who wanted to be generals are no longer there anymore. Since the Sereti barracks were attacked, which marked the beginning of the civil war, all those tin-soldier officers understood that it was going to be hard, that Castaneda's Lil Boys were going to cut open their prisoners' flesh, and they all got rid of their beautiful uniforms.

Today I'm almost happy to no longer have to determine my fellow citizens' lives for them. I have no more explanations to offer to anyone, and in this semiprison, I feel lighter, freer.

He thought about those palace meetings with the general staff once again, always angrily. Surrounded by generals all talking to him with deference, deliberately using words he didn't understand. The typical gobbledygook of military officers in the field. "Strategic depth." "Controlled fire." "Thermal signature." "Pyrophoric decoy." "Our forces are going to evacuate the ten-degree and four-degree north latitude and the ten-degree and zero-degree west longitude."

Nikiema often thought, if your profession isn't to kill your kind en masse, how can you know what all that means? For several months, he contented himself with listening to them and nodding knowingly. After all, he was the supreme leader of the armies. He couldn't, in all decency, send young people to their deaths without knowing what it was he was doing.

Their little game continued this way for weeks or maybe even months. One day, he had enough of them mocking him. During a general meeting, he turned to the deputy chief of the general staff of armies and said to him in an icy tone, "Hey, stop acting like an imbecile. Try saying things simply." Then, addressing the others, he added, "I am no fool, you know."

A deadly silence descended upon the room. Which indicated, for those used to the mysterious place often ironically referred to as the "high level," that it was one of those moments when everyone knows that a major event has just occurred.

In front of those expressionless faces, N'Zo Nikiema was more than a little proud of himself. He felt like the real boss, with all the cards in his hand. None of them dared to speak. In a way, their spinelessness didn't surprise him at all. They had important responsibilities even though they weren't the best at their jobs. Quite the opposite. All that was being asked of them was to serve and be quiet. It was simple: N'Zo Nikiema never claimed to be original in exercising his power. He didn't put up with any rebels around him. Pierre Castaneda taught him what it meant to be a puppet.

After staring each of them down with a glare, he said in a firm tone, "I let the common people call me the Omniscient or the Sun Giant of Mount Nimba. It's good for the work we want to do. All of us around this table want this country to move forward, right? It's good when the people think that the leader has magical powers, that he has dozens of degrees, and that he can conquer the most valiant enemy armies with a single little movement of his chin. But all of you and I know what the situation is, OK?" Then he added, with a brief deafening roar, intoxicated by his own rage, "Is that clear?"

I remember that after this meeting, I was responsible for the surveillance of all our superior officers. None of them seemed to want to mess around. I reported to N'Zo Nikiema. He just gave me a certain look: I understood that I had to bump off the deputy chief of the general staff. It was done. To come up with proof of a scheme isn't difficult. I would even say it's child's play.

—⁓—

I wonder why I'm talking to you about these people. They don't interest you, and you are right. Bastards, from fathers to sons. When I executed that guy under whatever pretext, his wife wanted to play the inconsolable widow. I told her to dry her crocodile tears. She raked in an unbelievable amount from the army uniforms, the detached helicopter pieces, and hey, why not, the officers' black well-trimmed and lustrous mustaches, everything. Billions. With all that, they calm down. And believe me, she calmed down very quickly, the little comrade.

—⁓—

Kaveena's maternal grandfather was, as I've already said, a modest taxi driver. Despite the tumult stirred up by the case and even though he was one of the people primarily involved, he had remained admirably reserved. And if nothing else, N'Zo Nikiema was happy not to be implicated in the murder of the man's granddaughter.

Of course, N'Zo Nikiema was past the age of sound reason. He was not so naive as to believe that men of the people were always dignified and honest. He had known many who were loathsome individuals. But he was forced to admit to himself: old N'Fumbang had known how to show real magnanimity given the circumstances.

We had discreetly offered him more money than he'd ever seen in his whole life. I myself had been responsible for delivering the little suitcase of bills to him. And, I must insist parenthetically to my reader, that's a delicate mission. You are entrusted with ready cash, withdrawn from "political" funds. If you're the nervous type, you can put a good part of it in your pocket without anybody noticing. I, Asante Kroma, can boast that I've never touched a penny of those fat sums.

Anyone in old N'Fumbang's position would have come up with some grandiose reasons for pocketing so many millions. He was content to refuse our offer without causing any scandal. Informed about his attitude, N'Zo Nikiema and Castaneda insisted on knowing if he was in contact with any of their political rivals. The day they called me in to talk to me about it, I saw that a real panic was starting to come over Castaneda. This Kaveena case was his secret wound. My department got right to work. We tailed the man, infiltrated his entourage, and even intimidated his employer. All that got us nothing. Still, Castaneda wanted him eliminated. Just like that. Each time he felt overwhelmed by events, he tried to regain control by taking those kinds of extreme measures. N'Zo Nikiema and I managed to calm him down.

It's worth recalling that the first fissures were already perceptible in the old collaboration between N'Zo Nikiema and Castaneda. As soon as I was alone with Nikiema, he started to denigrate Castaneda. "You see," he said to me, laughing, "if I let him be, he's going to make a martyr of that whole poor family! And of course, the newspapers all over the world are going to vomit their bitterness all over N'Zo Nikiema, the ruthless Negro tyrant!" The president was completely right in a sense. I said to myself that Pierre Castaneda had some nerve trying to make himself come off as the one responsible for respecting human rights in our country. On the other hand, I knew that Nikiema was a crook. I made no comment. When your two bosses get to that point, you simply have to shut it out or pretend to endorse the one who calls upon you as a witness. The important thing is to know who is going to win and to be with him. At any rate, N'Zo Nikiema was mostly just talking to himself.

It remains unknown why he had saved this anonymous taxi driver's life. At the time, I thought it was only to annoy Castaneda, who became very ill at ease as soon as Kaveena's name came up. Now I have enough information to provide an explanation for this indulgence that's a little closer to the facts. It's silly, and for what remains of my friendship with the late president, I would like Mumbi Awele to know it: N'Zo Nikiema was just convinced by N'Fumbang's sincerity. I found some handwritten lines in a notebook where he compares Kaveena's grandfather to Abel Murigande. "Those two," he notes briefly, "have the same spiritual power. One took up arms and died for a noble ideal, and the other for the rest of his life will remain an ordinary man, not even suspecting the high degree of his soul." The tone is perhaps a little too lyrical. That is understandable. Nikiema, lonely and being hunted down, feeling his end was very near, was not able to have a simple connection with the words. It's normal that he let them inflate, at times, to the point of excessiveness.

On the same page, N'Zo Nikiema comes back to the interview N'Fumbang agreed to give to a foreign television network. Remember that this was his only interview, and he literally appeared pious. To throw him off balance, the journalist had pounded him brutally: "The government gave you money, sir, everyone knows it. Is that why you refuse to talk to the press?"

"No, sir. It's not right to talk like that. I didn't get any money."

"But they offered you some, right?"

And N'Fumbang, looking the journalist square in the eyes: "No, sir, they never offered me anything."

In front of his television screen, alone in his office on the first floor of the palace, N'Zo Nikiema had gotten up and screamed in admiration, "Good God, what a man! What a man!"

The memory of that night had an unexpected effect on Nikiema: he felt, for the first time since his adolescence in Nimba, tears forming beneath his eyelids. That emotion didn't last long. He almost suspected he was playing sensitive now that all was lost.

—⁓—

As he came up from the basement, N'Zo Nikiema heard something like a light creaking above his head. Little by little, he had grown accustomed to the cracks of the wood planks in the ceiling and to the noise the snakes made in the tall grass around the house. But this one wasn't at all familiar to his ears. He remained motionless, his senses on alert. It was nothing: two pigeons snorting on the terrace. During those few minutes, he'd only had one idea in his head: if people came to arrest him, he would shoot at them and make them bring him down. He even thought about putting an end to his days. Although, he had trouble imagining shooting himself in the head or, as some bizarrely did, in the mouth. Even knowing he had no way out of his situation, it was impossible for him to consider such an extreme act. He always had real admiration for those who could reconcile themselves to doing it without being betrayed by their trembling hand at the last minute.

It was two o'clock in the afternoon and he had only just woken up. He knew from experience that the rest of the day would be difficult to bear. After his meal—always frugal: canned meat or dried fish, boiled vegetables, and a few fruits—he would have to sit there for hours, invaded bit by bit and then smothered by his past. It was even worse some nights. Not managing to get to sleep, he would toss and turn in his little bed until about eight or nine o'clock in the morning.

He saw a cricket slide between two poufs. He approached it slowly and, holding his breath, started to observe it. Suddenly he had the impression that the creature had just noticed his presence, because it stopped briefly before continuing its walk along the wall. Two little ants were on its path. N'Zo Nikiema caught himself paying extra attention.

70

If we judge by what followed, solitude at times had disastrous effects on N'Zo Nikiema's mind. The fact that the cricket and the two red ants were bound to cross paths seemed to him a unique opportunity, one he hadn't hoped for, to know how exactly such encounters take place in the animal kingdom. So many secret dramas, he thought, a little carried away, happen under humans' noses and they don't even know how to see them. Was the cricket going to eat the ants alive? Or were the ants going to trap him in their pincers or simply harass him until he died of exhaustion—like the gazelle Nikiema was remembering at that very moment? Impatiently, he started to watch for the fatal encounter.

—∞—

People like me like to believe that nature ignores mercy and that the cries of torture victims on our poor earth never reach heaven. The carnage didn't happen and I was a little disappointed. The cricket grazed the two little red points and rushed into a hole. Then, giving in to a sudden impulse, I crushed the ants under my heels. After doing that, I raved out loud a little. The ants were dead because I was there without wanting to be, because there was civil war. After all, I could have been somewhere else right now than in this small house. In New York, for example, pontificating in front of the United Nations General Assembly about strategies for accelerated development. That's been ambling along for centuries; African development, children dying of hunger or in wars and of epidemics. And everyone knows, the biggest problem with people who die is that they never come back to life again—and that's too hard. We can't just stand around with our arms crossed, so we look for solutions and, that's right, in Maren's air-conditioned offices, young economists with their broad foreheads have found the right strategy: to light a fire under development's ass and see how that speeds it up, ha ha. They would have written this speech from hell for me, and over there, in the Manhattan glass building, as the newspapers say, you read the confused words of ambitious counselors in a monotone voice—it's their life's cause, they're going to find you some unpronounceable words from old dictionaries!

And all those people stare at you with their dead fish eyes, not one among them believes even a word of your story, and when you've finished, they get up and give thunderous applause. There are hardly any dirty tie-wearing bastards in the world who actually ask you to save it for another time.

But I wasn't in New York, and the poor ants were two anonymous victims of History, and what's more, they were the only two whom I, supreme leader of an army taking flight, could have prided myself on having put to the sword. . . . Or perhaps the two poor creatures died because you have disappeared too, Mumbi. . . . That there is an infinite chain of causes and effects floating around in every direction which, ultimately, prove my innocence completely, even though my angry hammering kick was, I admit, fully intentional. You see, it's starting to go bad. I'm flying off the rails, so to speak. But with you, I can allow myself to. You're the only person who counts for me now. If I manage to find strong-enough words to convince you that I am not a child murderer, I'll be able to leave in peace. And I will find them, those words. And if you ask me why, I'll answer you quite simply: because I am innocent. Pierre Castaneda is your daughter's murderer.

And then, you became a pain in my ass. If I had killed Kaveena, I would have had good reasons for doing it and I wouldn't have regretted anything. And your father, this N'Fumbang who makes a fuss to us about being an incorruptible man, would have already been long gone to join her in the hereafter. I wasn't the kind to leave someone to hassle the entire country with his pain.

In my time, this country was still well governed.

Wait and see, soon they're going to miss me. I'm telling you.

―✵―

I can easily imagine their encounters in the small house.

N'Zo Nikiema in all his splendor. He comes about once every two weeks to reunite with Mumbi Awele. The young woman welcomes him reluctantly. As soon as the door opens, she stares him down with a hostile look and steps aside as he comes in. After saying a vague hello, she returns to her studio, an inscrutable look on her face. He pays no attention to her, more anxious about whether or not anyone has recognized him around the neighborhood. As she mixes her colors, sets her frames, or draws her sketches with broad strokes, he remains seated in the living room. He feels a certain awkwardness troubling her in the middle of her work. She blames him for it, but N'Zo Nikiema also knows that Mumbi is a deeply kind person. They just have to ride out the storm. She always ends up changing her attitude. While he waits, through the corner of his eye he skims through the dailies he brought with him. Photos of him are on every page. He hates the journalists who insult him and he scorns the rest, his corrupt adulators. It's no life, being a president.

After several minutes, she comes back and offers, "A coffee or something cold? I only have water . . ."

The question itself is a ritual. He feels her relax with the passing minutes. Their conversation, interspersed with long silences, becomes animated, little by little. Both of them are on their guard and she, it seems to him, is brooding endlessly with suppressed anger. One wrong word and she explodes. Kaveena is all around them.

I can add that they almost never talk about themselves. For this, he can only be grateful to her: anyone else would have tried to strip him of his secrets. In every country in the world, people know that their political leaders are lying to them shamelessly and that they— the leaders—are unable to do otherwise. So as soon as an ordinary citizen has you under his finger, he takes advantage of the situation to make you come out with a confession. He also knows just how much power fascinates. Each day he sees nobodies who have no reason to fear him go to pieces in his presence. But this intimate link with President Nikiema does not impress the young woman. She never breaks out of her proud, haughty air. Is it because of the unique circumstances of how they met? There is, too, the murder of her daughter. She seems to be saying to him, all this smooth talking is pointless; you are a child murderer.

Once or twice, however, he surprises her as she is undressing. What secret of Nikiema's is she trying to find out? No doubt only she can say.

She's a prostitute, she sells her body for nothing, to buy her cans of paint or a few meters of canvas. Back in Kisito, it's she who looks after the family. N'Fumbang, the father. Old aunts and some cousins. Nikiema takes a sly interest in what one could call her worth in the art world. Nothing special. Even he couldn't say he was blown away by her paintings. But he has the modesty to admit his ignorance on the matter. At times, he has been tempted to give her some money—insane amounts actually. A little out of habit: people ask him for it all the time and for years he has dished it out to his entourage. With her, he feels that it would be a disaster.

Some days, he wants to ask her if she receives men in the house or if she has a normal love life like any woman her age. Something, he truly doesn't know what, holds the question at the back of his throat. N'Zo Nikiema dreads that this might be, all of a sudden, the end of everything.

I have no trouble at all piecing together this bit of conversation:

"You want to know if I behave decently? Is that it?"

With her, Nikiema feels on the defensive right away. He answers sheepishly, avoiding her eyes, "No, of course not. You know it's not that. If I were anxious to know, I wouldn't have asked you any questions."

"I know that. You have the means to spy on everyone. In any case, my life is my life."

When she is mad—or is she only pretending to be, this time?—she is completely fake. He looks up at her to make her understand that she is being unfair to him.

There has never been the least ambiguity in their relationship. As much as they sit and talk about everything and nothing, she doesn't seem fully aware of her gender. In the beginning, four or five years earlier, she temporarily made him experience violent moments of distress. At the time, they made love much more frequently. She would yell, rambling. He thought this was unimportant then. According to what he believed he knew, it was banal human behavior: people make love throughout their entire lives, letting out the same confused cries, only for themselves, without the least pretension of being sincere. And honestly, the two are not alike at all. Between them, it is never a question of some amorous passion. But some days, she behaves like a madwoman and threatens to avenge not only Kaveena but also all of Nikiema's other victims. She hits him with anything she can get her hands on and blames him for the murders of Abel Murigande, a.k.a. Commander Nestor, and, furthermore, Prieto da Souza. "And in Warela and Mirinda," she goes on, "you and your friend Castaneda razed all the villages and massacred hundreds of thousands of innocent victims. No one in this country has forgotten that. Our people will never forget!"

In the middle of his own rant, he has a brief moment of lucidity: how can she mix up Kaveena's death in all of this? They are such different things! So, is she doing this for political reasons? That changes everything! "My little whore," he roars in turn, "let's talk about that—in Warela and Mirinda they launched an armed attack against the state and Castaneda and I dealt with it. Yes, as you say, my friend Castaneda and I!"

He tells himself that any minute now she's going to bash his head in. He persuades himself little by little that this has always been her intention and that she will do it, for a mysterious reason, while they're together.

Once back at the palace, N'Zo Nikiema thinks back on those crazy times and he is struck by this: if there is anything close to love between them, with this unforgettable carnal violence, it's only because Mumbi Awele's hatred toward him has remained intact.

One day, he pulls her toward him in the studio. They hold each other, their genitals touching. Their faces almost touch and their eyes meet but they avoid looking at each other. After a few minutes, they move away from one another, a little embarrassed. Never before had he sensed she was so fragile. It almost brings him joy. *She* isn't indestructible either.

—∿—

75

I heard that you were among the refugees gathering all over the country and heading toward the Saasun River. I imagined you walking along its banks for several days until you reached Niamina. Maybe you crossed to the other side of the border next?

On my end, I am starting to get used to my black hole down there; I'm even starting to like it a little. Last night, I stayed down there longer than I had to. It'll be difficult for you to believe but it was for pure pleasure. Or almost. Colonel Kroma and his men are searching for me night and day at the borders. I even thought it wasn't possible for them to find me one day. Or else it would be in three thousand years. There would be articles in two or three newspapers: A sovereign's tomb from the third millennium was found in Jinkoré, near the city of Maren. He had been buried with canned goods and bottles of mineral water. No gold or precious objects. Materialist civilization. Everything for the belly. Times have changed, right? But let's not get ahead of ourselves, the scholars would also say, because we've also found documents written in a very old language in the tomb. For that matter, some specialists think that the man wasn't a monarch, but rather a high-level civil servant, something like one of those austere scribes from ancient Egypt. Anatomists and archeologists would lose themselves in complex calculations. They would come up with all kinds of nonsense and its opposite, but no one on earth would know enough science to contradict them. And honestly, my dear Mumbi, everyone could really give a royal fuck.

—⸏—

After a civil war, the mercenaries are paid and go on their way. That's the general rule. Ours stayed to earn extra, solo. They know that, dead or alive, the fugitive can bring them a fortune.

I, Asante Kroma, am in a position to talk about it. They had completely infiltrated my secret service ranks. Our spies—and even some of my shady agents—were working off the books for them. And among themselves, those foreigners were intoxicated with outdoing each other. A real mess.

And as I write these lines, it continues.

They show off their warrior tattoos and talk about their exploits in Maren's nightclubs. Angola. South Africa. Liberia. Sierra Leone. They knock back an unbelievable amount of whiskey and muse on the day when they'll be able to call Castaneda. It will go something like this:

"Yeah, I believe your nasty nigger is in my area."

"Really? He . . . ?"

"You want to know if he's alive? He's a little odd! More or less, yes. I unhinged his jaw a little, but the rest is OK."

"Don't move an inch, man, I'll be right there!"

"That would be surprising. You don't even know where I am, big guy."

"But you're going to tell me. I have a written order from President Mwanke—the state demands that this prisoner be delivered."

"Have you gone crazy, my little Pierre? I'm in contact with the Red Cross. I'm going to turn over my package to them."

At that exact moment, Pierre Castaneda will stifle his mad laughter. "Oh, really?"

"This bastard's got to explain himself to the international courts. Human rights, that's what it's really about nowadays."

After a few minutes, Pierre Castaneda will say to the guy, "OK, we've had enough fun. How much?"

There will be a long negotiation. The video of Kaveena's murder alone would bring in hundreds of millions for the war hound. But Pierre Castaneda, who reigned over Cogemin's gold and marble mines, has the means to pay.

What happens next will definitely seem less funny to Nikiema. He is handed over to Castaneda. The man, cruel and vindictive, had been dreaming of this tête-à-tête for a long time. For days, he subjects him to the most unusual forms of torture. As long as he still breathes, a part of his body is cut off. An ear. His tongue. His chin. Whatever.

It's not easy to slice this chin, it's really too hard, boss.

You bums! It's certainly long enough—try with the metal saw, over there, on the little table, there it is, his fucking headstrong chin that juts forward, go on, put your hearts into it, go faster, sever it off for me I'm telling you and get a move on!

And all this time, Pierre Castaneda, sentimental as ever, doesn't stop reminding himself of the time when, as inseparable friends, they would go have their beer almost every day at the Blue Lizard, and you were mad about Heineken and I'd be gone on the Premium Club—I even called it my little brunette, do you remember? We were the best friends in the world. I'd have never thought that you could stab me in the back like that. We were making the future of your native country together. I helped you climb higher up the ladder, and as soon as you got to the top, you started pissing on my head. Maybe I should have let you climb up on the throne, over there in your lost hole? King of Nimba, my foot! You'd have become like your father, an old spoiled fellow, alcoholic and morose. A little port, a few small bags of popcorn, and he would sign anything we wanted, your royal pops! I pulled you out of nothingness and that's how you thank me, eh? You stick the murder of that little girl that you killed on my back! Is that it? Little bastard! Cut off his left leg!

Here, sir?

No, a little higher, let's see, moron, toward the knee! Higher, a little ambition, what the hell!

And while Nikiema howls with pain, Pierre Castaneda mops his brow with his handkerchief.

—◊—

I hope that things don't happen like that. I don't want to suffer. That would be useless. My destiny as a glorious martyr is a failed case. That said, maybe I'm going to surprise you: I can't manage to say Pierre Castaneda was completely in the wrong. Of course, I am surprised to see him mixing his emotions with everything. But actually, we had been like milk brothers. We simply cannot hate each other. The paths of our lives are intertwined forever. I'm sure that Pierre Castaneda also thinks about me night and day. No doubt with more rage and hatred, since he's the emotional one. For me, our break isn't the end of the world. Of course, it so happens that I can be outside myself when my memory opens old wounds. Solitude weighs on me more than usual in those moments and I dream of a bloody revenge. But I am not deluding myself: I played and I lost.

On the other hand, I admit that Castaneda understands Abel Murigande's attitude better than mine. Commander Nestor, armed, crossed his path. It was clearly a fair fight between enemies. I was happy to betray Castaneda. I also made a laughingstock of him. For years, all of his compatriots at Cogemin mocked him, but he had stood firm. He made a point of being seen everywhere with his Negro. He made a radiant political future for himself. People would say to him, those baboons are all the same, lazy and lackadaisical—be careful, Pierre, they are not like us. And as we savored Ta'Mim's grilled fish or saka-saka, we would both mock those little racist Whites from the colony. Then Pierre Castaneda would play the dangerous revolutionary, especially when he had drunk a little too much Premium Club. Yeah, it was too bad that a guy with such advanced ideas was stuck in such a place. He treated his own people like fools.

I see you smile—in a manner of speaking, Mumbi, because you don't smile very often. You are right: Pierre Castaneda's bravado is comical. I've seen him at it, our great liberal. The murder of your daughter, Kaveena, was nothing compared to his other crimes. Don't forget that I met the guy during the colonial period. A Negro had to stay in his place. We were forbidden to walk on the same sidewalk as Whites, to talk to them from far, to address them familiarly. Pierre and I were quite young then, but he already loved inventing the most refined torture methods. I saw him hang someone by his feet and ask some villagers to set his head on fire. I also remember the day when he ordered people to sweep all the paths leading to Cogemin. We went to inspect the grounds at the end of the afternoon. A single bit from the broom around there was enough for him to call all those in charge of the surrounding areas. He waved the twig around, high toward the sky, and said in a theatrical voice, "A child is going to be shot in the village closest to the spot where I found this. If I ask you to live on the property, it's for you, not for me. The execution of this child will be a good lesson for all of you."

And after that was the most difficult task: to know which village was closest to this famous twig. I saw Pierre Castaneda behave like a madman on such occasions. For several days, taking pride in his extreme precision, he did nothing but make stupid calculations, his map, notepad, and pen in hand. The residents of the concerned villages, under house arrest, waited anxiously. But incapable of admitting a fraction of uncertainty, he made everyone constantly retake the measurements. On about the sixth night, the chief of Mballa turned over a teenager to him, the son of an old woman who was said to be a bit of a witch. The child was shot in the village public square. The firing squad was under the command of an uncommissioned Senegalese officer. A little side note about this, Mumbi: In my opinion, we don't talk enough about these auxiliaries from all the colonial armies. The empire's bleak bulldogs! The dirty work was always theirs. When I see their country puff up its chest today and pass itself off as an example to the entire world, it makes me laugh! They're funny anyway, my Senegalese brothers. And what if they start by apologizing to the Vietnamese, to the Madagascans, to the Algerians, and to so many others? That wouldn't be a bad thing, I think.

Let's come back to our friend, Pierre Castaneda. You talk about an enlightened mind! I know all the little secrets of Maren's strongman. When he got here, he did what all the other Whites did, he slept with all the young women, blindfolding their eyes. And do you know why? They were not to see him naked. They all did it, too. The master's race. Isn't that true, my little Pierre? And that other time when a canton chief had slapped his wife, Hortense Dupaquier. Pierre was on a trip to France. The man was tortured to death. Upon his return, Castaneda was still so angry that he had the body dug up in order to have it whipped in front of the natives. I'm not telling you anything new, of course, when I say that this Hortense Dupaquier did not deserve so much infamy. But that is another story. . . . Not for a single day did that man think that our freedom was more important than Cogemin's gold and marble. You know, Mumbi,

those big words: self-determination, national destiny, independence—
independence, my love, oh boy!—they made Pierre Castaneda chuckle.
He never thought that we could take charge of our affairs by ourselves,
like other people on earth. And that's why, up to the moment when his
troops and mine started shooting each other, he refused to admit that I
had truly envisioned nationalizing Cogemin. In his mind, all I wanted
to do was blackmail him.

—᠁—

I've been to Cogemin more than once. As everyone knows, it's
the largest industrial company in our country. It extends across
tens of thousands of hectares if you take into account its gold and
marble mines. And since Pierre Castaneda has been its boss for several decades, Cogemin is central to national political life. Its em-
blem, a black eagle taking flight, is known throughout the entire
world. When foreigners hear about it, they imagine lavish buildings
standing in the middle of a thick African forest. The reality is quite
different. The mining company's offices are actually made out of
modest, rather unattractive barns. More than once, businessmen
who had come from far away were struck by the contrast between
these makeshift premises and those of the company in their own
country. Wild grass was growing around the buildings and you had
to jump over mud puddles in order to access the main entrance. In
the first years—during the colonial period—small businesses had
spontaneously popped up around Cogemin. Shopkeepers settled
into makeshift shelters made of cardboard and sold to the company
workers cigarettes, cola, ginger juice, and even packets of ice water
that were likely tainted; then came the cheap restaurants, and when
the bars opened their doors, prostitutes arrived. People would often see them on the arms of young workers in orange overalls and
gleaming helmets.

It continued like that for years. But a little before independence,
the director of the company was replaced by Pierre Castaneda, who
had been his trusted representative up to that point. For reasons
known only to him, Castaneda had all those establishments I just

81

described torn down. In his eyes, they were illegal. Undoubtedly, too, with this dramatic action, he wanted to show that he was a strong man. In a few hours, all the stalls were torn down, as were the surrounding villages. Some of those villages, several centuries old, were proud of their past. All of them were razed. Cogemin's perimeter expanded from one day to the next. That was one of the goals of the operation. Castaneda then had high barbed-wire fences put up around the mine. The residents of Nimba started to protest. But their king was Pierre Castaneda's friend. He was also, one must not forget, N'Zo Nikiema's father. The matter was quickly decided. Castaneda was a prudent man: he recruited young villagers from the western tribes to ensure security at Cogemin, which was located in the north of the country. Proud to wear uniforms for the first time in their lives, the stern faces of those who patrolled the mine were ready for anything. Very quickly, they got firearms. They liked to use them on the slightest pretext and they often had to be called to order. They later formed the shock troops against Commander Nestor's guerrilla force.

In a short time, Cogemin became equipped with better roads, clinics, and schools than any city in the country. Its white employees could go to the Belvedere Complex's two supermarkets to stock up on provisions shipped directly from France. They knew almost nothing about the indigenous town outside its walls. Not to mention, it didn't interest them at all.

In the early days of independence, people believed that Cogemin was going to be nationalized. Nikiema had made the promise several times in his meetings, but in very ambiguous terms. Pierre Castaneda didn't leave him any time to think about it. The new state signed a document with Cogemin called Nimba Protocol 212. It's a period in our history that I don't know well. I was preparing for my baccalaureate exams in high school and so I was far away from all that. In any case, only a few initiates knew from the start what was hidden behind that curious name. President Nikiema had just ceded, in the most legal manner in the world, the country's entire mine zone to Cogemin. The latter was obtaining the rights to police the area and to import or export whatever it pleased in the tens of thousands of square kilometers. Pierre Castaneda even had a small airport built. It quickly became impossible to conceal this fact: Cogemin had become a state within a state. There had been protests here and there. To no avail.

But as soon as he went underground, Abel Murigande reserved his most virulent attacks for Cogemin. According to him, Nimba Protocol 212 made it clear that the country was not independent. After Murigande's execution and the rallying of his senior lieutenants by the regime, no one ever took interest in the affair again.

On his end, Nikiema had hoped—as many African political leaders of his generation did—that independence, which was rigged to begin with, would slowly become a reality. Even if he didn't dare bring up Cogemin's nationalization, he secretly pursued the idea. He had to find the right opportunity. And, in his mind, it didn't have to be some sort of revolutionary rebellion. He just had to do it. But, far from declining, Castaneda's hold on political life only became stronger. And N'Zo Nikiema himself learned, much to his chagrin, that being a puppet is never an easy task. You constantly wait for your moment, each morning you're convinced it's finally here, and at the end of the day, it never comes.

During that period, I often got the chance to meet Nikiema. Every day, my police work allows me, as one can easily imagine, to observe people without their knowledge. And I must say that as the years went by, I detected a growing discomfort in the president. He became less and less tolerant of being Castaneda's puppet. The anecdote that I'm going to narrate is revealing of that mindset. A playwright had put up a play on this well-known topic—N'Zo Nikiema, a lackey of the Whites, etc. It was called *The Little Stone Dog*. Nobody was fooled by the play on words, "stone" being *pierre* in French. The text was loaded with mean allusions that triggered hilarity in the audience every minute. Sometimes, a few of them even chanted the name Commander Nestor or Prieto da Souza. Nikiema couldn't hear

83

anything about the author of this play without getting mad as hell. I rarely saw him hate someone so much. He used to say to me, "Listen, Asante, I knew this guy's father. His father was certifiably insane! He defecated in the street, he lived under a baobab surrounded by a dozen scrawny cats, he would talk to them all the time, he was a madman! And one day at dawn, people heard all the cats meowing. They went to see, and the cats were all sitting around the man's corpse and they meowed in a strange way, all together. He had died at night. And that, Asante, is who the father of our great writer was!"

I pretended to be scandalized, which is what he seemed to be encouraging. In fact, I don't think I played the charade well. I just did not agree with Nikiema. When a young man wants to become a playwright, he perhaps asks himself a bunch of questions—he may have doubts about his abilities or even the usefulness of literature. But the fact that the death of his father had long ago been announced by a concert of meowing cats early one morning is certainly not going to keep him from writing plays. In this case, I was above all a witness to N'Zo Nikiema's powerless rage. With *The Little Stone Dog*, this playwright was striking violently where it hurt and Nikiema couldn't even react. It was also a time when, according to what I understood, he was obsessed with the memory of Commander Nestor, who knew how to stand up to foreign powers and had the guts to do so.

At this point, the horrifying death of Commander Nestor gives us pause.

Despite his latest taste for confession—and, I will even say, his desire to remain sincere in all circumstances—we can't take everything Nikiema wrote at face value. When he told Mumbi, for example, about the end of Abel Murigande, we can suspect he exaggerated. And it's distressing anyway when a head of state writes, "I was furious when they killed my childhood friend, so I went on a little strike just to spite my French advisors." It's infantile, but also what a horrible confession! However, I am still convinced of one thing: N'Zo Nikiema was envious of Abel Murigande's fate. Commander Nestor did endure some hardship, but his suffering in some

84

way sanctified him. For all of us, his image is that of the golden eagle shot down in midflight. And Pierre Castaneda didn't realize what he was doing throwing him out of a helicopter into the Atlantic. He forever made him into a quasi-unreal being, a sort of archangel making a pact until his last breath with the thunder and lightning. In one of his letters to Mumbi Awele, Nikiema did not indicate otherwise.

However, without Kaveena's murder, he would never have dared to attack the all-powerful Cogemin. He thought he finally got Pierre Castaneda with this heinous murder. His father, the king of Nimba, had sold an immense plot of land to the foreigners for a few cases of whiskey and port. He himself had been subjected to the worst racist humiliation by Cogemin. He wanted, at all costs, to take his revenge on destiny, and he thought, for the first time in his life, that he had the chance.

—◊—

Don't listen to those who tell you with a whistle of admiration, "What a brilliant strategist Pierre Castaneda is!" In reality, his logic was quite simple. The boss of Cogemin knew very well what the exploitation of the gold mines in Ndunga and the marble mines in Masella meant. The sons of the country were working in there like slaves. They were forced to extract the subsoil wealth at the cost of great suffering. It was then loaded into boats and no longer concerned them. When you think about it, it's mind-blowing and even a little funny, this way of coming to the other end of the world in order to appropriate the wealth of others. Pierre understood that one day or another, the system would have to be made more flexible. That meant preparing the takeover. That was with me. There's nothing extraordinary about it. I almost want to say that for us politicians, our only truth is in our survival.

You know it too: I am introduced everywhere as Castaneda's valet. You yourself have spit this accusation in my face. Be wary of these obvious facts—they only lay the groundwork for serious errors. I was not putty in his hands. Those who say that don't know anything about the looks that Pierre and I exchanged in those days, sitting in front of our beers at the Blue Lizard.

85

We were genuine friends. The way two humans can be. If death leaves me the time, I will tell you all the little things that make me say this. Is it useful to come back to it? I'm not entirely sure. But on the other hand, with the life I've had, the remotest event only has meaning in relation to thousands of others, seemingly very far removed from it. In fact, you will only understand this confession if it leaves nothing in the dark.

When the time comes, I will inform you. I will know what to say to you and which words to let burst, like ridiculous little air bubbles, deep inside my guts.

—⁓—

With his finger N'Zo Nikiema pushed around the mangoes and bananas that were laid out on a red wooden boat-shaped tray. They were soft, blackened on some sides, and were giving off a sweetish smell. One of them was suppurating like an open wound. Not knowing where to throw them away, he put them in a small bag, closed it up carefully, and placed it in a corner. He was especially afraid that the rotten fruit would attract big green flies and red ants. His food withstood the basement's heat and frequent blackouts better than expected. That was good.

He had hardly eaten anything for two days and was beginning to feel weak. Barely used to preparing his meals himself, he did not manage to have a good normal diet. No doubt all those canned goods—tuna, pilchards, country-style pâté, etc.—killed his appetite as well. He could have opened a bottle of wine for himself and crunched on a few dry crackers, just to be able to stand up on his legs. The fact is, he had absolutely no desire to. I don't know if N'Zo Nikiema had decided to allow himself to die of hunger. He might not have been mad about this happening to him. I suspect he played a little, somewhat perversely, with the idea that he was a solitary ascetic, graceful and light, whirling around in the air like a kite, consumed slowly by profound and discreet suffering. Alone in the small house in Jinkoré, he was able to dream of a slow and noble agony.

86

He sat on the ground, his elbow resting on a leather-covered bench, legs stretched. He thought that he should do a little housekeeping at the end of the day because the dust had slowly built up on the rug. The latter had been made of four or five sheepskins sewn together. He'd brought it back for Mumbi the previous year from Chinguetti. For that matter, everywhere he'd gone on an official visit, he'd managed to get away from the security detail for a moment to go find a little gift for her. Naturally, he could have asked someone from his staff to do it. He wanted to take care of it himself.

He suddenly had a desire to devour the place with his eyes. Rattan armchairs were set on the rug, along with two crafted leather poufs bought at Ouaga's "handicraft village." On one of them, a bowl containing three enormous ostrich eggs from Zimbabwe was displayed prominently. His eyes took in the floor tiles—gray or a dirty white, he couldn't really remember anymore. On the wall, just above the sofa, hung a tiny drum from Burundi decorated with yellow and black diamonds, bright originally but already a little dull now.

At the end of the room, a wood Venn table filled almost the entire space. It normally could have been used to receive a dozen dinner guests. But the small house had never been filled with the laughter of happy friends gathering together for an evening. The table, at once too heavy and too long, had never been used for anything. At one time, it seemed to Nikiema that Mumbi wanted to make it her office. Seated at her used Macintosh early in the morning, she would only stop typing around two in the afternoon. Nikiema never knew what she was working on with that look of unflinching concentration on her face. In any case, it didn't last long. Now the Macintosh was out of service. From the printer, yellowed papers overflowed, also covered with dust.

Just in front of him, above the divan—which was where the sofa would usually have been—a painting attracted his attention. He had bought it for Mumbi, a few years back. He had to make a lot of effort to remember: Salvador da Bahia. The gaps in his memory, increasingly frequent, made him afraid. They meant that he had lost his bearings, that his past was also escaping him. He felt reassured by telling himself that this forgetfulness was normal: during that quick tour, he recalled, I had been in five or six countries in two weeks.

He remembered very well, however, why he'd been keen on going to Latin America that year. Kaveena's story had come to light several months before and war had almost been declared between himself and Pierre Castaneda. Castaneda had gone away to Ndunga, where the Cogemin headquarters were. Almost each week, he would create a so-called liberation army with hundreds of thousands of men. On top of it, he distributed huge sums of money to gangsters so they could start private newspapers or human rights associations.

Nikiema couldn't stand idly by. He traveled to Bogota, Lima, and other Latin American capitals to negotiate contracts of arms sales. Everywhere he went, he was received reluctantly by somnolent president-generals, their uniforms in bold colors, covered with decorations.

On the eve of his return, he went on an escapade in a popular neighborhood of Salvador da Bahia to look for the ritual gift for Mumbi. An old woman hanging out her window said something to him in an unfamiliar language; he stopped and shook his head to signal to her that he didn't understand. She then started speaking Portuguese. He ended up agreeing to join her. As he went up the narrow stairway, he wondered if he was making a mistake. It was a place where someone could rob him, slit his throat, and throw his body next to one of those big ponds of dirty water he'd seen everywhere. And that murder would make more noise than usual. But it wasn't the kind of neighborhood where one denounced the killers. In the end his casket draped with the national flag would be loaded onto the presidential airplane as military music played. In his country, he would be entitled to a grandiose funeral. The official word on his death would be a heart attack during fierce negotiations that lasted until late into the night with his hosts. Dead as he had lived: President Nikiema, in the service of the nation. But his enemies would start the rumor that he'd reached the next world in a despicable way, getting his private parts titillated, like such-and-such former president of Nigeria, by a dozen whores in some brothel in Salvador da Bahia or Montevideo.

Up close, the woman appeared less old. Despite some wrinkles crisscrossing her face, her skin seemed to have kept a certain firmness. She was barefoot and her white shirt was tied just above the waist of her garnet-red pants. She looked like a free swaggering intellectual and not at all like an old beggar. N'Zo Nikiema was entirely overcome by emotion, almost distressed, to learn that she was an artist, a painter. She seemed more concerned with explaining her work to the first person who came along—she really was talking nonstop—than with selling her paintings.

N'Zo Nikiema nodded his head in approval of everything she was saying, seeking to avoid that sort of naive amazement of a layperson that could have right away exposed his shortcomings. But all was in vain: the woman, of course, used to gauging the artistic sensibility of her interlocutors, knew right away that she was dealing with a total ignoramus. She communicated that to him through the ironic smile that lingered in her eyes during the entire visit to the studio.

"My wife is an artist and ...," he began.

She interrupted him as he searched for his words. "An artist ... ?"

"Yes," said N'Zo Nikiema. "Like you. She paints."

He was expecting an enthusiastic reaction from her. But it was quite the opposite, as if she'd been caught off guard, and she fell silent. Having only just met her for the first time, he decided it was useless to try to understand such an unexpected response.

"I want to buy a painting for her."

She suggested one to him for $250. It was called *The Little Butterfly Girl*. This was the painting that was now before his eyes, several years later.

Nikiema began to observe it as if he'd never seen it before. It appeared bland to him, probably due to its dominant pale yellow tones. That was, at least, his humble opinion—he, a fleeing ex–head of state

89

little versed in art's mysteries. In the center of the painting, a little girl in a long white dress was standing on the edge of a rock, just above a precipice. She was trying to catch butterflies that you could see gathering nectar and pollen on a rosebush. Fluttering capriciously around her, the butterflies didn't seem like they were really fleeing from her but just having fun dodging her net. The little girl, meanwhile, lost her footing, her left leg hanging dangerously in the air.

"The whole painting," the woman had explained to him, "is structured on this contrast between the candor of this little child and the cruelty of the world that surrounds her. One wrong step and she is going to plunge into the depths where a horrible death awaits her. Just underneath this charming scene that the painting portrays, a monster is waiting, thirsty for blood. He wants to devour this little girl. Do you see him? See how frightening he is, with his mouth open like he is calling out to the blood of the innocent child?"

Nikiema didn't see anything at all but didn't dare admit it. He merely nodded his head ambiguously.

The woman gave him an indulgent smile. "Of course, you cannot see this monster. . . . I drew it but it is not visible on this canvas. I painted it in black in the middle of the shadows. You understand that? Exactly like some of God's creatures that remain forever invisible to us, mister. Only imbeciles believe that the artist's work can be seen in its entirety by the naked eye."

N'Zo Nikiema noted that she had said those last words in a tense voice that rung with a poorly contained rage. He guessed that more than him, she was addressing her own enemies, undoubtedly other painters and critics with reactionary views. She added that she had to thrust her brush very deep into the abyss in order to find the right colors and that, for her, it was a completely unique aesthetic experiment.

That day, something very bizarre had also happened to him. After she'd sold him *The Little Butterfly Girl*, the artist had shown him a photo on the wall, of a young woman with thick brown hair, and said, "That is Magdalena."

"Who's that?" asked N'Zo Nikiema. He was all the more astonished because the young woman in the photo was completely nude. Sitting on the ground, her two arms around her left leg raised up and spread wide, she was looking straight ahead of her, her very attractive face glowing softly, her lips full. Between her thighs, her bushy hair burst out in a heavy dark patch. Nikiema only saw that, and for him it was an almost unbearable sight.

"That's my daughter. Magdalena acts in a café-theater down there."

More and more disconcerted, he pointed to the photo. "What's that?"

"It's the play. That's her acting in the play."

At that moment, N'Zo Nikiema thought that the woman was a little crazy. "But what play are you taking about, madam?"

She looked at him as if he'd just fallen from the moon. Magdalena Robles, her daughter, played the main role in *The Man Standing at His Window*, the most successful play in the theater circuit. She had been putting on the play for two years, and now her daughter, as beautiful as she was ambitious, wanted to do something else. All the movie producers were fighting over her. "You must have heard of her," she said, looking at him searchingly.

It was clear: she was starting to find him suspicious. He claimed to be interested in the art in this country and he didn't even know the name Magdalena Robles?

—⁓—

I had the urge to tell her that I, too, wasn't bad for my kind. The mean African dictator who'd come in search of weapons and to recruit mercenaries . . . she would have called for help. In the end, we are always someone's artist on this earth.

I must, however, confess to you that since then I have often thought of the nudity of this person I never knew, Magdalena Robles's nudity, as loaded with a completely terrifying violence. The conversation had piqued my curiosity and as soon as I left the studio, I bought Os Espectáculos in order to know more about The Man Standing at His Window. Os Espectáculos is the most famous literary journal there: novels, poetry,

91

theater. . . . In it, they talk about all the things that make you tick. If you understood Portuguese, you would have loved it. In the play, the man of the title watched the young woman, Magdalena, for over an hour. Nothing else happened, as in all the avant-garde plays that everyone is supposed to find sublime. According to what I understood, she didn't know that someone was observing her, in silence. She had just broken up with her boyfriend and was getting ready to put a bullet in her head.

I would have been able to go see her play the role that Friday; I wasn't heading back to Maren until the following day. But instinctively, I denied myself this. Magdalena's image was like a brief apparition in a bolt of lightning. On the stage, I would have only seen a woman's body, in the flesh a little sad. I would have depleted my memory, and my heart wouldn't beat so loudly each time I think of Magdalena Robles.

—⁂—

Upon his return from this unsuccessful trip to Latin America, he visited the house. Receiving the painting he had brought back for her, Mumbi thanked him coldly. She put it down—actually, she nearly threw it—into a corner of the studio.

It took more to hurt Nikiema. Had he been thin-skinned, he would have never accomplished anything in politics. Besides, he was in a rather teasing mood that day. At the risk of annoying Mumbi a little more, he repeated to her the explanation given to him by his distant sister from Salvador da Bahia. "It's marvelous, isn't it? The little girl on the canvas is risking her life on a noble quest for the Beautiful. That means that you artists are in the service of the Absolute."

Her face remained expressionless. She looked, he thought, irritated and amused at the same time. She said sharply, "That is not true. Those stories are full of crap."

"Oh yes!" N'Zo Nikiema insisted, suddenly coming alive. "The artist destroys her life in order to give others a little happiness—you are all generosity and sharing. You're the ones who always say so, aren't you? We should know!"

"Is that so?" Mumbi said with disdain.

Then their eyes met. She had once again put him in his place. When she burst into tears, he understood. He understood everything. And he was suddenly seized with sheer terror.

—⁕—

Kaveena.

I had brought back yellow and green ribbons mixed together for you from Salvador da Bahia, and here is what they really revealed, with a blinding clarity: the fate of your daughter Kaveena. I had been incapable of seeing that. My God, how my heart is hard . . .

I understood perfectly well what you wanted to say to me that day. The words did not come out of your mouth and yet I understood each and every one of them, one after the other, very distinctly: "When you're done joking about art with me, you will go back to your palace and there you're going to kill people who've done nothing to you."

And you were right.

It was a particularly bloody period of my reign. Pierre Castaneda did so much and did it so well that I saw people everywhere plotting my overthrow. Funny vicious circle. I had to kill incessantly. Not out of wickedness or any perverse taste for blood. Nowhere do people like that exist. Or out of ten million individuals, there are three or four of them, no more. And those people are ill. Idi Amin Dada. Hitler. Videla. The latter shoved live mice up the vaginas of young left-wing students. And compared to the two Duvaliers or Comrade Pol Pot, I was almost a noble and benevolent president. I just did at times what was necessary. I bumped off all those guys because I couldn't do otherwise, so to speak. For at least two reasons: One, I couldn't leave them alive. It was them or me. Two, they were helping me pose a threat to the potential plotters paid by Pierre Castaneda. That guy had too much money and he was set on using it against me. So all his people had to die, in front of everyone, in agony. I didn't have any other way to discourage the subversive urges of one or the other of them. From his stronghold in Ndunga, well protected by his paid militias, the boss of Cogemin let out horrific cries at each execution. Was I then going to be left to kill all those in the country who dared to think?

You have surely seen that photo on the front page of all the newspapers: Pierre Castaneda holding the son of an opponent in his arms and bawling his eyes out. In between two sobs, he says that he can't take these massive and repeated human rights violations anymore, that he is suffering personally because of them, setting aside any political considerations. He is asked, "Don't you feel a little responsible all the same, Mr. Castaneda?" After a long sigh, the sigh of a wounded man, cruelly deceived, he states, his voice breaking, "You mean responsible for having helped? Listen, he wasn't like that when I met him. I don't know when President Nikiema became a monster but it's a fact: he has nothing human left in him."

The trap, which worked beautifully, was slowly closing in around me.

—∿∿—

The month of May was coming to an end. How many days had he been locked up in the small house? Without a doubt, a little more than two months. Nikiema wanted to heat some water but some voices in the street caught his attention. They were so close he believed his end had arrived. Outside, someone shook the latch of the wooden gate. Nikiema rushed into the basement. He realized then that he could move around in there with relative ease. But even there, sheltered from any danger, he was still afraid. Not daring to either go back up to the living room or even close his eyes, he munched on crackers for a good part of the night. In the darkness, the words "hunger," "food shortage," "famine," "dying of hunger and thirst" suddenly came into his head. He let them make their little rounds in his mind and he set out in search of food. The dried fruits and canned goods were luckily on a shelf near the ground. He wouldn't have had the strength to climb onto a chair in order to reach them if he'd have put them away higher. That would not have been sensible: it was dark in the basement and everything could come crashing down around him. Nor was there any way to read labels. N'Zo Nikiema had to trust his own sense of smell in order to know whether the foods were spoiled or not. When a product seemed questionable to him, he would let a bit of it melt on his tongue, and depending on the outcome he would either throw the can in a corner or use his fingers to devour its contents.

It was on that day that N'Zo Nikiema was struck for the first time by the bad odor that was starting to emanate from the labyrinth. He would have liked to attribute it to the *kilischi,* the dried meat strips he had brought back a year earlier from Zinder, but he hated to lie to himself.

The next day, he woke up midmorning, bright-eyed and bushy-tailed. As often happens after a restless night, Nikiema had fallen deeply asleep at dawn. He stayed stretched out for several minutes, not really knowing what he was going to do with his day. As soon as he stood up, he listened all around. His fear from the previous night had disappeared but he was acting, childishly, like he believed he was still in danger. This way of being on alert especially helped him to conquer his boredom. The only things that bothered him—really what made him feel great shame and even a sense of moral degradation—were the dirtiness and the mess around him. Two open cans—one of sardines, the other of corned beef—were lying on the floor along with some bags of crackers. The garbage was full and he didn't know anymore what to do with the food scraps that were piling up in the basement. His clothes and his mouth were stained with grease. The oil from the can of sardines traced a thin black trench on the floor that was going to disappear under the library. N'Zo Nikiema scattered little peanut seeds on the ground that were actually poison. He had noted their efficacy as much on the rodents as on the cockroaches. Only he didn't know what to do with their bodies that stunk up the labyrinth a little more each day.

In the living room, everything was in the same place as the night before. He put his gun back under the bowl of ostrich eggs from Zimbabwe and headed toward the fridge. The pineapple juice squeezed between pieces of frozen chicken gave him a wonderful feeling of freshness. With his eyes half-closed and raised toward the ceiling, he purred with pleasure as he let the juice flow down his throat. He immediately felt like he was at home in the living room, which all of a sudden seemed more welcoming to him than it had ever been. When he had left to take refuge in the underground, he began to miss some of his everyday activities.

N'Zo Nikiema picked up a magazine from a pile of newspapers. It was *Nubia*. In his former life, he had had little time to read about art. Now, it allowed him to relieve his boredom. He went directly to his favorite section, *In Parentheses*. Each month, an artist was invited to, in a way, go off the deep end, and their delusions were reported in the newspaper. Nikiema read a title that made him smile: "Me, an African Artist? I couldn't give a damn, good God!" The painter first talked about the planetary village and the highways in the sky, with words full of tenderness. Then, out of the blue, he started scattering his text with curse words and with "Oh! Awwww! Oh!" under the pretext of having major pain in his shoulders. "How is it in your shoulders?" asked the interviewer. Yes, for the whole time he was carrying Africa and its wars and epidemics he had these really terrible pains, achy and stiff all over, contusions and everything. He added, in an even more bizarre manner, "Listen, mama, don't be afraid—I'm not gonna throw you into the trash like a bag of garbage. No. I have respect for the Ancestors, I do. I am going to lay you down gently on the ground and then . . . boom, a big kick in your big black ass and you'll manage like everyone does on this earth! Stupid bitchy abusive mother, go on!" It took N'Zo Nikiema several readings to realize that the mother in question, so harshly berated, was Africa. In the photo, the artist, a little chubby-cheeked, had dreadlocks, a youthful face, and a glint of mockery in his eyes. Of course, N'Zo Nikiema didn't have any opinion on what the young man was saying. It went over his head, all those celestial highways. But Mumbi's colleague was funny anyway.

N'Zo Nikiema leafed through a few dailies, too. He had fun guessing who had paid for which investigative piece, or even for a simple sentence fragment. The rates varied depending on the newspapers. However, such editorialists, moralizing and corrupt, had always seemed significantly overestimated. I gave him bags and bags of dough, that guy, Nikiema thought, and he couldn't even bring down Pierre Castaneda for me. This perhaps explained how this guy had become, from the very first hours of the civil war, one of Castaneda's most fervent partisans.

It was also very funny to see, in hindsight, to what degree everyone, including himself, could get it all wrong. The press had made such a fuss about certain events. Each morning someone would announce that the country would collapse by the end of the week. A few months later, as seen from the small house, all that seemed to him rather pathetic.

His photo was on the cover of all the abandoned newspapers in Mumbi's living room, naturally. He was troubled when he came across an interview he'd given in *Ebena*, the country's only fashion magazine. A businessman, who was also a notorious sexual pervert, had started the magazine as a shrewd way to attract young beauties to his bed. There were superb photos of models in *Ebena* and the guy said, enraptured, to whoever would listen, "As you see them, I screw them all, these little wonders!"

On that particular point, I can only say N'Zo Nikiema was right. I know Ludovic Mabeya's police files well—the boss of that luxurious colorful magazine. Each time I've seen information about him, I've asked myself how a person who is mentally ill—truly ill!—could have enough presence of mind to make so much money off public works or anything else. He was always talking about his female conquests and would almost always add, bursting into laughter, "It's just that I have balls of steel!" It's his expression. I bring it up merely for the sake of accuracy.

The interview with *Ebena*'s journalist managed to relax N'Zo Nikiema. She had asked him questions that were totally surprising, at times a bit inappropriate: Do you go cycling on Sunday, Mr. President? And the number thirteen—does the number thirteen make you afraid? And do you sometimes bring the Mother of the Nation her butter croissants and coffee in bed in the morning? Have you ever struck her in a fit of anger? She'd hesitated before asking him that. And of course, in order to lessen the impact of her audacity, she had added at the end, "in a fit of anger." A way of suggesting that a man like him, nearly perfect, could only behave in such a way if he precisely ceased being himself. The hand that ceases to obey its infallible brain and goes off on its own to smash the face of the Mother of the Nation! Dirty hand, I'm going to kill you! It was something to die laughing over, the goddamn stupid things that little journalist would do. But there you have it—in the past Nikiema had been admonished for a certain stiffness, even for his arrogance. So his advisors were keen to show the most human side of him. "Such bullshit," he railed to himself as he entered into the spirit of their game. To have to prove that one is still human! Well... the country had truly changed without him knowing because N'Zo Nikiema couldn't even imagine someone directing such questions at anyone. What was this, this story about butter croissants and coffee for the Mother of the Nation? Come on now! The Mother of the Nation! He had no idea they were still doing anything together, the Mother of the Nation and he.

Lost in his thoughts, he hadn't heard what the journalist had just said. "Excuse me, dear?"

She detected N'Zo Nikiema's irritation and repeated herself, her throat a little knotted. "Is there a day..."

At that moment, the memory came back to him at once. "Ah yes! A day that changed my life, you said?"

The young girl nodded her head, still just as intimidated. Her left hand was opening and closing nervously.

After pretending to think about it for a moment, his voice full of profound emotion, he recalled his first election to the presidency of the republic. At the time, he was no longer working at Cogemin and was living in the Artillery, a semi-working-class neighborhood in Maren. He spoke about how, in the middle of watching the popular jubilation fireworks light up the June night sky from his balcony, he thought hard and with a heavy heart about his mother. She was no longer in this world and that brought a drop of bitterness to that glorious day. N'Zo Nikiema added that, despite his sadness, he was happy to see a new dawn breaking on the horizon. And standing near him, Pierre Castaneda, his faithful friend, his old battle companion. . . . He and Pierre had overcome many hardships together! At every great moment in his life, he said gravely, he had felt the brotherly silent shadow of Pierre Castaneda by his side, this foreigner who was more patriotic than a lot of the natives of the country.

As he spoke, N'Zo Nikiema saw that the journalist was restless. This was the part of the interview that obviously interested her the most. So what does this girl want me to say? Nikiema thought. He promised himself he would have her watched. This was perhaps a new act of deceit on Castaneda's part, this interview. Their tiff was already public knowledge and all the newspapers were finding ways to throw oil on the fire. He paused for a moment, his eyes vacant, and he said, "After nearly thirty years, Pierre's loyalty to me has been unfailing."

"There have never been any clouds hanging over your relationship with him, Mr. President?"

N'Zo Nikiema easily guessed where she wanted to go with that. The same dirty tricks. Castaneda's loyal dog story. *The Little Stone Dog* . . . that famous play where they made a fool of him. He forced a smile. "As we say where I come from, in your mouth, tongue and teeth live together, but that doesn't keep them from getting tangled up once in a while."

"On what occasion, for instance, did that occur with Mr. Castaneda?" Clearly, she did not want to let it go.

He managed to not let himself get flustered. "Listen, Pierre always protected me against myself." After a studied pause, he added, "Yes, my dear, I am calm now, but when I was younger, I was an impulsive person. If you'd only known me back then! I hated above all taking the easy way out! I'd have been able to take my father's place when he died and sit on the throne of Nimba. It was so much more relaxing! But I knew the colonial system inside out, thanks to Pierre. At Cogemin, I had lived inside the belly of the hideous beast, to borrow

99

the great German poet's words! I wanted radical change! The people weren't moving fast enough for me and I loved this country too much to allow it to fail. We would fight about things, Pierre and I. I always wanted to rush at our adversary and he would say to me, 'No, Niko, let's be more shrewd than the enemy!' And do you know who the enemy was? His own white brothers! Can you believe that?"

He discerned a glimmer of admiration in the journalist's eyes. Well played. She was going to write nonsense that would be very useful to him. Naturally, it was out of the question to stop now that he was doing so well. "It was a great day, the day we achieved independence, for the battle had been long and rough. We had just won back our freedom after centuries of humiliation under the merciless yoke of foreigners. It was, above all, a challenge. When I saw all those children running through the streets of the city in boisterous groups shouting my name and the party slogan . . . yes, it's true, I could not hold back my tears."

Rereading this article in *Ebena* several years later, he couldn't help but smile. That young journalist must have been quite naive. She had swallowed all his lines enthusiastically. She had written things like, President Nikiema is a man like you and me. Even though she had added, in order to leave herself a way out, that N'Zo Nikiema wasn't completely like the others, that he had, rather, consented to reduce himself, with humility, to the level of his people. There were several pages of things like that.

There were also a lot of photos. In one, he was an adolescent among his brothers, at the royal court of Nimba. All of them were wearing berets with pointed edges, knitted sailor tops, and short trousers. He looked at his knobby knees covered with the dust of his native bush. In another photo, he was with Salima and their three children in the palace's vast verdant park. It was a beautiful Sunday and it looked like the presidential family had spent it together, finally happy and relaxed. But they were all only there for the photo. Over the years, Salima had become "Mother of the Nation" and their three kids the "Children of the Nation." That meant that his son and two daughters no longer had a father and that they were fine with it. At least they were not arrogant. They did not intend to terrorize the ministers and the senior civil servants. On the contrary, they called everyone Uncle or Auntie, out of both pretense and bashfulness. Having grown up far from the country, they didn't understand anything that was happening around them. Meanwhile, they literally siphoned the state coffers and put insane amounts into banks in the Cayman Islands, in Luxembourg, or in other such places. Their methodical and rational mindset at this game was a wonder. Nikiema realized that he didn't even know where they had gone to take refuge when the civil war began. Besides, he couldn't care less. They'd most certainly had enough of the country, not speaking even one of its languages, among other things. Nikiema imagined them changing their identities and perhaps even their faces so they could delight in reaping the fruits of their plunder in peace. This way, they would be back to square one. He had to admit, he'd messed up his children, too.

He reread a few parts of the interview for a third time. All of it was now right under his eyes, written in black-and-white. Yes, he'd had a little fun giving whatever nonsense for an answer. However, he hadn't lied to *Ebena*'s journalist about everything. About his mother, for example—that was true. He had gone to Nimba to spend some moments in silence at her graveside on the day after he took his oath. Back in Maren, he had realized that he'd forgotten to do the same for his father, who was buried a few meters away.

The event that had changed his life . . . ? He thought that the answer would have been very different if he'd been asked the question there in his hideout, far from the splendor of the palace. He had lied so often—out of necessity much more than out of perversity—that he couldn't even trust his own memories anymore. He believed nonetheless that he knew when it was that he'd experienced the most violent shock of his life. That was beyond a shadow of a doubt: everything became different for him the day when that young dancer came, right in the middle of an official ceremony, and whispered a few words in his ear. He relived that scene often, even at the most unexpected moments.

It must have been a party like all the others at the Congressional Palace. Fire-eaters, acrobats, and rappers performed one after the other in order to distract Nikiema and a half-dozen heads of state seated in the front row. The rappers told the presidents what to do, as they always did. You've got to respect the people, my homies! Yeah! You shouldn't hijack our billions! Yeah! They howled at Nikiema, and his guests practically delighted at him getting chewed out. As for the dancers, bells on their ankles and straw skirts around their hips, they mimed working in the fields, jumping in place. The drummers were circling around them, their eyes convulsing, imploring the sky to make the rain fall. According to the program, all those people were dancing the *Adad*, or the African Dance of Accelerated Development.

—๛—

All of that was rather astonishing, Mumbi. Were we intending to sort out the country by blowing shrill whistles? Watching that dance, I felt a mixture of shame and anger. It was pure farce. All those so-called artists with white diamonds, triangles, squares, and circles on their chests, drawn, it seemed, with ash. . . . And all those things they had on their heads, such complicated things, those tiger cat skins or other animal skins that no one has seen around here for a long time! There aren't any more tiger cats where we're from anymore, for Christ's sake! Who can attest that this is authentic African culture? Would you be willing to swear on it? Nobody knows anything about it and that's what's rather tragic in the end. An old madman whose memory was destroyed by alcohol came up with some peculiar fables and made them valid over the centuries. We trust him because we don't even know who we are anymore. If I'd been able to, I would have forbidden such antics. But people explained to me that had I done so, many fathers of families would be penniless.

It's always been like that. Each time I had the urge to tackle a problem, people told me the same thing: brave people will die of hunger. And when Pierre Castaneda's men started to make their bullets rain on the palace, I

thought that was the end, of course, but especially that my days had been
too short over the last years. But let's let that go. I'd rather talk about
you. About the first time we met. You were among that idiotic troupe of
dancers that was performing the African Dance of Accelerated Devel-
opment—you all were banging your feet on the wooden floor, calling
everyone in the audience up onstage. I have to admit, your troupe did not
cheat; it did everything to maintain its reputation. I was divided, because
while I found your presentation pretty grotesque, I felt like your energy
was lifting me off the ground. I even wondered how much you were being
paid to go through all that trouble. Or was it enough for you to perform
your number in front of so many heads of state? You would have been
mistaken. They are a fine selection of stinking hyenas! If I told you the
story of each of those guys, Mumbi, you'd vomit all night.

One of the dancers moved away from the circle and headed toward
him. As she walked down the seven red velvet steps, a million eyes
were fixated on her long black legs. Her body was gleaming with
sweat, there were pearls around her forehead, and she pulled off an
attitude of sensuality that was chaste and dangerous at the same
time. For Nikiema, the almost animal strength that emanated from
her especially drove the intensity of the moment. Maren's high society was there. Perfumed. Powdered. Repressed. There were also
numerous officials, those people who live in the shadows of the heads
of state and who panic at any little thing. All of them remained petri-
fied, and in that instant she appeared to be, of all those in attendance,
the only one who still had a breath of life. Also emanating from
her bold harsh eyes was a deaf violence and an impression of total
liberation.

He had thought, as undoubtedly did the other spectators, that the
young woman's gesture was part of the ballet. Already for quite some
time, that had been what was in style in the theater: the actors, sitting quietly among the public, rose suddenly at predetermined times
to say their lines. Everyone would then turn to them as the display
of lights tried to create who knows what effects. According to what

Nikiema had understood, it was supposed to show the link between Life and Art, the Real and the Imaginary, etc., but perhaps he hadn't understood anything, because he found this process a bit simplistic and frankly even dumb.

As for me, this theater technique reminded me of one of those spicy anecdotes that make the daily papers in all dictatorships. The first time an actor stepped in from the room, our security guards immediately carted him off. It's true that the guy's remarks were a bit of a rant. Real calls for sedition! I didn't hold an important position at the time, but I attended the interrogation. It was mostly decent, I must say. Shouting and threats at the beginning, but no violence. We quickly understood that it was a blunder. The actor was doing his job and we didn't insist. Luckily, the director didn't hassle us too much. He was a humorous guy and made people laugh by stating that the interpellation of his actor in the middle of the show was part of the play.

It's perhaps because of that incident that there was no attempt to arrest the young woman. When she planted herself in front of President Nikiema, he thought that she was going to start singing a song in his honor. Something about the Great Omniscient One, the Solar Giant of Mount Nimba, etc. There, in front of his peers, it would be a nice surprise for him. He was already relishing their resentment. You cannot imagine how much the presidents of the entire world hate each other. He then gave the dancer a fitting smile. But instead of dancing or singing, she remained immobile in front of him, an expression of mute reproach on her face. The drummers, visibly perplexed, stopped playing and the hall remained plunged in absolute silence. In a flash, Nikiema sensed profound contempt in the eyes of this woman unknown to him. And before he had the time to understand, she leaned over to his ear and spoke to him quickly. She spoke to him about her daughter. He muttered, "But what does this stranger want with me? What is this story about her daughter?" and then she slowly uttered the name he should have expected.

Kaveena.

The self-satisfied smile he was wearing on his face as a public figure froze. It was simple: he couldn't wipe his smile off anymore. He was deeply troubled and there was such silence in the immense hall of the Congressional Palace that everyone heard him ask the young girl, in a tone he would have liked to be playful but which was bursting with irritation, "What? What are you talking about?"

She leaned toward him again and calmly repeated Kaveena's name. From this first contact, he understood that this dancer was a person who was out of the ordinary. And as she returned to the stage dancing backward, the drums playing slowly for her alone, Nikiema applauded her, nodding his head with conviction, for the sake of appearances. That immediately lessened the tension. Everyone understood that the dancer had just given a bit of a special compliment to her Beloved President and hurrahs and laughter burst forth in the hall.

—∞—

You could have taken a gun out of your pearl belt and fired at me. By the time people understood that it wasn't theater, I'd have dropped dead. Your daughter Kaveena would be avenged, so to speak. And there was also that whole row of heads of state from I don't know what countries anymore—you could have bumped them off while you were at it, seven brigands with sinister faces, such corrupt and cruel guys it's unbelievable. That evening, Art lost its opportunity to do a little something for Africa. A whole lot of people on this continent would have been grateful to you! As for us others, the tyrants, we should be wary of certain theatrical innovations!

Pierre Castaneda was seated just behind the seven presidents. He did everything afterward to find out what had really happened. Luckily for you, I always refused to reveal to him what was really going on between us. Just by instinct. You know, it happens that my kind and I lie without even knowing why. We lie by omission or maybe because Castaneda's and my world is such that we never even know. Everything in our daily experience shows us to what extent the truth is dangerous. For example, that day I was saving both of our lives without knowing it. If Pierre Cas-

105

taneda had known that you had uttered Kaveena's name, you wouldn't have had a chance. He would have said to himself, OK, this chick is clever, but Nikiema has little interest in women in the end. How come he let her live? He would have ended up finding out about our secret relationship, and to do so, he would have made your life impossible. You would have had cops around you all the time, and maybe one day, for one reason or another or even for no reason at all, he would have concocted a little fatal accident for you without anybody noticing. And Pierre Castaneda would have acted, surprising though it may seem, instinctively. Compared to my friend Pierre, I'm practically a choirboy. But let me tell you, what truly left me awestruck is that after slipping that threatening remark in my ear about your daughter Kaveena, you went back to dancing with your bells that made all that racket, your straw things, your tiger cat skins around your buttocks, back to wiggling and shouting praises to the Good Old President. You suddenly seemed so idiotic that I understood that very first evening that you had two personalities, one clearly distinct from the other.

Remember, people in the country started gossiping. Once the first wave of astonishment passed, they made up whatever nonsense about that incident. That you had insulted the Mother of the Nation, that you wanted a date, that you were begging for a scholarship for your sister's studies. A clandestine newspaper even reported that you had suggested giving me a blowjob, right there in front of everybody. Literally anything. Pierre Castaneda said nothing. His men had lost your trail and he was very angry with them. My staff had more luck. They managed to find you rather quickly. It's true, I had a great asset: Colonel Asante Kroma. With that guy, you always win. He knows everything. He sees everything. And he only kills when you order him to.

And I can tell you this now: for several weeks, your life was barely hanging by a thread. And that thread was in my hands. Colonel Kroma and his guys were merely waiting for a sign from me. It didn't come. In general, those things don't happen like one imagines they do. I wasn't going to say to Colonel Kroma, "Bump off the young dancer from the Congressional Palace for me." No, it would be a shame if we had to talk in such a vulgar way. Your name often came up at our meetings or even at meals. What *audacity, that painter artist! Disguising herself as a dancer to come and coldly insult the president in front of his guests . . . that's serious! People resented you in my little entourage. If in one of those conversations I had shrugged my shoulders a certain way, it would have been about you. Colonel Kroma would have known what remained for him to do. You were lucky. I never wanted anything to happen to you. And—believe it or not—I don't regret it. You don't like me very much, but I think I did well leaving you alive.*

—॥‒—

Days earlier, my sweeping had missed a small piece of paper. Someone had scratched a few lines in red marker on it. I unfolded it and I immediately saw that the words weren't in N'Zo Nikiema's handwriting. Different from his, the writing was miniscule, angular, and slightly tilted.

I read part of a sentence aloud: "It happens all too often these days. A sad and vain transformation." On the back, a date: November 16. The year was illegible. On the paper was written, "This Thursday morning, at G's. I love him. He also loves me, I know it. But we are not of the same world. His parents are scornful. A girl from the poor suburbs. Not chic enough. Father a taxi driver. Plus she's a whore. Unwed mother at fourteen, they say to me. Violent, too, it seems. What do you want, my dear, they're all like that, no time to educate their children—poverty is still no excuse for this free-for-all morality. Basically, if I stayed in Kisito, everything would be in order. A young girl came from the next-door neighbor's to ask for some cardboard. A banal scene yet so difficult to describe if you want to render the profound truth of it. It was frightening. She said very little, but I saw everything, with terror and disgust: another person, very different from herself, had settled into her soul. The tone of her voice, her gestures, everything in her was saying, I am a young white girl, in spite of the color of my skin; I am not like the others. I thought: a reverse journey. The monkey is climbing back out of the Negro, under our eyes. It is so clear. . . . Everybody sees it and it's as if no one could do anything. We've truly been beaten. There is no more hope. It's perhaps even absurd to believe that it could improve in a thousand years."

I compared the writing with the signature on several of Mumbi Awele's paintings. As I expected, she was the author of those enigmatic lines.

—⁓—

Few people can boast about having really chosen their existence. I trust above all the wisdom of our neighboring people, where having a long nose literally means to live long. My fate too was determined behind my back. What does it mean to lead your life? No, it's actually our life that leads us where it wants to, by the tip of our nose, precisely. Since yesterday, I've been trying to discover when mine went to hell. I want to talk to you about it. Simple as that.

The same scene always comes to mind. Pierre Castaneda and I are sitting in the backyard of a restaurant. The place, modest and rather quiet, is called the Blue Lizard. It owes its name to the legend that you know well about Nimba's foundation. Our small table is cluttered with Heineken and Premium Club bottles as usual. I see Pierre again sinking his teeth into a bloody leg of mutton. I am happy with a few cashew nuts, because I prefer going home and eating alone. Pierre swallows large quantities of meat in such haste that the fat oozes from everywhere. He wipes himself with the sleeve of his shirt, sniffling and blowing his nose loudly. I say to him, "Hey, take it easy, Pierrot, you're eating like a pig."

Pierre shrugs his shoulders, as if to say, keep on talking, I'm starving.

We are alone in a corner, right by the kitchen. It's not far from the toilets—just a hole in the cement—from which a strong odor of urine emanates. Lizards are running noiselessly along the walls. I watch them stop, wave their flat heads all around, and then suddenly disappear.

In my memory, this scene is in very bright tones, dominated by the yellow of the desert and the green of the trees. In fact it has rained all morning and it's as if the leaves of the orange, mango, and papaya trees in the courtyard have been washed out.

It's all coming back to me, decades later. Perhaps you'll understand me better if I compare this succession of images to one of your paintings. My afternoon with Pierre at the Blue Lizard, but also that whole time at Cogemin, the most important time in my political career, blur into one moment. I guess I'm trying to find a starting point for this crucial moment as Pierre and I are walking along Ndunga's rutted streets to get to the Blue Lizard. It doesn't make any sense. It would be even more absurd to associate that scene with earlier events, for example my first government's antiguerrilla operations after independence. No, that scene is a block of time suspended in midair, laid bare to real life, with neither beginning nor end. In spite of its immobility, it is also the melting pot where the most diverse episodes of my existence come to be housed. It refers to the abundance of a life and not to particular realities; it refracts them all and transmutes them into colors and shapes.

The Prieto da Souza affair is at the center of the canvas. Prieto da Souza: remember that name. Our very first crime.

We must have talked about it for the first time at the Blue Lizard. Try to imagine the ambiance of a little shabby bar in a small mining town at that time. People were coming and going in the courtyard. Ta'Mim, the owner, whose real name was Émilienne Ganvi, was a strong woman, full of energy. She looked older than her forty-five years, because she'd worked her whole life the hard way. As far back as I can remember, I always saw her ordering her servers around, her face covered with sweat, a penetrating stare, a blue apron on her chest, and her right hand held out in front of her in an authoritative gesture. Émilienne Ganvi came from another country and there was a lot of talk about her. That she had stabbed her fickle husband and escaped from prison under incredible conditions, that a holy man passing through the town of Ndunga predicted her exceptional fate. For most people, that meant that she was going to become very rich, and they were all licking their chops, waiting for the fortune to be announced so they could partake. Ta'Mim, a fat woman who smoked a pipe and had reddened eyes due to lack of sleep, let people talk. I always thought she must despise these vain speculations. How can

109

you take those drunkards seriously when they sit around all day long telling stupid lies about her instead of going out to work?

In her early days, Ta'Mim was certainly deluded. She thought she'd be able to attract all of Cogemin's workers and even some European executives to her restaurant. You could see in the decorations on the walls— naive paintings showing, among other things, a ram about to be put on a spit to roast—that she had set up her business with careful consideration. Several years later, the only things that remained of those dreams were a few hunting trophies hanging above the bar, along with the sullen faces of her three servers.

I don't recall how we ended up making Ta'Mim's backyard our meeting place after office hours at Cogemin. In hindsight, I think that Pierre Castaneda and I chased away Ta'Mim's clientele. The last thing the African mine workers wanted was to be at the same place as Pierre after their workday. They'd really have to be forced. And at the time, I already had a pretty bad reputation. Cop. Collaborator. Puppet. The Negro on staff. You know, the dirty kind.

The bottles of Premium Club on the table were empty. Pierre forbade the servers at the Blue Lizard to touch them while he was there. It was one of his many quirks. Everyone ended up getting used to it. After joking about his piggishness, I said to him straight out, "You know what?"

He wrinkled his brow nonchalantly but I sensed he was very attentive. He asked me, "So, any more news about those . . . ?" He wanted to talk about the fliers that had caused a stir among Cogemin's European executives. When he uttered the word "fliers," he stopped. He couldn't stand to believe that he was disturbed by the fact that piles of these papers were found one morning on the tennis court at the Belvedere Complex. The Whites in the colony had seemed frightened by those fliers, which promised them all of hell's suffering. But I suspected they were just trying to scare them a little. Life at the Belvedere Complex was profoundly boring and they liked the idea that something was finally happening to them. In the days that followed, I heard them joking among themselves. One of them said, pretending to be horrified, "Careful, it seems they're going to throw us out to sea!" To which another replied, laughing, "That's *good—I never had time to go to the beach! Always busting my nuts for those layabouts." The same day the fliers were found, I came across Jacques Estival, the head of financial services. My direct boss, in fact. He was a bitter, racist, aggressive type. He said to me with a mean smile, "So, just like that, those brothers of yours are having ideas! They want independence, huh? I'd give anything to see that, a bunch of monkeys with a country on their hands!"*

As for Pierre, he would talk about those fliers with guarded fury every time. He felt personally betrayed. At the time, none of this was clear to me. In the heat of the action, I didn't have time to ask myself any questions. Today I realize that Pierre Castaneda backed himself further and further into a corner with a logic that was completely delirious: out of love for the blacks, he answered for them, he had protected them against the poor white settlers, and that's how they were thanking him! For him, those first signs of the struggle for independence boiled down to one odd question: how am I going to be able to put up with the mocking stares of the people from the Belvedere Complex? In that sense—and this was utterly incredible to him—our people's fight came down to a simple matter of self-respect. It never occurred to him that one day we could take our destiny in our own hands. He believed he was teaching us how to walk: the best of us could become, after being patient for several centuries, full French citizens. Castaneda had a rather crude mind, and when I appeared to doubt his theories, he sniggered, "My dear Niko, we are friends, but look, you have had billions of years to handle things. Instead of doing that, when we arrived here you were still in your trees. What has happened here over the last billions of years? Can you tell me?"

I did not answer. Of course, you'll think it was out of cowardice. It's possible: I had just been named assistant to Cogemin's deputy accounting officer. You can only imagine the battles Castaneda had to go through against his own so I could get that promotion. But I must especially point out that I was pretty shy; I had some ideas, yes, but I was never sure that they were good ones. Deep down, I told myself that perhaps Pierre was right. Maybe we deserved our situation with all those Whites treating us like dogs.

But what's changed today, Mumbi? As I am writing these words to you from the bottom of my hole, Castaneda is running the country. He thinks that we did not know how to seize our chance. Over in the palace, as he watches Mwanke guzzle down whiskey and redden his teeth from chewing on cola nuts, he must be saying to himself, it's no use burying our heads in the sand—all those damned independences brought them only misery and even more injustice. We're going to have to start all over again.

I'll get back to those fliers found that morning on the tennis court at the Belvedere Complex. Castaneda had asked Commissioner Garnier to be personally in charge of the investigation. It seemed that the Cogemin mineworkers were implicated in the affair rather quickly. Finding the names still remained. And that was what I wanted to talk to Pierre about that day at the Blue Lizard.

The beer I'd ordered when I came in arrived. He watched me open it and bring the bottle to my mouth. Then I decided to go all the way. The news that I was bringing him was hardly trivial. "The fliers.... You know, Pierre, our good old Commissioner Garnier got it wrong. It wasn't the mineworkers who pulled the trick."

For a fraction of a second, his face lit up. I sensed he was deeply relieved: his own miners, whom he had spoiled, could not have done that to him.

"Who, then?" he asked. "Are you trying to say that you know?" He pretended to be skeptical.

"It's Prieto," I said.

At first, he didn't seem to understand. Then he laughed as he crushed his Gauloise butt on the ground. Only then did I understand that it was a nervous laugh. After a few seconds he said, without raising his voice, "Prieto . . . ? Prieto? The same Prieto?"

"Yes."

"Do you take me for an idiot? Come on!"

"No, Pierre."

Prieto da Souza was one of Pierre Castaneda's many servants. He was skinny, very dark-skinned, and taciturn. He behaved so submissively in every situation that at times even I felt deeply uncomfortable. To every-

112

thing you would say to him, he'd invariably answer, "Yes, sir," or "Yes, madam," in a halting, obsequious tone. This completely strange tic, even for a servant to the Whites back then, at times had a very comical effect. Prieto, where did Hortense and little Gaétan go? Yes, sir. Did they go to gather sumps in the forest? In Ningas Forest? Yes, sir, no, sir, Madame and the little fellow went to Nyambwue. Stop saying yes, sir, all the time, please, Prieto. Yes, sir, I'm going to stop.

But we had noticed that in spite of this, Prieto da Souza was sharply intelligent. He never initiated discussion, but all you had to do was tease him about something for him to start saying rather astonishing things about it. He knew the history of the country well and was capable of narrating what happened in very ancient wars between certain tribes or giving his opinion about controversial events in the past. He would then say in a firm voice that throughout such-and-such battle, the traitor who had made a secret pact with the invading forces was one prince and not the other, whom people often wrongly accuse.

"But I don't understand you, Prieto. That prince is from your tribe and you're not defending him."

"Yes, sir, but you know, there are traitors everywhere."

"Even among your own? Come on, Prieto! Come on!"

"Yes, sir, there are even traitors among my own."

Such statements suddenly had a totally different sense in my memory than how I perceived them back then. Pierre Castaneda and I certainly thought the same thing.

It all pointed to the fact that the writing was on the wall, and it had been for a long time. I saw Pierre tighten his jaw. It was as if his mouth had suddenly filled up with bitter saliva. He had a nasty look on his face. We stayed much later than usual at the Blue Lizard, drinking our beers in silence. Prieto da Souza had fucked both of us and we didn't like it. We didn't like it at all.

I tell you that because Prieto da Souza was, so to speak, my true baptism of blood. I did have a little prior experience, but it was small fry. I was all out of sorts and I had nightmares after each hit. With Comrade Prieto, I had the intoxicating sensation of finally having become a man

113

of my time. Those are not things one forgets easily. When I strangled him, he didn't beg me or anything. He didn't even have a look of fear in his eyes. He died a hero, like in his stupid dreams where he was the chosen liberator of the oppressed masses. I saw him squeeze his fists so he wouldn't scream and he managed to maintain that look of contempt on his face, befitting a patriot face to face with the torturer who'd sold him off to a foreigner. No longer was he the servant boy who acted like an imbecile saying yes, sir, yes, madam, all the time. . . . It's true, he acted like a brave man. But what was the purpose of that? We were alone behind a bush; birds were passing over our heads singing indifferently. He could have screamed—that would have at least soothed him a little. It's no use getting smart about it. In time, they should have known anyway. For a Lumumba, a Sankara, or a Mandela, whom we still talk about, how many among those valiant men who resisted I don't know what had been frustrated by legitimate glory?

And Prieto da Souza was a puny man. I've noticed that most people who refuse to remain calm are the types that have skinny necks and emaciated faces. You can easily strangle them with one hand. When I saw he was no longer moving, I released him and I left. I had no remorse. I had messed up Prieto da Souza's destiny. If he'd gone on like that, he could have become president of this country one day, and I could just hear his flatterers chanting, "President da Souza is a true man of the people—when the Whites occupied the country, he was a servant boy for several years at one of their estates." People would have made us dizzy with that. There would have been films, pilgrimages, and all that stuff. I stopped him dead on the path to his glory, the brave boy. He had waxed the parquet floors at Pierre's and he'd gotten plenty of kicks in the ass, all for nothing. Crushed like a squirrel on a small path in the bush.

Getting back home to the Belvedere Complex, I heard a touraco cry out in the distance: caw-caw-caw. These troublemakers always imagine their departure to the hereafter as one of those grandiose events that moves the universe, and that the birds are going to whirl about among the clouds to bid them adieu. It never happens like that. The birds fly through the sky crying out like they always do, and that's it.

—m—

Their little matter with Prieto da Souza had worked out well. N'Zo
Nikiema was getting more and more excited. He told Pierre Cas-
taneda, "We should take this opportunity to do some cleaning up.
We have all the names."

Castaneda was more cautious. "We'll never have all the names,
Niko. These stories are not that simple." Then, as if thinking aloud,
he added, "All this is so new. Let it go."

He seemed more disappointed than angry. N'Zo Nikiema learned
a few days later that Castaneda had discreetly given some money to
Prieto da Souza's elderly parents. Even though he tried hard not to
let it show, Castaneda was very worried. And rightly so. We heard
the first rumblings of deaf revolt. Anger rose over the course of the
weeks. Where had this sudden rage come from? No one knew. Every
night, leaflets were mysteriously distributed in the city and they were
becoming increasingly virulent. They castigated the lifestyle of the
Whites of the Belvedere Complex, considered glitzy to the point of
indecency.

The Belvedere Complex was the name given to an area of nearly a
thousand hectares which housed Cogemin executives. Other than
N'Zo Nikiema, they were all foreigners. Belvedere, as it was called,
was well equipped. There were pools, two fancy restaurants that
were terribly expensive, and several stadiums for soccer, tennis, vol-
leyball, etc. And a movie theater. I have already spoken of its two
supermarkets with supplies arriving directly from France, which always astonished the visitors. They were also the pride of Pierre Castaneda. Some executives, like Jacques Estival, boasted of not having
been in the town proper more than twice during their several years
of living in Ndunga. Others still went to the African downtown,
especially when they wanted to escape the stifling atmosphere of
the housing complex. Although it was huge, residents felt crammed
on top of one another. Stories of sexcapades were rustled up like
nobody's business in Belvedere, as were fierce professional rivalries
and even some alleged political wrangling. Some of the newcomers,

young and still a little tender, often suffered from mood swings. We left them alone and they soon fell back in line.

It was during this troubled time that the inhabitants of Ndunga came back and built their slums close to the housing complex. Castaneda became very suspicious and saw it as a deliberately thought-out political act. In his mind, it was a quasi-military maneuver to stifle the European section of the city before attacking it from all sides. He was definitely exaggerating, but his fears were justified by the way it looked. The encirclement of Belvedere was indeed performed in a gradual and, so to speak, inexorable way.

In the beginning, a few young women came during the lull in the day to sell rice dishes or braised chicken to the miners for almost nothing. Then the shops opened, and soon there were bars which in turn attracted prostitutes, public transportation, beggars, and some homeless types. Many of the kids who offered sunglasses or bottles of ice water to passersby were pickpockets. Throughout the day, the sound of rattling old car engines filled the air, mingled with the cries of some illuminated people calling out to the common folk to follow the Path of Righteousness.

And little by little, Prieto da Souza's supporters joined the dance. They went from one group to another, repeating the same simple lines: Look around you, my brethren—is it normal that these Whites just take everything that is good in our country? And our children, don't they deserve to be happy? Don't they have the right to go to good schools?

That's how we got the first leaflets. Followed by more baby steps. At first, the demonstrations were a bit timid, but over the coming months they became more and more important.

Castaneda could have easily unleashed some bulldozers on the new native town, as he'd done before. But he was well informed and was aware that the times were changing. And that this was not happening only in Ndunga. Across the country, it was a time of revolt. And Cogemin was being criticized everywhere.

Underground and beyond!

Gold for them, death for us!
Our gold!
Our marble!
Pierre Castaneda, profitmonger!

Women and children were placed at the forefront of all the protests. It was clever because then the men had no choice: they followed. Miners with tuberculosis, pneumoconiosis, or other serious diseases were also prominently displayed. They had been reduced to the status of living skeletons, and the furious crowd screamed that it was Pierre Castaneda's fault: he forced the workers to inhale dangerous chemicals. A woman climbed up on a makeshift dais and asked, "Have you ever heard of a White in Belvedere having this disease?" And with fists raised to the sky, the crowd roared several times, "No!" The woman then screamed, "Freedom!" And everyone took up the chant: "Freedom!"

As for N'Zo Nikiema, he felt closer to the moment of truth. He was not a fool. He knew that despite some of the verbal excesses, the criticisms of Cogemin were well founded. To put it bluntly, he had always been on the wrong side, on the side of the foreign exploiters. It was not easy: hated by some and despised by others. He no longer dared to be seen among his own people around the Belvedere Complex, and with one or two exceptions, no Whites deigned to shake hands with him or speak to him as an equal.

As long as the situation was more or less normal, he could lie low. Right now he was at a crossroads. Of all the inhabitants of the housing complex, he was the only one who did not have the right to turn a deaf ear to the events. His reactions were being monitored and he felt obliged to show clearly which camp he belonged to.

But I don't think that even at this time, there was the slightest doubt in N'Zo Nikiema's mind. He was unambiguously in the foreigners' camp. His will, frustrations, or certainties had nothing to do with it. He had long been like an object floating in a void, and one day or another, the fall was inevitable. By this I don't mean that Nikiema didn't have a choice. I think people can still ultimately manage to remain worthy beings. But this comes with consequences that we must accept.

As evidence, I would like to open a parenthesis here and tell you a true story. Fortunately, it doesn't really take us away from our story since it concerns N'Fumbang, Mumbi Awele's father.

Here are the circumstances that led to my only encounter with this man.

The murder of Kaveena, his granddaughter, was turning the country upside down. I went to find him in the poor neighborhood of Kisito where he lived. I remember the shabby living room. He was sitting on the floor, leaning against a couch that was sunken in its middle, its cracked wood and springs visible. The rest of the furniture—chairs and a large wooden chest—was in just as bad condition and just as betraying, as with most poor folk, of the pathetic effort to convince themselves that their living room was at least clean and well-maintained and somehow masked their deprivation. The floor was waxed nicely but the paint on the wallpaper was completely discolored.

Mumbi's father must have had a skin disease, because he scratched his calves all the time. They were covered with a network of white tracks made by his nails. He didn't know who I was but he didn't ask me any questions when I arrived. He probably thought he had seen me somewhere, because he looked at me pointedly a few times with his glassy yellow eyes, as if trying to remember my face. A young woman—I remember she had a scar on one of her temples—placed two plastic cups of dubious cleanliness on the mat and poured some Orange Fanta. When she was done serving us, N'Fumbang told her to turn off the television. The man greeted me, and between the two silences greeted me once again and inquired about my family for the tenth time.

"Are the children well?"

"They are like little kings these days—it was different in our time, but things change, it's normal . . ."

"And your wife? Ah! Be careful, a husband and wife must be friends..."

He also spoke to me about his work as a taxi driver: he had managed to train a nephew who was going to replace him.

I brought the cup to my lips, took a sip, and after placing it back down, I said, "Father N'Fumbang, I work for the government and my bosses have asked me to come see you."

Still scratching his calf, he shook his head and grunted.

I told him about his granddaughter Kaveena. "Her death is a tragedy and President Nikiema understands your family's pain. Some people in this country are saying false things about Kaveena's death but the authorities prefer to let God Almighty mislead these evil folk."

"He alone has the right to judge our actions," the man said softly.

I added that President Nikiema and his dear friend Castaneda were certainly not involved in this sad affair in any way. Why would they kill a little girl? That is not the way to solve the country's problems. Their accusers were people of bad faith.

The man looked at me with a penetrating stare and asked in a quiet voice, "What do you say your name is?"

"I'm Colonel Kroma. I was sent by the government."

He smiled with an air of ironic superiority but with neither malice nor contempt. "I know. But eight days after your birth, your parents whispered a name into your ear. What is that name?"

"My name is Asante Kroma," I said, a little confused. The situation was beyond me. It felt weird to pronounce my own name for the first time in many years.

"Asante," he said slowly, "I know what's in the suitcase at your feet."

At that exact moment, I realized that everything was screwed. But I still continued. "Yes. The president's friend has asked me to give you this money. These few million will not bring Kaveena back..."

119

I am, like I said before, a regular with these confidential missions, and I've managed to grasp some basic techniques. For example, I never reveal a precise figure the first time around. You must first fling the magic word "million" in the air. You'll see that it immediately gives people an appetite and they become desperate to know the exact number of millions being offered to them. There are no rational rules in these cases—the amount can vary from two to eighty million—and their torment is painful to see.

Five million? Thirty-five?

Will I be able to build a decent house?

Or get into the transportation business?

Finally be on my own . . . ?

If he had been a normal person, Mumbi's father would have already seen himself snapping bills at a family ceremony in Kisito under the eyes of envious neighbors. Millionaire. Millions. It's terrible to say, but in such cases it's the only word people want to hear. It makes them crazy.

N'Fumbang was content to say no by shaking his head, even with a hint of embarrassment, which was quite disturbing to me. It was the first time I had seen this.

There was silence. I felt a little lost. Funnily, my attention was drawn to unimportant things: kids playing soccer outside the window, sheep bleating in the yard. There are, I believe, moments in life when a person hangs onto anything, in order to feel firm ground under his feet.

Now it was my turn to look him in the eyes. I said to the man, "I'm not gonna lie to you, Father N'Fumbang. President Nikiema and his friend are not giving you this money out of kindness."

He interrupted me: "Governing a country is difficult." And after a pause he added, "God knows it's hard, Asante."

I sensed something like compassion in his voice. I was confused and I could not wait to leave. But I wanted to understand. "Why do you say that, Father N'Fumbang?"

"Asante, come back alone another time and I will answer you."

"Alone...?"

As soon as I asked the question, I realized he wanted to talk about the case. This time I laughed heartily. The old man definitely seemed nice to me. Meanwhile, his eyes sparkled with an almost childish mischief. He was really an extraordinary man. It does not surprise me now that his daughter Mumbi ended up having so much power over the former president. From that time onward I understood that the conversation about Kaveena's murder would never really end. For one simple reason: Castaneda had been unlucky. He just didn't kill the right little girl.

The hardest part was admitting to Nikiema and Castaneda that old N'Fumbang Awele had refused our offer. I saw Castaneda sneak in a furtive smile. When the Kaveena case was brought up again, he became extremely tense, suspecting who knows which bad move on our part. His face was impassive, but his eyes moved from Nikiema to me with extraordinary vivacity. He seemed to be saying, "An old taxi driver in this country who spits on millions? Try telling that to someone else!" For Castaneda, things had started to unravel. He proposed that we eliminate old N'Fumbang. It was a typical reaction of his. When one of the three of us said, "So-and-so is dangerous," the other two knew exactly what it meant. Castaneda mostly used this formula when he didn't know what to do. In his mind it was, strangely, a temporary solution. Basically he got rid of a few unfortunate ones while waiting for some clarity.... Castaneda made me kill people the way trees are felled in the forest to open a path.

A side note: With each passing year, Castaneda had the feeling that he was more alone, and, I also believe, more vulnerable, despite the extent of his powers. He thought he was surrounded by plotters, and more importantly mockers—which for an "African" like him was humiliating. For example, it was more prudent to speak French in his presence because he imagined that he was being denigrated in the other languages of the country.

In any event, I did not see myself doing harm to Kaveena's grandfather. Nikiema agreed with me, and everything went back to normal in the end.

N'Fumbang was an unusual man. He lived in poverty. He could have said, "It's true, my granddaughter is dead and perhaps what I'm going to do is not good. But it is God's will. His ways are inscrutable, and in my situation I cannot help but accept their money."

The fact that N'Fumbang had the strength to resist the temptation did away with all of N'Zo Nikiema's excuses. The reader will allow me to put it in simple terms: Shortly before our independence, two paths were open to N'Zo Nikiema. He took in all consciousness the one that led to treason. He knew very well what he was doing. And we both well deserve whatever happens today.

—∞—

The disappearance of the Kamber family—Arnold, Verena, and their two children—caused a big stir in Belvedere. The Kambers had gone camping, as usual, in the Nyambwue Forest. Not seeing them return late that Sunday afternoon, their boys sounded an alert. It was not possible to look for them in the evening. A big search was organized the next day. I must say that the Nyambwue Forest was a dangerous place. To camp there was to risk being attacked by lions or leopards. There was also talk of a gorilla—one in particular—that attacked unaccompanied women. He paraded before them showing off his manhood with somewhat ambiguous grunts. They didn't understand his advances at all, and he ended up raping them. I don't really believe this tale but such anecdotes at least go to show that the Nyambwue Forest was not a resort.

The four bodies that were found after a week of anxious waiting were not a pretty sight.

A group that called itself Commando Prieto da Souza had just signed off on their first violent political act. We had entered a new era. The days of gently dropping leaflets onto Belvedere's tennis court or of slightly disruptive demonstrations around the mine were over. It was war now.

For Nikiema, this quadruple murder was almost a family tragedy. The Kambers were the only people in Belvedere with whom he had succeeded in having more or less normal human interactions, apart from Castaneda, obviously. Arnold was a brilliant geologist in his fifties, a willing comedian and totally unprejudiced. He and his wife, Verena, were simple folk and they did not live with that sort of intellectual tension that so often ends up corrupting the soul. N'Zo Nikiema could not help thinking that if Commando Prieto da Souza had struck another family, he probably would have rejoiced in secret.

Two days after the funeral ceremony at the Ndunga Church, Pierre Castaneda brought Nikiema into his office and told him bluntly, "You are going to stop, Niko."

"Stop . . . stop what?"

"You heard me."

N'Zo Nikiema could not understand what he was talking about. Such a sentence could mean a thousand different things. He just stared at Castaneda in silence.

"You're going to leave the company. There is too much talk here and it's not good for you."

"I don't know what you mean, Pierre."

"You're the only black officer in the company and those people are saying you're a spy."

"And you? What do you think?" Nikiema said, surprised by his own spirited question. He wasn't in the habit of speaking to Castaneda this way. He felt an anger rising within him, as well as anxiety mingled with shame. You betrayed your people and at the first opportunity they are throwing you in the trash, he thought. Now you're all alone.

The word "scum" began to spin all around his head. At that moment, in a flash, he realized that his whole life had been built around Castaneda. The latter had held his destiny in his hands for a long time without him really realizing it.

Anticipating his concerns, Castaneda leaned forward and spoke in a low voice. "Listen to me, Niko. You and me, we'll remain friends.

But let's get this straight: the day I stop trusting you, you're a dead man. There are some excited folks in Belvedere who want us to play Fort Alamo—they are shitting in their pants right now, and are talking about organizing patrols. There have never been so many firearms circulating in our housing complex. This is serious."

Reassured by Pierre Castaneda's tone, N'Zo Nikiema just nodded. He was also confused about having been so quick to doubt his friend.

"Go and wait in Nimba," Castaneda continued.

In the end, Nikiema was not upset about getting away from Belvedere. He told himself it would give him time to get his thoughts in order. After all, maybe he still had a chance to recover.

They arranged all the practical details. He enjoyed a long-term leave and kept his salary and benefits. But a few days later, at the Blue Lizard, he told Castaneda, "My life is here. I don't want to go bury myself in Nimba."

Castaneda was silent for several minutes before replying to him in a definitive tone, with a sort of brotherly irritation. "You need a plan? Well, you're going to get one."

He then spoke to him frankly. Nikiema noted that Castaneda's voice, almost reluctantly, became more and more complicit.

"Furthermore," Castaneda said, "I'll accompany you to Nimba."

"When should we leave?"

Castaneda thought for a few seconds. "Look, I have to go home in three weeks. First to Alsace to offer condolences to the Kamber family, then Paris. The Kamber deaths were a terrible shock there. They already see us all as little squares of meat in the boiling pots of cannibals. Everyone wants to understand. I must go explain everything. Arrange for our departure in six days, will you? That will give me time then to return to Ndunga and prepare for my trip to France."

"That's fine," Nikiema said.

"One more thing, my man: people may try to provoke you—you have to stay calm."

N'Zo Nikiema was already up and ready to start his holiday. He nodded in agreement before saying, "If I understand this clearly, Paris wants to respond to this?"

"Seems like it worries you," Castaneda said.

"You're a friend, Pierre, and I'm not going to lie. I didn't want to get caught in the crossfire. It's already complicated enough."

"I hear you, Niko, but these people have gone crazy. They want to make an example—they always say that in these situations."

"I know what that means."

"Yes, burning down two or three cities, poisoning the livestock, shooting the leaders, et cetera. I will try to reason with them. What was done to the Kambers is hateful, it's incredibly cowardly. On the other hand, this is the price to be paid once in a while if we are to remain here. Trust me, I am going to speak to these politicians."

At this point in my narrative, the reader will allow me to slip in an observation, and he can perhaps gauge its importance later.

N'Zo Nikiema's return to Nimba fueled a controversy that has not died down since our independence. The three years he spent there were decisive in his rise to power, as everyone knows. It is tempting to think, as some do, that he knew it was time to move back so that he could make the leap. It was indeed in Nimba that N'Zo Nikiema established the people's Convergence Party and began to criticize, with unusual virulence, the foreign stranglehold on our economy. Nikiema's supporters like to describe this period of his life as one of open revolt against colonial oppression. According to them, N'Zo Nikiema had until then been working for Cogemin—there he had studied his enemy up close, and then from his stronghold in Nimba he delivered unstoppable blows.

I am convinced, as indeed are the majority of our citizens, that this is just absurd and dishonest gossip. The truth is much simpler. This was the era of big moves, and these two friends—Nikiema and Castaneda, his mentor—had devised a fairly effective tactic: shout out hymns about black freedom just a little more forcefully than the other jackals did. I am not one who will blame them for having been more cunning than their opponents. However, as Nikiema further suggests in one of his letters to Mumbi, you've always got to tempt fate a little. He might have played a much more important role than we can admit today. With the passing years, we all tend to believe that politicians are far more subtle—or cynical—than they actually were.

—∞—

On the morning of their departure, they saddled the horses and decided to start before daybreak. They hoped to reach Nimba the same night or maybe the next day. At the beginning of their trip, it was so dark that they walked for nearly two hours in silence. They were also a little worried because it had been a long time since either one of them had been on horseback. They were too busy with Cogemin to find the time to go riding in Belvedere. Because of the way the hooves sounded on the ground—dry, almost metallic or stifled—they knew they were on a path covered with gravel or an otherwise grassy surface. In Ndiben, the first large village in the west, the sky began to clear. Everyone was still asleep. Shortly before Ndze-Ndze, they stopped under a banyan tree. Once the horses were tied, they went to pee behind the bushes, then moved around to stretch their whole bodies. Castaneda held his butt, rotated from left to right, and deliberately let out some comical groans. Making fun of him, N'Zo Nikiema punched his fists in the air, like a boxer warming up. He then rubbed each shoulder and knelt down to stretch. They laid out two mats on the floor and set up their rather modest breakfast. They had coffee in tall thermoses but it was already lukewarm. While Castaneda placed a pan on the oil stove, Nikiema delightedly inspected the large ham and Emmental cheese sandwiches that Pierre's wife, Hortense Dupaquier, had made for them.

Well before the next village—it had to be Tinko, the site of a famous battle between the Kingdom of Nimba and a coalition of its southern neighbors—they started crossing the paths of farmers go-

126

ing to their fields or women returning from the well. The two travelers were not strangers. Soon the rumor spread that Prince N'Zo Nikiema, heir to the throne of Nimba, and his foreign brother were riding on horseback to the kingdom's capital.

"We were stupid to think we could surprise my old man!" N'Zo Nikiema said.

Castaneda sensed the pride in his friend's voice. "It's the African drum!" he said with a laugh.

N'Zo Nikiema knew that Castaneda didn't mean any harm when he said this but he didn't like this way of speaking. He couldn't articulate why, but these kinds of jokes irritated him.

He pretended he hadn't heard, and gestured toward the landscape with his hand. "So beautiful here! I had forgotten about this world," he said dreamily. "I didn't even remember anymore that I was Prince N'Zo Nikiema. All my adult life spent crunching numbers . . ."

"We still need accountants today," grumbled Castaneda.

At Tinko, the chief sent horsemen to meet them. It was eleven o'clock in the morning and you would have thought it was market day in the village square. Young girls held out calabashes and knelt in front of them. The water was clear and pure and the two friends quenched their thirst. In his residence, the chief held out a spear to N'Zo Nikiema, then kissed his feet as a sign of allegiance. Then there were very long speeches. Usually the leader spoke in a low voice to a griot who then repeated his remarks to the audience. But this time, only N'Zo Nikiema, future king of Nimba, had such a privilege. He was not prepared for this exercise. He managed quite well, though.

The leader then said, "Your houses are ready."

When this was translated to him, Castaneda barked, "Our houses are ready! What does that mean?"

"That means we will spend the night in Tinko."

"Thank you, I understood that! Only, that isn't going to happen."

The people of Tinko listened without saying anything and N'Zo Nikiema wondered, embarrassed, if any of them understood French.

Anyway, it wasn't necessary to know French to understand that he and Pierre were fighting. He looked at Castaneda as if he were seeing him for the first time in his life. Castaneda's brusque manner clashed almost unbearably with the silent and reserved notables of Tinko.

"Look, Pierre," he said, "we don't have a choice. The chief has had a hundred oxen, a hundred goats killed—"

"He's also had one hundred guineas killed and there will be at least a hundred liters of palm wine!" Castaneda interrupted sharply. "The chief is really great!"

"Absolutely. The chief is really great," N'Zo Nikiema said icily. He saw quite clearly the kind of comments that Castaneda had in mind but he did not want to prolong the discussion.

"We'll stay here tonight," said Castaneda. "After that you're going to figure something out so we don't have to deal with any more of this shit." Seeing that he had offended Nikiema, he then added gently, "You have to understand, Niko. If we carry on like this, it will be a month before we arrive in Nimba. I came along with you because of our friendship but I can't be away for too long. I also have to take a trip to my country."

The next day, they were too tired to leave at dawn after a night of drinking. As soon as they were out of Tinko, Prince N'Zo Nikiema ordered the horsemen responsible for escorting them to turn around. He spoke to them more harshly than he would have liked and read the fear in their eyes. It was as if they were afraid of being killed on the spot by Prince Nikiema. He felt a drunkenness he hadn't known before. Gazing out at Mount Nimba, which could be seen from everywhere, he thought, this is my kingdom . . .

Villages filed past them. Tigri. Zara. Mindanewo. N'Zo Nikiema kept his promise, and each time someone wished to host them, he spoke to the chief who, a little fearful, came to kiss his feet. It was the same in Kitenge, and when they were alone, Castaneda exclaimed, "Well, Your Majesty . . ."

N'Zo Nikiema, suddenly annoyed, refused to let him go on. "You cannot joke about this, Pierre."

Pierre Castaneda immediately realized he had made a blunder. He paused and after a moment said, "You're right, Niko, one doesn't joke about this. But there's a question I can't ask anyone but you."

"What's that?" Nikiema said, surprised by Castaneda's seriousness.

"Well, I want to know, why do people empty their cellars and slaughter all their cattle just for two people passing by?"

N'Zo Nikiema almost said that he was the heir to the throne of Nimba and not just a passerby. Naturally, it would have made no sense to offer that as a response to Castaneda.

"I don't know why." Then he paused and said emphatically, "No damn idea why, Pierre." He felt the anger rising in him.

"The year's provisions! Of course they're going to starve after that," Pierre Castaneda continued, as if to himself.

They walked in silence along the Nemeni River. Each was lost in thought. After a quarter of an hour, they passed a group of women burning dry grass near a large pit. One of them left the group. To N'Zo Nikiema she seemed young and old at once.

She said a name and asked them if they knew him. Nikiema translated for Pierre, who said immediately with conviction, "Tell her that her son is well and that he's the bravest miner in Ndunga."

"So you know her son?"

"No," Castaneda said. "But it will make her so happy—it's obvious that she only lives for her child. Why would you want to deprive her of that joy?"

The woman said that she never forgot the Cogemin chief in her prayers. Thanks to Castaneda, her son sent her money at the end of each month. It was also not the first time that a villager spoke to the two travelers about Cogemin. The company had a presence in the land of the Nimba kingdom and Pierre Castaneda had hired most of the youth in the area.

Sometimes at the Blue Lizard, Castaneda would mock N'Zo Nikiema too. "You're part of the local recruitment, my man!"

To which Nikiema would reply, "That's my father's fault, that old jerk! I have no idea why he gave you all these lands."

"Well, we asked him!" Castaneda laughed heartily.

N'Zo Nikiema then thought, a little bitterly, you bought it with a little popcorn, yes. Some popcorn . . . Well! Oh well!

He couldn't believe it.

—∞—

At the entrance to Nimba, the king had a group of dignitaries greet them. Prince Nikiema had always seen them around him during his adolescence. They were as dignified and stiff as before. However, he noticed their greedy and suspicious eyes. There was a vulgarity in their gestures that he had never perceived before. No doubt he had left Nimba too young: only adults could have this perspective. Mansare, who had died a few years before, was not with them. He had been his mentor. How he would have liked to see him again! Mansare was a righteous and proud man, one of Nimba's best.

The two travelers passed through a line of griots emphatically singing the praises of the prince. Young girls waved palm leaves in their faces. Several people shouted, rolling on the ground and throwing handfuls of sand all over their bodies.

The king received them seated on his throne. His *pagne* had big green and red squares and came up to his ankles. On his bare chest one could see dozens of amulets, and he wore a large hat of ostrich feathers on his head. N'Zo Nikiema remembered his childhood. He used to be fascinated by all the colors that made the king look like a giant butterfly. During elementary school in Nimba, he would often try to count them with his fingers in that new language he was learning: red, blue, green, orange, violet. . . . After a few seconds, the colors would blend into one another. He would count again but they would always blur as they seemed to be dancing on his father's half-naked bust.

Guards stood behind the king looking stubborn. The king, pensive and vaguely severe, stared at length at N'Zo Nikiema. The prince had the impression that the king was looking at another person behind him, and he felt ill at ease. With great difficulty, he suppressed

130

his desire to turn around. He knew: royal etiquette forbade him from looking around. It was the first thing that old Mansare had taught him: "You are a prince, N'Zo Nikiema—you must not shout or stamp or look left and right." As if, in Nimba, in order to govern, it was first important to show that one could stand still for as long as possible. N'Zo Nikiema could not understand either why a father who had not seen his son for nine years had to receive him as an outsider. He regretted having stayed away from his family for so long. In his little two-cylinder car, he could cover the distance in less than seven hours, even if he stopped occasionally to rest the engine. He promised himself that he would explain to his father, when they were alone, that it was not easy to leave Cogemin to come see him. It was not his fault. Castaneda could attest to that. His father had a soft spot for Pierre. Or maybe the old man was punishing him for not having returned for his mother's funeral. He stood there, everybody watching him silently, and he felt guilty. He felt guilty without knowing why. He also had to admit he was their princely heir and he felt ashamed of them. What had happened over the last several years that made him feel he was no longer at home among his people? He did not know that his life, day by day, had slyly slipped away from him. He dared to look for Castaneda's eyes and saw that he avoided his gaze.

His father finally motioned for him to come forward. When he approached, the king asked Pierre Castaneda to do the same. All of it had only lasted a few minutes but to him it felt like an eternity.

The griot was supposed to scrupulously repeat the king's words, but sometimes he adorned them with little historical facts or a dash of humor. N'Zo Nikiema, who could hear both his father and the griot, was struck by the griot's political sensitivity. The king especially spoke of the old friendship between Pierre Castaneda and Prince N'Zo Nikiema.

"You are," he said, "blood brothers. You two are blood brothers, and even Fomba, the Ancestor of Ancestors, has come to accept that."

The dignitaries shook their heads and chins, and the two friends guessed that this enigmatic remark had not been made by chance.

Over the course of a few seconds, Prince Nikiema and Castaneda became more and more enthralled. Basically, the Ancestor of Ancestors had been testing them for a long time. He had seen that the hearts of the two men were free of hatred for each other. But Fomba was not someone who relied on appearances. Upon the foreigners' arrival, Fomba was convinced that the Evil Forces had sent him to Prince Nikiema to enable the loss of the kingdom. He had searched again and again among the stars of the night, the wind of dawn, and the ocean floor, and had seen nothing wrong.

"For several years," the king said, "Fomba has followed you, watched you, set traps for you. He has heard every word you've said, and has even heard your most secret thoughts."

He then asked Nikiema to translate for Castaneda all that had been said. As he spoke in a clear voice and with fluency in the foreigners' language, the prince read an expression of immense pride on his father's face. He almost got up, although like any monarch he was forbidden such indulgences in the presence of his subjects. It really seemed as if his heart might explode with joy at any point. The words sang and danced as they came out of the mouth of N'Zo Nikiema, who maintained complete self-control. The mere fact that his son was capable of such prodigious acts seemed to forever legitimize the power of the old king over the people of Nimba. In spite of this, N'Zo Nikiema felt somewhat embarrassed. In his own eyes, this discomfort remained a mystery. After all, he had always carried himself well around foreigners without any qualms.

When N'Zo Nikiema had finished translating the king's words, Castaneda said, "Then . . . ?"

"That's all," replied N'Zo Nikiema.

"Are you kidding me?"

"I'm serious."

"Your Ancestor discovered that you and I are blood brothers. OK. And what else has the Ancestor decided?"

"Maybe the old man will us tell later."

"What do you mean, 'maybe'?"

"It's just a way of speaking. I know he has an important revelation to share with us. Please Pierre, let's not make a scene." N'Zo Nikiema was becoming increasingly irritated by Pierre Castaneda's rude behavior, and Castaneda noticed that.

Nikiema's father summoned them at dinnertime. When they arrived, they immediately noticed the king, whose appearance was entirely different. He was sitting on the floor on a simple mat. A pagne made of *faso danfani* fabric covered half his torso and he had on a gray and brown hat, tilted to the right. The room he was in was large and pleasantly cool. Nikiema's father was still smoking his pipe, and the smell of the tobacco brought Nikiema back again to his childhood. Without his ostrich feathers and rows of pearls around his neck, his father looked somewhat ordinary and even a little lost. Nikiema regretted having come to Nimba with Castaneda. No matter what he did, he saw his own father through Castaneda's eyes: skinny, with hollow cheeks and wrinkled skin, and eyes reddened by palm wine. And even his hat, tilted to the right, made him look like a clown. He was an insignificant man. Nikiema's father was the king of Nimba and it meant nothing.

He wondered why this trip had caused him so many little pangs of anguish that he hadn't felt before. If he'd been asked to sum up in one word his feelings and thoughts from the previous few days, it would definitely have been this: *defeat*. It was a terrible feeling and he saw how much defeat had infected their souls and destroyed everything in its path. Yet he could not tell—any more than the people of Nimba—when and where the war had actually taken place. It was strange. They had been defeated and yet they had never realized that there had been a war.

He saw in the king's eager eyes—just like those of the dignitaries—that he was watching for the moment when they would bring him, according to the unchanging ritual, gifts from Pierre Castaneda: crates of whiskey and cans of sardines. And also boxes of

133

popcorn. The king loved popcorn. He loved cracking handfuls of it between his old teeth with childish delight, a bit of drool flowing from his lips down to his chin. N'Zo Nikiema thought that this time he could not endure such a spectacle. Castaneda probably sensed his shame, because he gave the king some money and promised that the gifts would be delivered in kind later.

In Nimba, too, cattle had been slaughtered in honor of the two travelers. But their stomachs were tired and they were happy to have some millet porridge with green tamarind sauce.

When they retired to their rooms, Pierre Castaneda said to N'Zo Nikiema, "So?"

Nikiema looked at him quizzically. "What are you talking about?"

"What did the Ancestor say?" Castaneda looked very worried. N'Zo Nikiema finally understood that he was especially worried about Cogemin. The company was benefiting from a concession to extract gold in Ndunga and marble in Masella, a little further southeast. Having a rational mind, Castaneda had always thought it was a little too good to be true. He anticipated difficulties at any time. For him, it was inevitable that the people of Nimba would eventually begin to grumble, "Why do you come from so far away to make money with the riches in our subsoil?" And he knew that they would say that Fomba, the Ancestor of Ancestors, didn't like that very much because all those foreigners turning over Nimba's bowels were disturbing his rest below the ground. Castaneda had no intention of letting it go but he knew that such a story could make things terribly complicated.

"It's good news," N'Zo Nikiema offered, almost despite himself. "Father senses his end coming. He's decided that we will both be the sacred kings of Nimba. A throne for you and for me. It's great, right?"

"You don't look too happy, young man."

N'Zo Nikiema was suddenly overcome with a deep weariness. He remained silent. For his part, Castaneda would have liked to know what this story of him and N'Zo Nikiema being crowned kings of Nimba meant in practice. But he didn't ask any questions. He could clearly see that Nikiema was not in the mood to answer him.

—⟋⟋—

One day, after the first rains of the winter season, we found him sitting on a stone at the entrance to the cave.

We believed that the traveler was trying, without fearing for his life, to slip into the depths of the earth. This required courage which only the Gods can give us. But he came from the cities of the West. And people in the West, as we know, do not know fear. Over the centuries—or so it was at least claimed, though there is no need to provide proof—thousands had been swallowed by the abyss. And it always happened the same way: sitting, their heads bowed, where they had found the foreigner, they awaited dusk, their favorite time, to go to that place where darkness was perpetual. And the shadow hovering around them would slowly envelop them. No one was surprised not to see them return. We knew that there was a labyrinth that spanned the underground and about the things that happened there, and the horrors had reached the point where it was impossible to bring them back even if you weren't particularly hard-hearted.

But the man we saw toward the end of the day at the entrance to the cave was not getting ready to go in. Instead he was coming out. When people realized that, there was an outcry. The news spread throughout the entire Kingdom of Nimba.

The foreigner stood there, frozen, and the first sons of Nimba to arrive on the scene told senseless stories about a clay statue. After we'd circled the man cautiously, we approached him.

He was alive and well.

"Who are you?" someone asked him.

He did not answer, and the question was repeated with all kinds of gestures. He remained silent and, obviously annoyed by our insistence, waved us away.

When they began to back away slowly, worried and confused, he uttered the name of the Ancestor of Ancestors three times and pointed to the entrance to the underground.

It was only then that we recognized his voice. He threw off the coat that was hiding his whole body, and his goatee and blue eyes erased any remaining doubts we had.

For a moment, the silence was total. Everyone looked at each other without saying a word. Each of us could see that over time, dressed in his rags and zigzagging backward like an old drunk, he had lost his mind.

Then I saw the crowd make way for an old, noble man to pass: Mansare. He said, "I, Mansare, come from beyond, and I am telling you, stop your foolish lying." His face was hard, as it had been long ago, in the days of my childhood.

I said to him, "You, old Mansare, my former Master, I cannot shed your blood. Go away. I beg you. Master, go away. Leave us among ourselves—we are like dogs howling at twilight and you have never been part of this world."

And Mansare answered, "I'll remain here, I came from elsewhere without having even moved my feet. Here is where my roots are and my place of exile. Fomba's earth is gone."

The foreigner stood up. We heard cries of anger: "To death! To death!" A shot rang out. More and more shots spat out from the mouths of old rifles. The foreigner, frightened, stopped sticking out his chest and took refuge behind a recess of the cave. From there, he started looking around for somebody.

Me.

I felt dizzy in this moment of absolute power. I held his fate in my hands. I could have crushed him like a bug on the black rocks of Mount Nimba. All I had to do was want it.

Everyone waited for the signal to turn the foreigner into an ephemeral bloodstain.

At that exact moment, the future was handed to us on the blade of a knife. We could have cut the stranger's throat. I said, "Let's make a place for him in our hearts." In truth, we had a choice. We would never have been able to pretend otherwise. We cannot accuse destiny of having imposed this foreigner on us. And you, my father, shame on you, who for a little whiskey put lies into Fomba's mouth—Fomba, the Ancestor of Ancestors.

Does the foreigner now remember the moment when I held him at my mercy? Does he remember when he screamed insanities against me, holed up in his palace, and asked the Lil Boys to bring him my head on a bayonet?

I am not telling you about what our friendship was like before, when he was like an older brother to me. No, I am talking about the throne of Nimba. Fomba gave it to him willingly. I am talking precisely about the moment when he was already almost dead, when the crowd, led by Mansare, although still silent, was in the grip of a massive rage, was ready to disown Fomba and my father, and I went over and rose up in the middle of the circle and said in a strong and clear voice, "No one is going to hurt this man."

A young man yelled, "But we know who he is—he's the head of Cogemin! He treats our people like slaves there. He's a dog!"

This was the type of guy who had a picture of Prieto da Souza in his bedroom. I knew who he was. He wore sunglasses and had a small limp.

I said firmly, "No one is going to hurt this man. The Ancestor of Ancestors has split his heart between him and me."

They began to recede.

The foreigner came out of his hiding place and came to stand by my side. He was still pale with fear and trembling slightly.

We took the road to Nimba together. Everyone followed us. I made a gesture and everyone started to sing and dance.

Those fools.

Fools.

Mumbi Awele, in my solitude, I yell out again: Fools!

Do you hear me, Mumbi?

So quick to dance to the beat of the drum, they get screwed without even realizing it.

When they do understand, it's one or two centuries later. Later? Too late? I don't know.

And I: infamous for generations, long before Fomba's time. I was not their hopeful prince. I was the chief accountant at Cogemin. What a great promotion. Hey, who's the crazy one, Fomba? I even had a little two-cylinder car.

After a few days, we started seeing bodies floating near the shores of the Kartani. The bodies of those who had fired the shots. The bodies of those who, at dusk, had treated the foreigner like a dog. Among them, the young man with the limp and the sunglasses. He did not even have time to remove them before he was beheaded. A head without a body, with sunglasses on.

They deserved it. The audacity to challenge Fomba's lies!

—◊◊◊—

Late yesterday afternoon, after reading the thick file on Pierre Castaneda's induction into Nimba, I found myself muttering, "Well, here's a coronation that hasn't gone unnoticed . . ." It was a straight-up global event.

This is how I started to go a little insane. How can I keep a clear head with the kind of situation I am in? I am starting to feel the effects of my confinement in this cramped place, in the company of this corpse—now completely dried and almost presentable—of the man who for so long has been, after God and along with Castaneda, the master of our destinies. My own death lurks all around me because I don't see how I will be able to escape unharmed. Aside from all of that, the documents I am unearthing every day are so fascinating, it's intoxicating. All our history of the last seventy years is right here. Of course, we need to go even further back.

A line from N'Zo Nikiema—or, less often, Mumbi Awele—is sometimes enough to take my mind on a ride to the moment when, for our people, Time began.

But I get back to reality soon enough.

In 1955, there were a thousand and one things happening in the world that were infinitely more important than those I'm going to tell you about. There were wars, masterpieces of world literature were published, and surely many great scientific discoveries were made. I'm just assuming this since it is impossible for me—as each of you will see—to find traces of these events in the archives.

It is therefore understood: that year, the world didn't suddenly start to revolve around Nimba.

Yet, judging by the press clippings, Castaneda's coronation did pique the interest of some major newspapers at the time. Some of them had sent special envoys to the kingdom's capital. I have in front of me a piece of photojournalism expressing the shock felt by a Japanese magazine on this occasion. If I had to create a single image from all the articles I read yesterday, it would look something like this: "Pierre Castaneda, a white colonial, becomes a black king." Incidentally, this same sentence appears, with slight variations, in many other texts. It shows that the whole issue appeared in a style meant to entertain the readers. In fact, only the unusual side of it was highlighted. I must say that throughout my present solitude, I've often enjoyed this style of writing, full of light irony and almost dancelike. There were, of course, several mistakes. It was inevitable: in Europe in the mid-fifties, few people pretended to believe in equality between races and nations. Thanks to these articles, I learned the names of a certain Joseph Conrad, and because of Gaétan—Castaneda's son—Rudyard Kipling. Castaneda was being compared to Mowgli, the jungle boy. He had also been introduced as a "hero of our time" who made the choice, completely crazy but wise nonetheless, to "leave our civilization and return to the sweet ardor of the primitive world." This lyricism had a knack for infuriating one columnist renowned for his bad character. I read remarks in his writing that seemed to me, even for the time, somewhat excessive. He claimed he had no desire to go "screeching through the trees together with the savage baboons."

In hindsight, all of this just makes you smile in an amused, almost tender way. You ask yourself how all these supposedly educated people are so stupid.

Ethnologists had also made the trip. They questioned all the residents of Nimba, who had received orders not to talk with the foreigners or else be severely punished. Just like the reporters, the ethnologists eventually fell back on N'Zo Nikiema and Pierre Castaneda.

N'Zo Nikiema explained things to them very simply: "Fomba, the Ancestor of Ancestors, wants the power to be shared between Castaneda and me."

Someone insolently asked him to spell Fomba's full name. One journalist was surprised by such a long name. "Don't you think it would be easier to just call him 'Ancestor,' Your Highness?" she asked.

"There's a reason we address him this way, ma'am."

"Which is, Your Highness?"

"With us, there is a reason for everything," N'Zo Nikiema repeated.

"And so with others too? But you haven't answered my question, Your Majesty!"

"Well, go fuck yourself, madam! How's that?" He had had enough of these people calling him "Your Highness" in a mocking way. He was not going to be polite to them.

"Your Majesty, what did he say exactly?" asked one reporter.

"He said, 'If Nimba does not fulfill my wish soon, then its people will disappear.'"

He was ashamed as soon as he said those words.

"Excuse me for insisting, Your Highness, but can you confirm that you heard the ancestor distinctly utter the name Pierre Castaneda?"

"Not me, sir. My father heard it, last year, shortly before his death."

"But you, his son, have worked in Cogemin's accounting department?"

"Yes, sir."

"You were under Mr. Castaneda's orders?"

N'Zo Nikiema did not understand why someone would come from so far away to mock him. Faced with the foreigner's laughing eyes, he had the urge to unleash his anger but was suddenly overcome by sadness and a strong feeling of powerlessness.

140

Actually some of those reporters and ethnologists had not come to Nimba for fun. Among them were hard-core hired assassins, and never had Nikiema and Castaneda come so close to being machine-gunned in public. Were the two friends aware at the time that they might not have survived that situation? Although I have no proof, I believe that they had no idea. However, it has been established that Cogemin's competitors thought that they were hiding something. All the gasoline, cobalt, and diamond mafias, and I don't know which others, were on a warpath. For them, the coronation of Castaneda and all the other nonsense were part of a huge diversionary tactic by Cogemin. They suspected the company of having designs on the vast area that lay to the central west of Nimba. And what had they discovered in these territories? They had come for the sole purpose of finding out. They were not about to let Castaneda hide such an enormous project from them.

The ceremony itself was, as one might say, colorful and flamboyant. Television did not exist at the time, though some photographers insisted on being present during Castaneda's initiation. They behaved like spoiled kids, saying that they had come from far away, almost risking their lives, just to get to this shithole. It would be great for Nimba's tourism, with the slogans and everything, if they showed the world some unedited images—for example, of Castaneda dancing like a black king in the sacred grove. N'Zo Nikiema showed himself to be intractable. Hatred rose in his heart like never before. He was capable of having those foreigners who ventured beyond the determined boundary killed, and, indeed, he really wanted to.

To N'Zo Nikiema's great surprise, Castaneda handled himself quite well during the first part of the initiation. But he did not seem to be equal to the task of the Ngunzi dance. They had made him wear heavy clothes, hundreds of amulets, small mirrors on his forehead, and copper bells on his ankles. All of that, in addition to the straw belts, made him look rather grotesque. Forced to fit in and failing at everything he tried, he began to lose patience. Red with confusion, he whispered in Nikiema's ear, "Fuck, I'm never gonna get it!" He was mad at himself but somehow also at the Kingdom of Nimba for having such complicated coronation rituals.

N'Zo Nikiema pretended not to hear him. He was actually preoccupied with himself. He continued to feel, in a confused way, the weight of his mistake. *And so, you had the audacity to lie to Fomba.*

The next day, Pierre Castaneda said to him, "I'm married, as you know."

N'Zo Nikiema knew his friend's practical mind and had anticipated this comment. He said, "Hortense Dupaquier will be the Queen Mother." And he added, with a slightly contemptuous smile, "That goes without saying." He almost felt ready to embrace the bright side of the situation. He was still single.

Hortense Dupaquier had no place in Pierre Castaneda's life. Nor did he ever speak of her or their son Gaétan. N'Zo Nikiema hastened to clarify that Gaétan from that point on would bear the title of Crown Prince of the Kingdom of Nimba.

Castaneda took his new responsibilities very seriously. "Estival will replace me when the time comes. Maybe in two years."

"Estival?" Nikiema said. "He's mad. He will make their life tough. I'm glad to be away from the company during that time."

"Yes, he's going to give them a hard time. He's an asshole. But I need to stay here to learn all your royal stuff."

Castaneda's goodwill surprised and sometimes even moved N'Zo Nikiema. Castaneda asked questions about everything and, conscious of arousing a lot of curiosity, voluntarily took a back seat to Nikiema. He also took notes to make sure he wouldn't make any gaffes. One day he sheepishly said to N'Zo Nikiema, "After all this time, I should have been able to talk directly to the people.... I don't know your language. It's shameful."

"That's OK. I'll be your professor."

After a few lessons, Castaneda decided to stop.

"The student is bad, the professor is no good.... Could this really have worked?" N'Zo Nikiema asked cheerfully.

They had always worked in total cooperation. At Cogemin, Castaneda protected him from their French colleagues. But this was the first time they were truly in tandem with each other. Even to make the smallest decisions in Nimba, they had to discuss everything for hours. N'Zo Nikiema remembered the day the king's advisors made Castaneda extremely perplexed. The issue was about deforesting the area around Nemeni in order to build—with Cogemin's funds—the first health clinic in Nimba. And the advisor had said, in his usual pointed way, "Before pulling out the roots of a tree, noble sovereigns, raise your head and look carefully at the top."

After the meeting, Nikiema explained to Castaneda what it meant. Then a sort of passionate philosophical joust ensued between the two friends. They spoke in French, using words that nobody around them could understand, and this brought them even closer to one another.

One day, Castaneda said, "Niko, I've been observing you since our first trip and since my return from Europe."

"Yes . . ."

"You've changed."

Nikiema was aware of this but asked anyway, "How?"

"No offense, but . . ."

"Go on."

"Here it is. . . . It seems sometimes that you are ashamed of your people."

"It's not that simple," said Nikiema after a quick moment of reflection.

"I agree," said Castaneda thoughtfully.

Castaneda wanted to be the king who built and grew the kingdom. After a short while, he had holes drilled, encouraged young people to establish firms for mutual savings and credit, and initiated education programs to prevent ethnic conflicts or promote human rights. He erected a building—three rooms in a row—where the housing project was accommodated. We learned that it was implemented under the joint authority of the two sovereigns. It was in a way Nimba's government building. Everyone started talking about capacity building and local development. Nobody really knew what all that meant, but they all were suddenly enthusiastic about the matter. It was a way for young people to earn a living and simultaneously break the monotony of the long days of idleness in Nimba. The old folks noticed that the younger ones no longer had an empty and uncertain look in their eyes. Instead they saw them running in all directions, stopping only to say hello. In short, with the new clinic, the new elementary school, and bold initiatives on the ground, Nimba regained a taste for life. Nothing seemed too good or too expensive for Castaneda when it was intended for Nimba.

From what I understand, this attitude provoked, at least initially, distrust in N'Zo Nikiema. Especially since in order to fund these so-called self-reliant development activities, Castaneda used his own money and was anxious to let that be known. But eventually Nikiema, a keen observer, chalked this ostentatious generosity up to the desire, though poorly controlled, to do well. Much later on, he himself must have understood this neophyte's reforming frenzy. During his first term, immediately after the country had achieved independence, he used to take long walks alone in the middle of the night through Maren's streets to ensure that everything was in order. He noted every detail: the buildings built in spite of common sense, the broken embankments, and the heaps of filth at the intersections. A few days afterward, he summoned the culprits to his office and lectured them for a long time, like a parent. But he did not hesitate to discharge several repeat offenders from public service. He believed he had also found a way to reduce at least a quarter of the spending dedicated to public health: by encouraging all the administrative officials to exercise for two hours every day.

However, N'Zo Nikiema did not uphold any restrictions when it came to the subject of the throne council members' salaries. On this occasion, Castaneda indeed had the elegance to advance his friend's interests. The decision to increase the salaries set off a veritable storm throughout the Kingdom of Nimba. The kingdom began to buzz with rumors of endless intrigue, clan rivalries, and stories that those whom the two sovereigns favored were being poisoned. The neighboring people started to show their jealousy and aggression, and Nimba, although better armed with Cogemin's support, had to flex its muscles to calm them down. We see that in this case, the youth were ready to shed their blood for their country.

The Queen Mother—Hortense Dupaquier—began making speeches about everything and anything. It was not usual in the kingdom for the Queen Mother to be so talkative in public. But she thought that the patterns within the kingdom had to be changed at her own discretion. She also prided herself on the natural bond she had with the women of Nimba. She used to get them together under the sun and make them suffer endless harangues. "Don't let your husbands get away with it," she told them. "You're human just like them. If any of you are being mistreated by your husband, come and tell me. I'll know how to talk to this little domestic tyrant."

She stood before them, ruddy, with a khaki helmet on her head, and said, "If you want to avoid disease in your children, be less dirty! Wash your hands before eating! Wash your hands with soap after eating!" And she added, in a sudden fit of rage that surprised even her, "It's not so difficult to wash your hands with soap, damn it!"

You could say that Hortense Dupaquier was really taken by this game. But it had not been easy to convince her to accept the title and function of Queen Mother. I'll tell you how it happened.

For Pierre Castaneda's wife, living in Africa was already enough. And when he talked to her about his becoming the king of Nimba, she thought he had gone mad and she forbade him to involve her and their son in that story. She was a small woman, with full lips and a pockmarked face. Whoever saw her for the first time was struck by her lively gestures, her slightly innocent eyes, and her sour demeanor. Maybe people expected the wife of the almighty boss of Cogemin to be more serene and mild-mannered, to have more style.

Nobody knows how Pierre Castaneda managed to make her change her mind. Hortense Dupaquier first made several short trips to Nimba, living almost exclusively on mineral water, for fear of catching a tropical disease. However, she did not delay feeling reassured. She, who at first found it ridiculous to be called Queen Mother of Nimba, became strict overnight regarding questions of etiquette. She gave the griots the names of her ancestors and asked them to compose songs for them. They did so without complaining. But it was reported that in between two songs of praise, the griots would shower the Queen Mother and her ancestors with coarse insults. She would nod, pleased, and give them money.

When N'Zo Nikiema heard they'd done that, he laughed about it for several days. When the griots, hugging their *kora* to their chests, passionately yelled out the names of Hortense Dupaquier's ancestors, his ears would prick up and indeed sometimes heard somewhat unexpected lyrics. The griots of Nimba were real magicians. They could, with a simple inflection, completely reverse the meaning of their words. N'Zo Nikiema's eyes shone with malice and he shook his head in quiet approval. He was aware that it was a derisive revenge but he didn't have anything else at hand. He was, in any event, happy to see that he was not the only one who hated Hortense Dupaquier with a vengeance.

Naturally, there was nothing more than these pleasant personal resentments in the Kingdom of Nimba. Pierre Castaneda, always on alert, saw that some young people did not approve of what was happening. They secretly mocked the housing project and the new ideas, which their companions repeated like incantations intended to bring down the sky on the self-reliance programs.

They didn't dare to say a word in public against Nikiema and Castaneda. They just watched Pierre Castaneda in silence. At least that's what he believed. He felt drawn into an abyss of shame by their silent and disapproving faces. When he could not bear it anymore, he spoke to N'Zo Nikiema about it. There were ten young rebels. All were killed, one after the another.

I had been head of the secret services in our country for a long time. I knew that Castaneda and Nikiema were bound by the blood

146

they had shed together for years. But I had ignored the damage they had caused during their monarchy phase.

—⁂—

As of today, as we approach the time of the final departure, I still don't know who you are for real.

At the time, Colonel Kroma's department investigated you. They had nicknamed you the Artist, out of spite. It's typical: stalking is a dirty job that they don't necessarily like, and this is why they turn it into a game and come up with somewhat funny nicknames for their victims. And that brings a question to mind: how did Colonel Asante Kroma, who held people's lives and deaths in his hand, manage his own conscience at the end of the day? For Pierre and me, this terrible power was executed from a distance: eliminating an opponent meant removing a piece on the chessboard. Nothing more. We never saw blood. But he who had to live with it constantly, how did he do it? Here is what I imagine, though maybe I'm exaggerating a little. Colonel Kroma, the methodical policeman with records that are marked with the date and time of the death of this or that person. The guy's on TV, does his thing, and, looking at him, the colonel thinks, that one's got four days left. Or something like, keep talking, my boy.

But they lost your trail. I am the one who sabotaged the investigation. I made them dizzy by sending them on a wild goose chase. The colonel is smart. But this time he didn't smell the smoke. It's not that complicated with us politicians: being smart doesn't happen in the head but with the hands. It's the hands that hold the cards. All we have to do is have more cards to play than the other side. We weigh the pros and cons all the time but what balances our scales are the facts and not ideas.

Castaneda had his suspicions, he thought I was not legit in this story, but he could not prove anything. I took some risks for you, you know.

This Artist investigation was like a recreational activity for the colonel's men. It made them discover that world, quite an extravagance for them—actors, filmmakers, sculptors. In short, the world of those who present themselves, in all modesty, as creators. Our agents used to go to this café, Chez Mado, and after hearing poems being recited there, they

147

laughed about it for days afterward. Back at the office, one of them would look up at the sky, evoking a comical version of the "ardent singing stars of the future," while another one mocked the "flames consuming the winter in the darkness of my heart." Everyone would burst out laughing. But the day they were impressed was when a writer, a little bit drunk, got up onstage and said, "Well, I'll tell you how I write my novels. Here you go. I stand at the door and ring the bell politely. Then I go inside and greet my hosts politely, always politely, right. As you know, ladies and gentlemen, I work with words. I will find them wherever they are. It's all stupid, and I sometimes wonder, just between us, dear friends, why people think all this complicated stuff about writing. Words are just sitting there, doing nothing, a little sleepy, a little stupid even; when there is no one to shake them, they yawn from boredom, the poor little things, and they're not really sociable so they don't talk among themselves. Without me, they are good for nothing, they rot in hearts and minds, they wither between the pages of dictionaries. But I chat with them and they listen to me, and I tell them what I expect of them. They are all there. The funny ones, the beautifully dark ones, the ones the color of blood, playful, dismal, etc. I do my shopping, you know; I pay and then I'm off. After I've mixed everything, I mix it again and again and then I serve it. There you go, that's how I write my books, and if you don't want to read them, that's a shame but I can't do anything about it, you poor fools, just carry on."

From what Colonel Kroma himself told me, his men, without understanding much of this half-crazy gibberish, had succumbed to the magic of the writer's words. The colonel had surprised them while they were talking about him with respect, saying, if I remember correctly, "This guy's words are really powerful!" Tall, half-starved, and very sure of himself, the writer had dyed his hair red and green, and he had, it seems, a piercing look and near-perfect elocution.

This proves that Colonel Kroma's guys are not that stupid. They understand the value of art and all your stuff. Only some things are beyond them—for example, when someone decides he's going to write books or make films and show them to the entire world, even if it means starving. Not trying to offend you here, but these artists are braggarts. When

they threaten us in their works, we pretend to be scared and they feel
pleased with themselves. But we the tyrants know well: they are com-
pletely harmless.

As for you, Mumbi, your little friends from the art community do not
like you very much, it seems. They jabber away in the bars without know-
ing whom they are talking to. You should be careful, if I can give you a
little advice here. The gossip we picked up about you! The colonel gave
me the list—very thin at the time—of your exhibitions and some articles
from so-called art critics. One of those wackos presents you as one of the
greatest painters of our time. Nothing less! Bravo.

But Colonel Kroma did not find what would interest me the most:
a political opinion or something that resembled it. You are not what I
believe is called an engaged artist. In the National, you had been very
clear at the time: "I am only interested in the beautiful things in life.
Politics is too ugly."

Precious words, especially from the mother of Kaveena. I was reassured
by them.

I was the only one who knew the truth at the time. If Castaneda and
the colonel had guessed even just a little bit, it would have put the whole
republic in a stir. And let me tell you once again: you would no longer be
in this world.

—※—

Nikiema's bleached-out skeleton now seems quite banal to me. I
almost want to say it looks attractive, but it is just that I don't find it
repulsive anymore. I often observe it in silence, without feeling anything. Little by little, it has begun to take on the quality of ancient
human remains exhibited in the glass boxes of museums, indifferent
to the visitors' eyes. I have to admit that though I am not inclined
toward mysticism, I find it absurd that N'Zo Nikiema just lies there,
resting peacefully in his grave, as if for eternity. It feels logical to
think that his body and soul are, in some way, *waiting*. I am convinced that N'Zo Nikiema's body will be discovered in the weeks to
come and that something will finally happen. I imagine, for instance,
an angry mob of people walking his skull and bones through the

streets of Maren, chanting with hatred. Maybe Pierre Castaneda will make arrangements for a grand national funeral to further his political interests. One way or another, Nikiema will be buried in Nimba, then wept for, insulted, and forgotten. No different from anyone else really. The rest, meaning the matter of N'Zo Nikiema's second life in the hereafter, will be between him and his God. It isn't my problem. I find it hard to come to terms with the fact that the individual story of N'Zo Nikiema has ended forever, and almost by accident. And that he is just asleep in his room with his eyes closed, waiting there until Judgment Day. It doesn't make any sense. There are so many religions on our vast planet of men, and none of them has ever claimed that such a thing is conceivable.

He drifts through the air like a subtle fragrance. And this waiting, filled with anguish and uncertainty, has a name: Mumbi Awele. Which is why I wasn't surprised to see her in the studio one afternoon.

That day, I had stayed a little longer than usual in the basement. Incidentally, the air had become more breathable since N'Zo Nikiema's feces had become like cow dung exposed to the air for a few days: although they once had been expelled from his presidential bowels, they were now dry, dark pellets, somehow small and trivial. Around four in the afternoon, I went back up to the living room. Someone was singing and listening to music. I could also smell tobacco. I realized immediately that Mumbi Awele was back: if the door had been pried open, I would have heard the noise downstairs.

Mumbi was busy tidying up the studio. A mop lay by a small puddle on the floor and a broom leaned against the wall. I stood in the doorway not knowing whether I should make a sound or wait until she turned toward me. She continued to wash the dishes, singing along to the music in a voice that sounded vaguely absent to me. I thought, this is the dancer from the Congressional Palace. I was now the only person in the world who knew about her relationship with N'Zo Nikiema. She may have sensed my presence but she did not let it show. She was barefoot and wore jeans that stopped at her calves and hugged her ample bottom, which was too wide for the rest of her body. The tap squirted water on her face now and then. She kept arching back to avoid getting wet and seemed to take a sort of childish pleasure in the whole thing.

There should have been something intimidating about this whole encounter. This was, after all, someone I had been on the verge of eliminating when I was head of the secret services. Perhaps she knew it. I could imagine Nikiema telling her, "Castaneda and Colonel Asante Kroma had planned on liquidating you. I stopped them in the nick of time." Judging from his letters, the former president was like a small puppy bouncing on Mumbi's lap. No doubt she was a very strong woman. Anyone in my situation would have liked to know her better. I knew two or three small things about her, but they didn't matter. Prostitute. Failed artist. Irrelevant. If that was all she had been, I would have known what to do with her. But it was clear that her real life was elsewhere. Her real life was not even in this small house.

To reach the forks on the round table, she had to turn to her left and show me her profile. In that moment, I knew she had seen me. I coughed discreetly. She quietly gestured that she was coming back, but then she apparently decided to wipe her hands first.

Finally, she walked toward me. Her white shirt, tied at her navel, was wide open and showed her firm, gleaming breasts. Her whole upper body seemed to project itself forward and gave all her movements a small arc. I was in front of her for a few seconds and had not yet looked at her face. All I saw was her body, and the drops of water on her breasts. I felt like she had emerged from the sea, and this bothered me. Yes, I have to confess: for some inexplicable reason, I only saw her body. She noticed this and made it known to me with a subtle and quick movement of her lips. It was something like, "Pull yourself together, my friend . . ." Suddenly a little embarrassed, I found myself wondering what she was going to think of me. It was a bad move, and everyone in Maren will tell you that I am not the sort of the guy to lust after women. *Colonel Asante Kroma? You're kidding.*

We always wonder who fathered his children! Such spiteful rumors sometimes made their way back to me. The logic was simple: people were afraid of me because I was not interested in money or sex. It's just my nature. Or maybe the result of being raised by a very strict father. I am not going to talk about this now because it's irrelevant to this story. It is this mastery over my mind that has helped me climb the ladder. In my profession, sobriety in all its forms is the only advantage. One of my younger colleagues saw his promising career cut short: he used to accuse pretty women of conspiracy so he could rape them in the Satellite cellars on the pretext of duty to the state. That's all he did for years, and everyone got sick of it in the end. We arranged for a little accident just before he was due to get married. Poor old Timbo. Rest in peace, anyway.

Mumbi Awele held out her hand to me and said, "Hello, Colonel."

I replied with the same ease, though I felt a slight tremor in my voice.

"Don't be surprised that I recognized you," she said. "There's no mystery. I was there when you came to see my father in Kisito."

"Ah?" It was not something I wanted to remember. I had gone to see old N'Fumbang with a suitcase full of banknotes. The mission had been miserably thwarted. My professional reflex quickly regained the upper hand. "So then you . . . you were there?"

"Yes. My father spoke well of you after you left."

I tried to hide my embarrassment. "He should have chased me out with a stick. I was trying to buy his silence with a few million."

"He was a fair man. If he'd thought it was the right thing to do, he would have killed you and then turned himself in to the police."

Odd family, I thought.

I immediately had the impression that the portrait of Mumbi in N'Zo Nikiema's letters did not correspond to reality. I was expecting to meet a young woman who was belligerent, arrogant, depraved, though still a misfit in our miserable little real world. I also assumed that she might be marked by a long-lasting grief, ever since the death of her daughter, Kaveena. An almost eternal pain that might show on her face and in her every move. On the contrary, she had a singing voice that made her especially charming, and I also felt that she was acting a little; she didn't want to appear defensive in front of me at any time. Of course, we hadn't said much.

But I believe that the first moment of contact between people is important, especially in situations that are somewhat strained or abnormal. This is also something my job has taught me. Every time I've had to interrogate a tough guy, and what I mean by that is a mentally tough guy, it all played out within the first quarter of a second. I could always tell the moment our eyes met if the prisoner was going to talk, or if he would choose to crack under our hands. Obviously, this is not how it's going to go with Mumbi. She has nothing to confess, and I am certainly not going to be the one asking questions. I just want to say that, contrary to all expectations, she seemed to be a totally normal person who was pleasant to be with.

"I'm here for several more days," I said, "just to test the waters."

"Several days . . . several weeks, I don't care. Anyway, you have nowhere else to go."

"I will be forced to leave at some point."

She took a pack of Dunhills from a bowl and said, "Can I?"

I nodded. She lit a cigarette, inhaled the smoke, let it out of her nostrils, and looking searchingly into my eyes said, "I didn't offer you one because I know your reputation. The colonel doesn't smoke, the colonel doesn't drink, et cetera. They just say 'colonel' as if there were only one in the whole country."

"In my earlier posting, yes, I was the only one."

"With your striped cap. A legend."

I smiled, somewhat touched. "Right. There was all this fuss, but it was just a cap."

"People still talk about it."

I shrugged. Mumbi seemed to be mocking me with every word. I felt that she had a cynical attitude toward everyone, or she was convinced of her superiority to the rest of the world.

"What's the news outside?"

153

She chose not to answer directly. "The most important thing," she said, changing her tone, "is to not let them find you. They're looking for you everywhere, and they've burned down your house."

"My family is already far away."

"That's fortunate. Pierre has only one goal in life: to destroy you both." She made a slight, almost contemptuous gesture toward Nikiema's body.

I started. "Excuse me?"

"Yes. He is convinced that you are building a liberation army."

"It's not that, madam. It seemed to me that . . . Castaneda . . . you called him . . . Pierre?" Without intending to, I had spoken in an icy, suspicious tone. It was exactly the same tone I used to use when I suddenly had the feeling I'd finally cornered a tough guy.

Mumbi smiled. I was especially struck by the harshness of her expression when she said, "Well, get this: I am sleeping with Pierre Castaneda." She paused studiedly, and without giving me time to react, added, "Take it any way you want, but don't make a big deal of it, please."

In situations like this, I never say anything. I am like an animal being chased by the pack, looking all around to see where the danger may be coming from.

What Mumbi had just told me was not only likely—certain even—but absolutely stupefying. All of a sudden, too many things were coming out at once: N'Zo Nikiema's corpse, right there under our noses, little Kaveena, her father refusing tens of millions, my guys who never managed to nab her, and now her story with Pierre Castaneda. All this for just one person? Of course, I was dying to know how long she had been with Castaneda. I knew very well that I had no right to ask questions. *Take it any way you want, but don't make a big deal of it, please.* It was infuriating for me to think that this woman might have been hopping around from Nikiema's bed to Castaneda's while I, supposedly a detective, was on her trail. I don't know about her relationship with Castaneda but I can attest

154

to the fact that she never felt anything for the wretched Nikiema. With them, it was mere sex, just sex, nothing but sex, sex night and day, morning and night, like a couple of addicts. I allude to it rather discreetly later in this account, but to tell you the truth, the notes and letters from N'Zo Nikiema are filled with vile obscenities. He talks to Mumbi about her splendidly spread-out legs, describing the young woman's private parts with striking realism. And just like my agent, Mike, he says stuff like, "Your pussy's on fire." Literally. Such are the crude terms he uses to address her. I didn't really want to reveal this aspect of N'Zo Nikiema's character. It's not good for him or for our country: when a man his age speaks like that, you cannot repeat his every word. Especially if he has embodied, for better or worse, the ideals of our great nation.

"Listen," I said, "I don't want to get involved in your private life. I've seen it all, as you can well imagine. But after what you just told me—"

She interrupted me. "I thought about that. Don't worry about your security. I can assure you of one thing: if you stay here, you will be under my protection." She spoke with incredible authority, and in a tone that tolerated no argument.

"OK," I said, not knowing if I really agreed.

She relaxed a little. "You cannot imagine the torment they have in store for you and the other one."

There was silence. Both of us were thinking of N'Zo Nikiema. His skeleton was right behind us on the living room couch.

Mumbi said, "I'm going to tidy up the house a bit. I've started with the studio because I am preparing this exhibit."

I thought that the best solution was to buy myself some time in order to see things more clearly. I said very casually, "I'll give you a hand."

I expected her to protest. She accepted. "Fine."

We did the housework without making too much noise. Mumbi informed me that she liked to work with music on, excused herself, and promised not to disturb me.

She didn't live exclusively in the small house. Sometimes she stayed for several days in the city. When she returned, she would bring me fruit and newspapers and prepare food for both of us. We almost never spoke. She liked that: to do her own thing without involving anyone. I understood and I lived happily with it. I was never very chatty myself either.

—⚏—

Little memory exercises, more to relieve him from his ennui than out of necessity, allowed N'Zo Nikiema to remember the number of days of temporary calm: thirteen, and not one more. He muttered, "Oh, thirteen days though..." It came to him, too, that it was an early Wednesday morning that he had seen the last line of tanks move toward Jinkoré. The last battle, people everywhere were saying, was in sight. After they had passed, thick black smoke darkened the sky for a while, making the city even sadder and the air more suffocating than usual. He thought that the tanks would come back at some point during the day, at dusk perhaps, and that the fighting would be particularly violent around the palace.

But there was nothing.

From his window that day, he saw some dull but unusual sights. The residents of his neighborhood, the chicest in the city, could not decide whether or not to flee before Castaneda's troops arrived. Some men, clearly the fathers of families, went out first and looked around as they talked among themselves. He could tell from the sound of their voices that they were afraid. Then they all went back into their houses. They were going to have to leave. They cursed Nikiema and hoped he would have to leave as well.

He held on to his power. And yet he knew very well that he would be defeated.

An egg, beaten against a stone!

How conceited!

Yes, but he already had Mother of the Nation secured, and their children....

156

Those kids are foreigners. Surely they feel better where they are. The president's children!

Each of their luxurious residences cost hundreds of millions. They had finally left, although by force. When you think of the number of people who don't want to make war, N'Zo Nikiema thought, you are always amazed that war is happening anyway, and so often, just about everywhere in the world. He wondered if the people who were fleeing knew where they were going. Most likely not. Still, they were lucky: they could save their skins by doling out bank bills, Indian hemp, or cans of beer to Castaneda's Lil Boys. This way, they would manage to reach the border town of Dombe down south. With each passing day, Dombe found itself to be at the center of greed. The rest of the country was ransacked. Armed factions with eccentric names, under the command of cruel and at times demented leaders, shot anyone who crossed their path and then slashed them with machetes.

—◦◦◦—

Tap-tap.

Rat-a-tat.

Tap.

Little clicks and popping noises in the light of the morning.

He approached the window and slowly, with pressure ever so slight from his right index finger, moved the curtain that lined the bay window. The street below was calm, deserted. Exactly as he had expected.

He could make out a vague dark figure zigzagging toward the balcony of the palace. Then a young man appeared at the end of Blériot Avenue. He must have been between eighteen and twenty years old and was dancing around alone on the ridge, his eyes and Kalash pointed up at the sky. He shot several bursts in the air then watched the bullets form a curve above the blaze. It was as if he was trying to get drunk off of the odor of the powder. His weapon made a small brief clicking noise:

Tap-tap.

Rat-a-tat.

Tap.

The young man was wearing a white or yellow bandanna under a cap and his shirt was ripped up to his chest. Alone in his refuge, N'Zo Nikiema particularly remembered the guy's sneakers. They were what made him seem like an adolescent tap dancing or playing roulette. It didn't seem to be a scene from a country at war. He could have abandoned himself to the same little dance in a semideserted street in Marseille or Zurich holding a bottle of Coca-Cola in his hand instead of a Kalashnikov. But on this wide avenue, on those days when the outcome of the war was being decided, there were no fast food restaurants serving cold drinks and hot dogs; instead there were carcasses of charred cars and corpses that no one thought anymore about coming to pick up.

It was hard for him to believe that this was one of Pierre Castaneda's Lil Boys right before his eyes. Everyone referred to those adolescents' cruelty in a fearful, hushed tone. They weren't the only ones: each camp had such kids in their ranks. They liked to make their victims' hearts and livers throb in the palms of their hands.

The difference with the Lil Boys was that they weren't very good fighters. The one he was watching come and go along Blériot that morning, a red Walkman stuck on his ears, hadn't smeared his face with blood. Nor was he wearing his victims' bones around his neck. He moved laterally around the ridge with a certain grace and one could sense how happy he was that the country was being ransacked and pillaged. Chaos suited him quite well. There was all-out lawlessness and, unlike him, the powerful of yesterday were afraid of death. Pressing his heels into the cobblestones, he swiveled his waist around, like a rock n' roll dancer. His black baseball cap, too big for him, made it hard to see his eyes and face. N'Zo Nikiema could only make out the outline of his jaw. It was somber and square. Although the boy was rather weak, his whole body exuded strength and wild energy. He felt like the master of the universe. In that posh neighborhood, dozens of people kept their eyes fixed on him, too frightened to even think of hating him. Guys who wanted to live for a long time because for them life before was good. And plump or thin women, nonchalant and wearing perfume, who were so desirable.

N'Zo Nikiema nodded his head slowly. He almost understood the Lil Boy: when all this is over, he'll have to run after those ladies outside the supermarket to push their carts full of nice things. Then they'll distractedly throw him a few of their measly leftover coins. N'Zo Nikiema thought with a mean smile that the kid had definitely made the same comment as him: in times of peace, the rich outside the supermarket are often distracted, they don't look at anybody, they never see the kids crawling around them like maggots on a piece of fruit.

The cartridge cases across the boy's chest glimmered in the morning light. Having reached the altitude where N'Zo Nikiema was, he stooped down and pretended to unload his Kalash on the palace windows.

N'Zo Nikiema returned to his office, where he began sorting documents. His ministers and some senior civil servants were waiting for him in his council chamber for a meeting. "No doubt the last," he muttered.

—⁓—

His last meeting with Pierre Castaneda.

He had tried to negotiate and Castaneda had said to his emissary, "Go tell your boss that I will receive him at Cogemin."

"The . . . the head of state is coming . . . here?" For the emissary, a completely ingenuous young man, President Nikiema was a god. He asked his question again, utterly stupefied. It was unthinkable to him.

"Don't worry, sir," Castaneda said softly. "He will come."

Nikiema didn't have a choice: it was the rule of the game. With a little luck, he would save what he still could. After all, he and Castaneda had lived through very intense moments together. And that creates connections.

Castaneda made him wait for thirty minutes at Lil Black's, the most frequented bar in the Belvedere Complex. Although it was the middle of January, the air was warm and dry. Alone at his table, he had a view of the park and the pool, a few yards away. Except for the boys dressed in yellow and brown livery, N'Zo Nikiema was the only African in the café. One of the waiters noticed him and nearly dropped his tray, he was so shocked. N'Zo Nikiema had known the young man's father back in the day when he himself was Cogemin's deputy accounting officer. He said hello with a friendly wave. The waiter wanted to wave back at him but couldn't manage to, which troubled him. Nikiema could easily guess the questions that were jumbled in his head. How could it be that President Nikiema was sitting there all alone, like any other customer, at a table in Lil Black's? In the newspapers, people would sometimes say that the war between him and Castaneda would erupt in a matter of days—what could the head of the enemy army be doing there? Nikiema turned his eyes toward the park to give the server an opportunity to disappear. He didn't need to be coaxed.

The Belvedere Complex hadn't changed much. True, some new buildings had been put up. Shiny new SUV Troopers or Pajeros had replaced the old two-cylinder cars and the black Peugeot 203s from the 1950s, but it seemed to him that the spirit of the place hadn't changed. Three young French women, half-naked with slender bodies, passed in front of him without looking at him. In any case, there was little chance they'd already seen him on TV. Him: a motionless shadow above the chasm. An old warlord already defeated. Them: the movement and carefree attitude of ripe fruits in the sun. The joie de vivre. They were living in the same country, but on different planets.

Behind the bar, the servers couldn't take their eyes off him. He thought they would talk about this scene for the rest of their lives. *I saw him. He was alone. He stayed sitting by the pool for two hours, he didn't seem proud—yeah, it was a little before the war. They're all the same, yeah. They're so afraid of the Whites. He stole our billions and then*

160

left to have an easy time of it, and with all this, people want the country to develop. Development, my foot.

N'Zo Nikiema saw an old man coming in his direction. He was walking with difficulty, one step after the other, leaning on a cane. Right away he recognized Jacques Estival. Having reached him, Estival stopped in front of him and came out with, "People told me you were here. I couldn't miss it. Schmuck."

Estival was always so spiteful. He was once a young, ambitious, energetic man, ready to commit any despicable act to pass from the B1 category to the C3 class. He was said to have come from a good family, and his tall stature, unruly hair, and blue shirts with open collars gave him a domineering look. He boasted, in a play on words, about fixing his sights high and having a critical eye. But already at that time, N'Zo Nikiema knew that Jacques Estival would be a lonely and bitter old man. He was one of those people who wear the marks of decrepitude on their faces from very early on. Nikiema was happy to see he had not been wrong. Jacques Estival was all out of sorts: mentally unbalanced, out of breath, disconnected and a little crazed. "And you don't even have any teeth left, you dirty son of a bitch!" he uttered under his breath, his heart full of hate. Dribble, all white, accumulated on Jacques Estival's swollen lips, and he was incapable of being articulate; his words ended up being a continuous inaudible buzz. To hide his anger, N'Zo Nikiema forced himself to appear contemptuous. Estival shook his head, and as he moved away, he said, "Well . . . Well!"

The day N'Zo Nikiema had come for an interview at Cogemin, Jacques Estival had been in charge of receiving him. How many years had it been? He tried to count and gave up very quickly. Jean-Luc Dardenne was the boss of Cogemin at that time. Pierre Castaneda, one of the advisors that he most listened to, compensated for his lack of education with his taste for action and his familiarity with the African cultural milieu. Nikiema had just come out of adolescence. A happy and protected childhood at the royal court of Nimba. Until that day, he'd seen only fear and respect in the eyes of

161

men and women. For the first time in his life, he was left to his own devices. He had been sent from office to office with a sullen tone. In Cogemin's dusty hallways, he had crossed slovenly Whites who sometimes stank of alcohol.

Jacques Estival seemed uncomfortable with the meeting. He was supposed to address an indigene like a normal human being and he had never done that before. Anyway, the test was only a formality. Everything had been arranged with Jean-Luc Dardenne and Nikiema's father, the king of Nimba. Estival asked him simple questions, though at times rather disconcerting ones. The number of wives his father had. What he had heard around him about Cogemin. The period of France's history that interested him the most. If, in his opinion, the Africans had a civilization. What he thought about friendship. If he believed men and women were equal. Did a leader, according to him, have the right to kill to make people obey him.

As he tried his best to answer, Jacques Estival's colleagues came and just planted themselves in the middle of the office, observing him with a pensive air, and then went on their way without any comment.

Nothing about that shocked him. All he knew about life was what old Mansare had taught him. But that world, the one of the French of Cogemin, was totally foreign to Mansare.

He was going to get up when, as he turned his head, he saw a man with a massive face and olive skin standing at the window, a pencil stuck behind his left ear and a Gauloise between his lips. He must have been there for several minutes and he was watching him and Estival, much more than he was listening to them. N'Zo Nikiema recognized Pierre Castaneda. He had come a few days earlier to visit his father, accompanied by Jean-Luc Dardenne.

Nikiema said hello with a little wave. He knew, however, that that wasn't done.

Later, Castaneda had to admit to him, "I liked your nerve, but the others found you quite arrogant. Some of them were furious. The boss had to use his weight so that you were taken in spite of it."

Thinking about that several decades later, he was still staggered by the foreigners' arrogance. After their long occupation of the country, they had more or less gone back home. But before they left they'd forgotten to explain why it was such a grave offense to greet them from afar, even politely.

Another question whose answer I'll never know, he said to himself, following Estival with his eyes. The latter headed toward one of his compatriots, who was playing ping-pong with a boy about ten years old—clearly his son. Estival said a few words to him and both turned toward Nikiema. The man, tan like all the Whites in the company, in his paunchy fifties, didn't appear very interested in Jacques Estival's words and went back to his ping-pong game. One of the young slender women, an orange towel around her waist, went to join the two players. The sunglasses resting on her forehead gave her a very chic look. She must have seen that in a fashion magazine, thought N'Zo Nikiema. She played ball girl and each time she bent down, you could clearly see the outline of her black panties on her tight buttocks for a few seconds. He saw right through everything that was false in the gestures of the woman in the orange towel. As often happens with people on vacation in the tropics, forcing her laughter and jumping around like a little girl, she attempted to convince herself that she was enjoying wonderful family time among half-savage people who had no history, far from the dullness of her country. They stopped the game from time to time to talk low enough that he couldn't even hear the timbre of their voices. Their lips formed words. Just like on TV sometimes, when you watch a film and decide to mute the sound.

Pierre Castaneda sat down across from him. They observed one another in silence, no doubt to size each other up, but maybe above all out of curiosity. They were a little intimidated, like couples who see each other after many years of divorce, each one trying to guess how the other had lived without them. Castaneda's face was impenetrable and he had the same prying eyes. N'Zo Nikiema was nevertheless reassured that he didn't sense any aggressiveness in him.

163

Having to wait alone for him at Lil Black's was humiliation enough. He was not in favor of putting up with more.

"You see, nothing has changed," said Castaneda, running his fingers across the table's surface.

N'Zo Nikiema kept quiet, annoyed. He didn't want to pretend he'd come to the Belvedere Complex for a banal visit just to be courteous. "I'd like us to get right to the point," he said. His voice was a little more distant than he'd have liked.

Castaneda seemed to reflect for a long time and then shook his head. "Do you know why I asked you to come here?"

"That's not important anymore, Pierre. I'm here, that's all."

At that moment, N'Zo Nikiema sensed just how much he despised himself. He was tense, his voice lacked confidence, and he was avoiding Castaneda's eyes. His coffee was getting cold and he didn't dare touch it for fear of seeing his hand tremble.

"We can sort things out," Castaneda said suddenly. "You can avoid war in your country."

He felt a little shock in his chest. What was Castaneda cooking up? "I came to see you to hear out your proposals."

"You came to see me because everything is lost, Niko," Castaneda said dryly.

He was struck by Castaneda's tone, suddenly colder, more insolent. Swallowing all his pride, Nikiema declared, "This country needs us both."

Castaneda threw himself back, his arms crossed. "You wouldn't have spoken like that if your little dealings had worked out in Latin America. You wanted weapons, but you didn't have anything more to pay with. Your coffers have been empty for a long time."

Cutting to the quick, N'Zo Nikiema suddenly said forcefully, "No one has the right to speak to me like that."

A few clients turned toward them. Nikiema's eyes met those of the young server, who was bringing a little bottle of Marwa for Castaneda, and he lowered his head.

Castaneda looked sorry and after a moment said, "It would be a shame to tear each other apart in public. Time to finish our drinks and we'll discuss as we walk. That work for you?"

He acquiesced discreetly. Castaneda was throwing him a line, anyway. He was the head of state and making a spectacle of himself wouldn't earn him anything. He wasn't wrong, however: that magnanimity was that of the victor.

They were both pretty good actors and they managed to speak with ease about this and that. They reminisced about the Blue Lizard together. Ta'Mim had died a few years earlier, bedridden and penniless. Castaneda informed him that he had quit smoking and drinking but sometimes treated himself and got majorly plastered. Nikiema was about to tease him: "Yeah, you've always thought that alcohol would help you get your whores." He didn't, though. Both of them knew very well that this final meeting came at a very bad time and that certain lines could not be crossed. They brought up the Kingdom of Nimba in an almost relaxed way. A little while after independence, they'd done away with all the government positions known to be traditional. Each of them, without too many regrets, had thus accepted losing his royal title.

"It's been a long time since you've been in Nimba," Castaneda said.

"Much too long, yes."

Actually, N'Zo Nikiema was almost forbidden to stay in Nimba. Both of them knew it was a delicate subject and they stood up to start walking.

It was nearly dusk, and it started getting a little cool. They moved into a large sandy alley lined with fruit trees—mandarin, pomegranate, orange, and so on—as far as the eye could see. Their foliage, a somber green, was in some cases covered in red sand. A large part of the complex had become an orchard, making Belvedere an oasis of peace and happiness.

"It's a real passion now, and I'm trying all sorts of crossbreeding with fruits from the Antilles or even Australia."

"And it works?" Nikiema asked, incredulous.

"Not really. But we just hired a young agronomist engineer. A hyperintelligent guy. He's going make a little miracle, I can feel it."

Cars were forbidden in the area, and the two men almost didn't meet any other living soul. At the other end of the long alley, about a hundred yards away, they could only see the Cogemin workers going back home or watching an evening soccer match. Most of the young executives behind the wheels of cars with the black eagle were Africans. He made a comment about it to Castaneda, who proudly gave him the example of the financial services. "You remember, in your time you were the only black guy over there. Today, out of more than a hundred positions, there are only about fifty French guys."

"Things happened very quickly," Nikiema admitted.

For a moment, Nikiema might have felt that he was a normal head of state getting overzealous explanations from a factory director in a town deep inside the country. Castaneda insisted on clarifying, however: "I am sure that you know there are fewer expatriates in the company, but they hold the most important positions. I know my Africans too well; I'm not going to trust them with the keys to the safe! Who's that crazy, right? As our Ivorian friends say."

He had always heard Castaneda happily accept that type of racist talk. In the palace, when he was angry, he treated his collaborators like monkeys with glasses. Nikiema was surprised to notice that he himself had never taken offense at such insults. Now he couldn't even react. Castaneda would have simply shrugged his shoulders. Nikiema couldn't hide it from himself: his whole life, he'd behaved like a flunky with Castaneda. It wasn't the time to put on airs and graces. It was time to pay.

"Now that we're alone," said Castaneda, "I'm going to talk to you."

"What are you expecting from me, Pierre? For a while now, I've been trying to figure out what's in your head . . ."

"I advise you to disappear. That's all."

His voice trembling, not out of anger but out of fear, Nikiema said, "I don't understand."

"It's simple. One morning, people wake up and the president is no longer there. I can give you some time to prepare yourself. Three weeks. A month. Maybe two . . ."

Nikiema found the strength to forge a slight smile. "What happens then?"

"Nothing. I'll be able to help you out from time to time. I'm not promising anything."

He almost managed to be ironic. "Really? You don't want to promise anything, is that right? Not even one or two billion?"

"You're wrong to joke about it. Listen to me: it's about knowing who's the strongest. And it's me. Remember what we used to say: only imbeciles go through the trouble of thinking things over. The two of us were too smart to take the time to think. Do you remember?" He waved his finger around, toward an imaginary point in front of them. "There are obstacles ahead of us: we jump over them or we walk around them . . ."

". . . Or we fire into the crowd," N'Zo Nikiema finished. That was our credo, he thought bitterly. Two real action men, unshakable and effective. "I know that that was our credo. And after that? This country is mine, Pierre." However hard he tried, he couldn't manage a hint of warmth in his voice or any conviction.

"Get out of here and don't talk about it anymore," Castaneda went on, getting seriously infuriated. "Look at yourself! You're at the end of your rope. You have a chance, take it. I won't give you another one."

Night had fallen. The insects were circling around the streetlights. They stopped near a long gray building. Nikiema read a sign: "Test garden. Experimental station." Huge metallic engines—plows, he thought—were scattered around. The odor of manure, right next to them, was bothering his nostrils. He turned to Castaneda. "This country is mine, Pierre, and I will fight until the end. And you want me to tell you? I am the strongest. You've never understood this: whatever you're able to do, you are and you will always be a foreigner among us."

167

He couldn't say where his strength suddenly came from. He saw Castaneda go pale. His cheekbones trembled as they did each time he got this angry. Nikiema had aimed accurately. He knew where to hit to make it hurt.

"I am ashamed for you," said Castaneda. "You think you can make this war with a videocassette? A little dead girl years ago, what's that worth? What's a little Negress worth, huh?"

N'Zo Nikiema retorted sarcastically, "You're the one talking about it. I haven't uttered Kaveena's name even once."

Castaneda let out a little nervous laugh. N'Zo Nikiema understood that everything had just ended between them at that very moment.

Cheers rung out to their left. One of the teams must have just scored a goal. A brown insect—Nikiema wondered if it was a winged ant or a mosquito—stood still for a few seconds on Castaneda's forehead. He swatted it away with his hand, then shot daggers from his eyes into N'Zo Nikiema's. "Listen," he said, "I knew that our meeting would be difficult. I've often wondered over these last days if we were going to behave like old accomplices who are a little mad or like two rams rubbing their horns together before battle. Neither of those two attitudes appealed to me. I've been telling myself, 'Young people are going to die for us, and a few days before that we're going to be laughing remembering the time when we were living it up at the Blue Lizard and elsewhere?' That seemed obscene to me. On the other hand, you and I have passed the age when we're all talk. And actually, that's why I too was determined to see you."

Pierre Castaneda's voice was unusually calm. Later, alone in the small house, N'Zo Nikiema thought about it again many times. The words that were coming out of Castaneda's mouth were violent, vulgar, hateful even, but his voice was beyond anger, friendship, or any other human sentiment. Undoubtedly they'd never felt so naked face to face. In the end, all their old passions and all their crimes were for nothing. Before they even had their war, both of them were defeated. Pierre Castaneda was talking about a faraway world, without raising his voice even once: "I'm going to remind you of this: this country is yours, but for a long time I've been its master. It's entirely up to me to be its president. I never changed nationalities. I am French. French from France, you hear me? But here, no one gives a damn. There may be some teeth-grinding among some, but believe me, people will quickly forget. Your philosophers will say, 'It's globalization, you see, anybody can be president of any country. Once again our great nation gives a lesson in tolerance to the rest of humanity, and may no one tell us that this man is white—careful, no racism, that's what is written at the entrance to the Global Village.' Bullshit. Blah, blah, blah, there you go. These people are my little dogs, Niko; I've always been the hand that feeds them. Yesterday Hortense Dupaquier was the Queen Mother of Nimba—she will become the First Lady. Everyone will fawn over her. Talk to me about a proud people, my dear Niko! They chase you out of every country on earth, they throw you in every ocean into the mouths of sharks so you are not even capable of saying, 'We are at least our own masters at home!' All those lusty fellows, turned away at all the borders in the world, insulted, treated like black locusts in Morocco, dirty Negroes in Spain, well, back in Maren they won't hesitate to kneel down before a white woman and kiss her feet! And the white woman in question, my wife, is a real stupid cow, if you'll allow me to reveal this distressing family secret. Hortense Dupaquier is a total imbecile!

"Let me tell you something else, my dear N'Zo Nikiema. A few years back, your father made me the king of Nimba. I didn't give a damn but it worked out well for my company. So I played the game. To the end. Former Pierre the First of Nimba, great reformer before the Everlasting! Sustainable development and all that. You must be joking. A few months later, I brought you to my little town, over in Haute-Savoie. You never knew anything about it, but for a long time after you left, people threatened unruly kids that they'd be served as food for the black at the Castanedas'! You understand?"

Castaneda asked his question again, then paused momentarily, his eyes still fixed on N'Zo Nikiema. The latter thought for a moment

169

that Castaneda was waiting for a reaction from him, but quickly understood it was nothing. No doubt it calmed Castaneda, in some way, to talk like that standing up as night fell. He didn't even seem to be addressing him. In any case, what could Nikiema respond? He totally agreed with Pierre Castaneda. He recognized himself in each of his sentences. And he knew it too: if he had the urge to say his four truths to Castaneda, Castaneda could do nothing but listen to him in silence. In that, their complicity remained intact. And perhaps they'd never even been friends so deeply as they were at that moment.

"Do you remember," Castaneda went on, "that guy who came one night to Montparnasse, Belvedere's cine-club, with his film under his arm? A real pistol no less, that highbrow so-called proletarian, with his pipe and his striped cap like Colonel Asante Kroma's. He had demanded that our workers be present in the movie theater to see his film, otherwise we could go to hell. He had character anyway, yeah! Before the screening, he'd treated us like monstrous colonialists, he said we were going to be swept away by the wind of the revolution, et cetera. Fine, that was nothing. For me it was just talk. But at the end of his film, there's a scene where all the beggars in the city surround the main character. The latter is a rich businessman. He's completely naked, and the lepers, the clubfeet, the hunchbacks, the blind, all those people hurl heavy wads of spit and pus at him as they insult him profusely. His wife and two children are there, they watch it and can't do anything. The director then explained, 'It was a purification ritual—that man betrayed his people, so they had to humiliate him like that in order to cure him.'

"Well, the character in question was a guy like you. He was sticking out his chest claiming to have kicked us out, us the colonizers, after a long heroic struggle. A real bastard, in fact. He had been all for us and continued to love us madly. He loved our great wines, the little shaded streets of Paris, de Gaulle's Appeal on the eighteenth of June, and all the rest. A dirty pleasure-seeker, too. Beautiful women and whiskey. At the time, I'd been disgusted by the image of his nude body covered in vomit. But these last two years, when it started to heat up between you and me, that scene hasn't ceased to haunt me. And today I believe that the filmmaker was right: those of you who've always been at the top in the African countries, you sell off your brothers cheaply to us, like old scrap iron. It's as simple as that. And if I've understood correctly, you sell off your brothers to us out of pure hospitality. In the end, the foreigner mustn't lack anything. One more lie.

"You, for example, convinced yourself that we were friends and you put yourself at my disposal. I don't know why, but you've always done everything I've wanted. That doesn't make any sense. We can be friends, OK, fine. But to what extent? I have never lost sight of my country's interests, nor those of my company. I could have taken you down at any moment if I sensed any threat to those interests. And I'd have done it as a friend—that goes without saying. That's how life is, and I'm surprised that you seem to have had doubts about that. You have a serious problem in your head here! Do you even know what a merciless world we all live in? I've often wondered: so why are they like that? You're always talking about the Global Village, but you're ready to slit children's throats from the neighboring villages under the most crazy pretexts. And when strangers come from far away, you lie down at their feet, you sing, you dance for them, and I play the drum for you and I throw you up in the air and I shout wild screams at you, things like, I am a black man, I'm not like anybody, I know a thing or two about rhythm, I've got plenty of it in my blood! You don't see that we don't have anything to do with your rhythm? Why should your brothers dance for me? I come from a place that's called elsewhere. You hear, Niko? *Elsewhere*, that's to say almost from nowhere, it's so far and so different.

"The truth is, my dear Niko, you are your father's son. He had given us Whites all the land we wanted, for a few cases of bad alcohol. And you, ever since you moved into the palace, you confirmed that infamy with Nimba's Protocol Two-Twelve. Didn't you know what you were doing? You condemned your own people to starvation. The

171

children of these people relied on you for their health and for their education, and you, you never thought of anything but your own personal comfort. You would do anything to maintain that power. You're both sick, your father and you. Before, we used to call you the civilized ones. What's your new name? Doesn't matter. You dream of becoming Whites, you dream of our love, and no matter what you used to say, everything from your homeland brings you shame.

"And since we will never see each other again, let me tell you a little story, Nikiema. Last October one of our little youth, fresh off the boat from Mulhouse, said to me, 'This continent is an insane asylum.' I replied to him, 'Say what you want, but then it's an upside-down asylum . . .' He opened his eyes wide and asked me what I meant by that. Here's what I said to him: 'In this asylum, the only crazy ones are the psychiatrists! They wear white coats and thick glasses, they solemnly question the sick and prescribe medicine, but they are the only crazy ones!' To listen to you, famine and corruption keep you from sleeping, you, the elites of this continent. In fact, the only problem is you. And that filmmaker, once again, was so right! You know, my dear Niko, we've killed many people together. But you don't seem to have noticed: we've never killed a white man together, we've only killed your brothers. Abel Murigande. Prieto da Souza. The ten kids from Nimba who'd had enough of our disgraceful masquerade. The hundreds of millions of others massacred by our dogs of war and later by Colonel Asante Kroma. All those who refused to bow down. Now you treat me like a foreigner. Too easy. What can that really do to me? And the lame guy with the sunglasses, who found it shocking that you and your father made Fomba lie, maybe I wasn't a stranger when you were smiling as you watched me strangle him on the banks of the Kartani? And then you slit his head open?"

N'Zo Nikiema watched with amazement as Castaneda mimed the gesture of strangling someone with his hands, his jaw clenched, his face suddenly all red. That was the only time it had seemed to him that Castaneda had lost his cold-bloodedness.

"I don't have to answer you," he said.

"I know. But I wanted you to hear all that once and for all."

Pierre Castaneda followed him with his eyes in a gesture of defiance that seemed absurd to him and, maybe more than anything, uncalled for. For a few seconds, Nikiema could only pull at the skin of his neck, pinching it between the index finger and thumb of his right hand. That often happened to him when he didn't know what to do or what to say.

"I believe it's time to go."

He'd almost said, "Well, then, adieu, Pierre." That would've been quite theatrical. Luckily, he'd pulled himself together at the last moment.

"About that little girl Kaveena...," Castaneda said.

Nikiema was surprised to see that Castaneda was less and less able to control himself. That story troubles you terribly, my man, he thought.

"Yes...?"

"You'll have to manage to win the war."

He smiled reluctantly. "Of course. The little girl's murderer is the only loser. Is that what you were going to say to me?"

Castaneda didn't respond.

They said goodbye to one another with a quick wave and each went his own way. When he was about twenty yards away, Nikiema turned around and saw Castaneda slip onto a path that he hadn't noticed before. Most probably a shortcut. For a few seconds Castaneda's shirt shined in the light of the streetlamps among the orange and coconut trees, and then he disappeared.

The big march on July 21 Boulevard happened a little while after their meeting in Ndunga. For Castaneda, the reader may recall, it was the opportunity for a real demonstration of force. By the following week, a little commando was launching an attack against Sereti's barracks.

That was the beginning of the civil war.

—⚏—

173

Woke up with a bitter aftertaste in my mouth.

All night long the same words resonated in my head. I can't remember what the words were. "Mwashah" is on the radio. With my eyes half-closed, as if in a dream I see a caravan moving through the desert. Suddenly Hamza El Din's voice stops. Someone says, "Dear listeners, stay tuned. We've just received some important news."

I hear my heart beating. Has someone discovered and surrounded the small house without my knowledge?

It was nothing, really. Some workers uncovered a mass grave above the Satellite. Castaneda and President Mwanke went over to the site right away. They're disturbed by what they've seen. Instruments of torture from another time. Heaps of corpses of women and children. Luckily, it's a bygone age; the Tyrant has been rendered harmless. The Tyrant: me, N'Zo Nikiema. But I'm hardly concerned. The most trifling words push me, like so many discreet and powerful impulses, far from the present.

Among a thousand flaccid memories, I search for anchorage points. But only insignificant details emerge, unexpectedly, from my past. For a man being hunted down like I am, the future doesn't mean anything in the end.

I asked him his name. The man's eyes lit up but he didn't answer. Then I understood he was waiting for me. The vagina of nothingness. I had the urge to repeat those four words. In vain. My strength was leaving me. It was too late. The history of nations is not a narrative full of fantasy and elegant swag. It is not written backward. It does not begin with the end.

Mansare had told me that.

—⁓—

Coming through the door of the small house, I've often found you listening to bossa nova. Almost always the same track: "The Girl from Ipanema." In the beginning, I had a hunch that that melody expressed Kaveena's pain. It made you more human. I thought, a little girl martyred. It's happening in Brazil or not far from there. Although the song seemed so cheerful to me.

As time progressed, I understood: a love story.

In the end I reveled in the slightly airy melancholy. Little by little it had become the echo of my internal rhythms. I often wanted to ask you why you liked that song by Moraes so much. Is it a part of your life? I don't know anything about bossa nova. I imagine a young man pacing up and down one of those long beaches suitable for more or less fatal passions. The women are so beautiful there. No doubt she'd wrapped up all her sensuality in a bikini with pink and blue flowers, perhaps also a pair of Ray-Bans with yellow frames that were curiously aggressive and chic resting delicately on her nose. Years earlier, a shadow had passed close by him, swaying her hips. And he'd been haunted day and night by the memory of a woman he'd never seen.

My end is near. I reexamined my career and its holes with gaping shadows. A succession of abortions.

My life has not been well lived after all. The ideal has passed me by: to have never lived. Yes, this would have been the best thing to happen to me: nothing. Definitely the most beautiful of dreams.

—⁓—

I'm surprised there are so few photos of Kaveena hanging on the walls. There are drafts of your portraits lying around all over your studio. You never told me this but I'm convinced that you became an artist so that you could paint your child. I imagine how far back in your memory you have to go. It's far and painful.

I was struck by the power of one of those unfinished paintings. Each time I stop in front of it, it opens up a vast emptiness underneath my feet. Kaveena dares me to face her. The oil drawing, placed on a chair, is covered in dust. It's clear that it had been based on a photo. Yesterday I thought about bringing it down to the basement. I know I'll never do it.

You drew little Kaveena carefully, probably for months. She's three years old with chubby cheeks. She's lying on her stomach, her eyes closed. A light brown teddy bear with a black snout and red eyes is wrapped in a pagne tied to her little back. Kaveena fell asleep sucking her right thumb. You can see she was a pampered child. I imagine you photographing her while she was sleeping. You activate the flash with a triumphant little smile. There's an indefinable glimmer in your eyes. You stay silent for a moment, as if fascinated by so much grace and innocence. A moment of affection stolen each time destiny played its dirty tricks.

—ᴍ—

In Tomorrow's Times' very first articles, they referred to your daughter by her initials.

Nothing then indicated that the Kaveena case would take on such magnitude. The reporter had written his text with a certain casualness. He was outraged and definitely wasn't entirely putting on an act. It just seemed to me that his anger came more from a professional reflex than from an authentic human sentiment.

It was a classic situation.

People in high places commit a heinous crime, and a journalist talks about it in an outraged tone that is accepted in a democracy and promises that, according to his sources, the investigation will not stop there. And the investigation stops there. All the articles in Kaveena's case had the ring of a sort of deaf resignation to injustice. The ends of the months must have been tough for the young reporter. In order to survive, he really had to forget Kaveena. Besides, our country has never been one where the murder of a six-year-old child can cause much trouble for a man as powerful as Pierre Castaneda.

I'm not telling you this to make up for my own past misdeeds, but I remember well having been sickened reading the narrative about Kaveena's death a few years ago. It was horrible. At the time I wondered which of my men had been able to do it. At first I didn't think of Pierre Castaneda. But by the following day I'd forgotten about the case. And then it suddenly came back as a top story. And can you believe it was Pierre Castaneda who warned me first, in an almost mocking tone, "Be careful, Niko. The higher-ups claim to not understand anything about this story. I know its all bullshit. They say you should stop with your excesses."

I said to him, "My excesses? Are you fucking joking, Pierre?"

He shrugged his shoulders. "I don't know why, but this little Kaveena story means a lot to them."

I tried to remember. Your daughter's name didn't ring any bells for me. So I said to him, "Listen, Pierre, we all have a lot on our minds. So it's normal that we forget sometimes. What's this about? Who is this Kaveena, as you say?"

He jogged my memory about the case and concluded in a willfully false tone, "I know it's not your fault . . ." That meant, don't worry about it, we'll manage this together, I've always been there to clean up your messes. No one had yet spoken about the famous video.

I remember I was very clear: "Listen to me, Pierre. I'm as bloodthirsty as can be, but I'm not into killing little girls knowing neither why nor where nor when. Agreed?"

He sneered and I sensed a mix of disgust and skepticism. I didn't like that. I didn't like it at all. It was a fight. It started slowly. That day, I asked Pierre Castaneda, "So, then, where exactly are these higher-ups . . . ?" He smiled as if to say, "Stop acting so naive."

As I expected, at the first opportunity they brought up your daughter's murder to me again. A journal benefited from a review of the year's politics—it was the end of December—so in between two pontificating analyses they could slip in a discreet allusion to the "unexplained crimes of the republic." Among them was Kaveena's murder, "particularly shocking," they wrote, "to human consciousness": "What seemed at first to be a sordid news item could be, if certain information is confirmed, a real time bomb." Such an expression in such a newspaper was the equivalent of a death sentence for me. Only Pierre Castaneda could be the instigator of that article. All I could do was prepare myself for the storm. It would be terribly violent.

—∞—

Why did I decide to give free rein to all my memories? I really have no idea. Maybe the Lil Boy I saw yesterday from the balcony of my palace tap dancing on Blériot Avenue has something to do with these lies and confessions. Or is it simply the fact of being where I am at this moment?

In the small house, there isn't a single mirror. You could never stand mirrors. Clocks either, for that matter.

One day, I wanted to understand why. According to your laconic, irritated explanations, there was nothing to understand. I let it go. It wasn't worth a fight.

—m—

A car passed over the bridge. A truck. Or maybe one of those new Volvo buses from the national transportation company. Only they were capable of making the walls of the basement tremble. In the beginning, those noises—even muffled—hammered in his head. But rather quickly, he came to miss them. He used to go up to the living room and wait to see the yellow-and-green buses through the thin cracks of the window. Their tires would lift up the ocher dust at the end of the avenue. He couldn't even see the passengers' faces through the bus windows. He imagined their dreams and their frustrations. Some of them cursed him in silence. Others denigrated him openly.

That man dared call himself the Sun Giant of Mount Nimba!

He was mad!

So where is he now? I say, where is the man who filled our husbands' hearts with fear?

I'm asking you, sister! Tell us!

Only God's greatness is eternal!

Wherever he is, I don't envy him, that man who did so much evil to us!

I say, only God's greatness is eternal!

Wallaay!

Each day, new desires. It could be anything. To bite into the pink acidic flesh of a guava fruit and feel the brief crunching of its seeds between his teeth. But there weren't any guavas in his hideout. We always forget something. It made him a little sad.

Luckily, his hikes with Mansare at the foot of Mount Nimba came back to him. He was the heir to the throne and the old man was naming the world for him.

"That bird, as small as it may be, still has a sacred significance. It's a hummingbird. People tell a story about him."

178

Coming from afar, Mansare's voice resonated discreetly through the silence of the house.

"One day, my prince, oh so long ago, this entire forest you see was engulfed in flames. Such a fire, along with such furious winds, no one on our earth had ever seen anything like it. So all the animals, frightened, fled far from the blaze. The lion, the hippopotamus, the warthog, the leopard, the jackal, the big and the small animals, all of them took shelter. All of them, or almost all.... Because the hummingbird decided to fight the fire. With his tiny beak, he drew water from the Nemeni River and threw it on the flames that were so high they were turning the sky red. He did that several times, then, exhausted, he decided to rest a little. Then the other animals lashed out at him.

"'Conceited little fool, go on!' said the rhinoceros.

"'Ha! Ha! Keep going,' the hyena giggled in his nasal voice. 'A hero never tires!'

"They took turns mocking him this way, all of them laughing heartily. The hummingbird let them laugh as much as they wanted and then he said to them, 'You're right. All alone, I'll never be able to put out this giant blaze. I know it myself. But remember this: *at least I am doing what I can.*'"

At that point in his story, Mansare stopped. Had it ended? That was impossible. Breathless, the prince waited for him to continue the story. He wanted Mansare to say that the rhinoceros and hyena and all the other animals in the forest were ashamed after hearing the hummingbird's words. That's what was good about Mansare's stories: when someone was misbehaving, sooner or later he made them die a painful death.

Nikiema asked hopefully, "Old Mansare, what happened to the other animals? Were all of them devoured by the fire?"

The old man smiled and simply shrugged his shoulders. Since Prince Nikiema was insisting, he said to him, "Noble Prince N'Zo Nikiema, one day you will be our king, and when that happens, for the good of Nimba, do not forget what your ears are going to hear now: the stories I'm telling you now sometimes have an ending much later." He paused, then added, " ... Or too late. Don't ever forget that either, Noble Prince."

Remembering this, the fugitive shook his head.

He'd been a lively, happy, and mischievous child. This was surprising even to him when he thought back on it, since so much of his adult life had been full of sadness and bitterness.

He decided to get clean.

When he'd arrived at the small house two months earlier, he had no self-doubt. The cold yellowish water flowing from the faucet disgusted him. He preferred to stay dirty, as if driven by a subconscious desire for punishment.

But this morning, he wanted to shave and take a nice shower. He wanted to feel his pores breathe like they did after a massage at the *hammam*. He poured five bottles of mineral water into a blue plastic bucket and picked up the olive oil soap coated in a mesh cloth. White foam formed and he scrubbed his body for almost an hour, with fierce diligence. As he dried himself off, he pretended not to see the stains—thick black filth—on the white towel. Incidentally, that was what discouraged him from splashing some cologne on himself. He feared not being able to tolerate the mix of odors: excrement and urine in the toilet and eau de cologne on his clothes. Better to start over again. Kill time one way or another. He went back into the bathroom and scrubbed his whole body again, taking his own sweet time. He rubbed the mesh cloth again and again over every millimeter of his skin, except on his face. He didn't know why there was so much filth on his arms and legs, especially on the inner sides of them. He didn't stop until he was sure he was really clean. The filth, now slimy from the olive oil soap, had accumulated again in the bathtub. He contemplated it with slight disgust and made it disappear down the kitchen sink. It had been a long time since he'd felt so good in his skin. He even felt some sort of cheerfulness coming on.

He made himself coffee. From Kitalé, his favorite. He was amused to read what was written on the package: "Fine and lightly spiced. 100 percent Arabica. From the mountain plantations in the region of Kitalé, near Mount Elgon, this Arabica owes the magic of its aroma and finesse to the richest volcanic soils of Africa." As he sipped it, he started putting his papers in order. Since his arrival at the small house, he had left things lying around almost everywhere. In his utter confusion, he thought he had little time to live.

He placed the album on his knees.

He had always gotten an ambiguous pleasure from ripping up the photos and letters of certain people he'd forgotten about. Going through his calendar and throwing addresses and telephone numbers into the fire made him feel like he was bursting boils on his body one by one. Almost a way of killing people he'd thought he liked and whom he'd ended up hating with all his might. He hesitated when he came to his honeymoon photos. Mother of the Nation. Or "Ma Nation," as the poor used to say to mock her. They had never been happy together, not even the day when, young, radiant, rich, envied by all, they rushed onto the stage of the open-air theater to start their wedding reception. At least that was clear. The rest, a mystery. No use stopping there. Good old Ma.... All your photos in the hole. Couldn't give a damn, he lashed out silently with a little smile loaded with violence. Besides, one day Mumbi had said to him. "Doesn't this Mother of the Nation have a real name?"

She certainly hadn't asked the question out of sympathy for the president's wife. She'd always despised her. And he had thought, without really believing it, that she was jealous. To humor her, he'd replied, "Oh! That one.... Always talking about the good Lord. She's a visionary."

"Not even," Mumbi then said meanly. "She stuffs her pockets, yes."

Nikiema had preferred to stay quiet. He didn't know where she was trying to go with that. They weren't in the habit of talking about his family life.

She went further: "Much too young for you. And you know she's not virtuous."

It was his fault too. He wanted a wife who looked good on TV. For his political career. She was always talking about the good Lord but she had the devil in her.

Other images.

He and Castaneda are standing on top of a mountain. It's winter. They look really young. They're wearing yellow coats with thick collars and he, with his hands in his pockets, seems to be shivering. He's always been very sensitive to the cold. Are they in Haute-Savoie or somewhere else in Castaneda's country?

They were the best friends in the world. Nothing would make him believe that Castaneda had calculated everything from the beginning. Of course, Nikiema had been called to reign over Nimba, a region exploited by Cogemin. It had been more prudent to count on him and Castaneda had done that. And afterward? That wasn't all there was between them. Castaneda had brought him to spend a vacation with him in his native village. A peaceful little town. He saw himself again sitting on a stone bench facing the lake. People walking had been passing in front of him since the beginning of the afternoon. They're in no rush, walking. From time to time he focuses his attention on a runner in a jogging suit or on a cyclist. He follows them with his eyes until they disappear into the distance. He turns to look at the lake once again. All the beauty of life, all the sweetness of the world is on its smooth surface. Ducks glide noiselessly from one bank to the other. People throw the white parts of bread to them, or some other food, and they grab it with their beaks almost without moving, agile and elegant. For a moment, he imagines himself shooting at them. Lake reddened with blood. What a commotion! The inhabitants of the little town would talk about it for a long time. *Don't you remember? The year their son Castaneda brought this Negro here and he killed all our ducks. They're not like us, they don't like animals, those people. You all are young, but you've got to ad-*

mit, it isn't the first time those Castanedas started showing us their true colors.

He remembers something he read in his youth. An American thriller. The story of a student who was a serial killer. Every week, they would find a corpse hanging from a tree. His victims were the campus squirrels and he would rip out their eyes before killing them. The plot thickened through the pages—some screamed their anger and others said OK, and what about the Indians, what did we do to them, better not exaggerate, dirty hypocrites.

On the other bank, we can make out the contours of a small town through the fog, known for its whale station and casinos frequented by billionaire princes from the east. He's alone because he's waiting for a girl. It's his very first date ever. In the beginning, he was terribly intimidated by Nicole. For several days, Pierre hadn't stopped pushing him: go on, Niko, don't be an idiot, a girl so screwed up, they're hot around here, she's crazy about you, my man Niko, I'm telling you. Pierre made people's enjoyment a point of honor in his little town there.

All that was a long time ago, Nikiema said to himself suddenly, with a hint of melancholy.

If someone were to ask him what his idea of happiness was, he'd know what to answer. A deserted street in the morning, in a little town. Over there, of course. Like that day an eternity ago, sitting with a young girl who was a little shy on the terrace of a café, watching two garbage collectors dressed in yellow suits with wide green bands rolling some garbage cans to their truck. Nicole Lombard. Suddenly disturbed, he remembered the man seated in front of them opening his newspaper, a look of ennui on his face. Just that had upset him so many years afterward.

It was time to go to bed.

As he was turning off the lights, he noticed an unfinished portrait of Kaveena leaning against one of the chairs. And even that couldn't spoil his budding happiness.

He thought, oh! Mumbi. . . . Let her refuse to believe me if she wants. I'm not going to drag that out all the time. I've finally had enough, my little bitch. And besides: We are innocent or we are not.

Then, out loud, in a semisarcastic, semiangry tone: "We know them well, the murderers of little girls, eh!"

My God, how he hated Pierre Castaneda!

—⚬—

Mumbi Awele is an amazing young woman. She's the center of everything but she builds a wall of absolute silence around herself. What can she be doing with Castaneda? I've never heard her utter her daughter Kaveena's name, or N'Zo Nikiema's. She spends each day in front of the mortal remains of the latter, seemingly without even paying any attention to him. I've learned to read faces. Hers signals very clearly, "I don't have anything to say about that man or about anyone else."

As for me, I sometimes forget that I am, as was N'Zo Nikiema a short while ago, a fugitive. A few days ago, I suddenly understood: I'm also waiting. In this small house, Mumbi is the only master of her destiny and perhaps even of ours. N'Zo Nikiema is waiting for a burial and I am waiting for death. Or exile. Or the truth. I don't even know the meaning of the last word. I believe I hold a part of this truth and I want to say to Mumbi, "Your hate is blinding you. N'Zo Nikiema did not kill your daughter." May the former president's enemies pardon me: I want to testify to his innocence. It's understood: Pierre Castaneda and N'Zo Nikiema, each is as vile as the other. I know it because I've worked for each of them. But if there's a case I followed closely, it's that of little Kaveena's murder. And I must say this: Castaneda managed to commit this crime all by himself. And also to make a complete mess of it.

Each time Mumbi comes back from town, I think, this will be a good time. We're finally going to talk about what happened. In fact, I'm not expecting her to take the initiative. I simply hope that I'm finally going to dare to lead our conversation to that topic. Nothing ever happens. She comes and goes for days, takes care of me with

kindness—as if I were one of her family members who was conva-
lescing in her home—then leaves again without saying when she's
planning to come back. The rare times we speak, it's about really
trivial things. Like the discussions we've had for a long time about
some soccer match between our country and Cameroon. It's true we
came close to a riot with that game.

I don't understand Mumbi Awele's stubborn silences—which in a
way quiver with a thousand secret words.

This morning, after being absent for several days, she comes back
much earlier than usual. It's not yet nine o'clock. I say to myself as
I watch her head toward her studio, Today I will not let her leave
without trying something.

"I stopped by Donka's," she says as she lays out some cakes on a
small rectangular Venn wood plate.

I admit to her, as I serve myself half a chocolate croissant, that I'd
wanted a solid breakfast. Then I go make coffee for both of us. From
the kitchen, I hear the sound of crackling and a succession of voices.
It's one of the first things Mumbi does when she arrives in the small
house: play with the dial on the transistor radio and look for the
music she likes.

"I brought you the daily press," she says, still fiddling with the
radio dial.

That, too, had quickly become a ritual. I get a selection of dailies:
the National . . . Hope . . . Echoes. . . . I scan them very quickly at first,
as if to let myself get intoxicated by the odors of the city of Maren
by the perfume of its gossip and its scheming of the highest order. I
love that. The printer's ink, in the morning, is like good warm bread.
I like those newspapers right when I open them up. They provide me
with a great fleeting pleasure. I have the impression that the world
is coming to life before my eyes and that each day their titles bring
me a brand new future. Later, after my nap, I will read them atten-
tively. They will have already lost their secret magic. In fact, I'm going to decode them. A thousand and one pressure groups are milling
around scheming in the little articles destined to pass unnoticed. If

you'd been the first cop in a country, you would no longer believe in anyone's innocence. Neither in yours nor others'.

I tease Mumbi at breakfast: "You're right to have no interest in politics."

"It tires me. People always say, 'The situation is explosive, the regime is going to crumble.'"

"Yes, it's funny. And nothing ever happens."

"Do you know what people are saying about your disappearance, by the way?"

"What?"

"More of their nonsense, Colonel." Her tone is complicit, even a little affectionate. Clearly, she makes me uneasy. That's pretty new in my life. It seems to me that I've always provoked fear or hatred in people and never really friendship.

I ask her, "When do you plan to go back into town?"

By the quick, furtive look in Mumbi's eyes, I see she's noted my change of tone. "Today's Thursday. Maybe Monday. . . . Or maybe Tuesday." I expect her to add, "Why do you ask?" She doesn't say anything. I think, this woman is definitely strong.

Then I charge forward without warning: "We have to find a minute to talk, Mumbi."

Sounding almost sorry and at the same time firm, she replies, "I'm going to be frank with you, Colonel. Since I've returned, you're waiting for some explanations from me and I'm amazed about this because I don't have anything to say."

I hang onto the end of that sentence to set things in motion in a way. Such an opportunity won't present itself again for quite a while. "You might have also wondered what I'm doing here," I say. "Do you know why I spend the majority of my days decoding all these documents and drinking coffee?"

She looks a little surprised by my remark and ends up stating, almost to herself, "It's true that you're supposed to be hiding but you don't seem very worried about it."

"It's very simple, Mumbi: I have the right to know the truth."

I sense her suddenly closing up again, becoming harder on the inside. "Let's drop it, please."

Instead of letting it go, I appeal to her common sense. "Do you really see me staying here doing nothing, face to face with the corpse of our former president? I'm going to leave; I know how to cross the border. It won't be easy, but I'm going to try. I'd just like to know the truth before I leave."

She agrees to leave it like this: "We'll chat one of these days." I see her hesitate. What she wants to add is important for her. One can sense that sort of thing. She says, "I'll bring the body down to the basement."

I'd like to believe that she wants to do that out of respect for the dead, but there's such contempt in her voice that it curdles my blood. I want to reply to her, "We'll bring it together." It would be quite normal to say such a thing in this moment. I don't dare open my mouth, though. Given the state of mind Mumbi Awele seems to be in, each word can mean its opposite. I decide to keep quiet, to let the events play themselves out and bring me in the end wherever they may. I must admit it: I've never felt so powerless. The passage in one of N'Zo Nikiema's last letters comes back to me. In it he was praising my loyalty and my investigative talents and was saying more or less this: Colonel Asante Kroma knows everything, he can do everything. Well, that's not true. I am completely lost.

Two days later, Mumbi comes to find me. "The body is downstairs."

I tell her in a neutral tone that I'd realized that.

She'd arranged for a transfer of the mortal remains at some point without my knowledge. I had seen that the divan in the salon was empty, dented in the middle by Nikiema's body. Some skeletal remains were scattered on the carpet and on the bed itself. I'd then imagined her pulling Nikiema's body by herself to the underground.

After a pause, she says, "Don't be shocked, Colonel, by what I'm going to say, but you're the one who talks all the time, actually. Well, here's what I did: I, Mumbi Awele, put the remains of this man in a bag and I threw them into the trash can."

187

I think I keep my head down. There you have it: Mumbi picked up N'Zo Nikiema's remains, like the pieces of a broken canary, and threw them onto a heap of garbage.

She goes on: "That's what I did and I wanted you to know."

As I listen to Mumbi talking, I detect a kind of fear—or sadness? or shame?—that has been totally unknown to me. It's strange: it's especially my fingers that refuse to stay still. It's the first time they tremble like that. I cross my arms to appear as natural as possible. My throat is a little knotted. "Mumbi, you're wrong. He didn't kill your daughter."

I don't dare utter N'Zo Nikiema's name. He has become "He." He's not only dead. He never existed. Someone we remember in our dreams.

A shadow falls over Mumbi's face and I say to myself that she is going to burst into tears or let her rage explode. To the contrary she says, detached, "I saw the film, Colonel. Your famous video. . . . I saw it at Castaneda's place, if you want to know. I saw what that man did to my child."

I think back to the last time N'Zo Nikiema and Castaneda had met. The latter had shouted out to him in the guise of a final goodbye, "You'll have to manage to win the war."

To which the former president had retorted, "Of course. The little girl's murderer is the only loser."

N'Zo Nikiema didn't know how right he was.

Mumbi Awele had been cheated and he had to accept that. It wasn't worth trying to repair the damage. Although, thinking of N'Zo Nikiema's distressing letters, I can't keep myself from finding it all dreadful, almost unbearable.

—⁓—

He didn't even need to hide his face. His beggar's rags were enough to let him pass undetected. Besides, he was already someone else after more than three months in the small house. As he pushed open the door to the courtyard, he blinked and tipped his cone-shaped straw hat forward a little more.

He started by pretending to pull up the weeds near the fence as he surveyed the surroundings. A kid passed through the alley with a pile of newspapers under his left arm. "*The Independent*! *The National*! *Progress*!" he yelled, turning his head all around.

Seeing Nikiema following him with his eyes, he slowed down. Nikiema called out to him, "Do you have *Hope*, little guy?"

The kid searched quickly through the package of newspapers and handed him one. *Hope* was the only title to have continued to appear during the war. A pretty well-done newspaper but paid for by Castaneda. Pierre Castaneda's photo, black-and-white and a little blurred, took up the middle of the first page. The editorial questioned "the end of the state of grace," and the headline read, "A New Challenge for the Country's Strongman." Stories like: he brought down the tyrant, but will he also be able to win the war for peace? Pierre Castaneda had gotten a little thinner since their famous last-ditch meeting at Cogemin. With his left hand pressed to his temples, he seemed absorbed in deep meditation. His eyes were heavy and he looked serenely serious, which suited him well. Nikiema gave the paper back to the seller and the boy showed his irritation by slamming the gate. He expected to be treated like an old skinflint, but the kid didn't linger around.

Times were tough.

Almost all the newspapers he'd quickly scanned in the pile were talking about the war. To think, it hadn't really ended. Military patrols continued to actually crisscross the southern part of Jinkoré. They crossed the neighborhood at great speed, and the soldiers, relaxed and sure of themselves, put on airs of being liberators. Passersby sometimes waved at them and they responded by throwing their red berets up in the air. Nikiema listened to what was being said in the streets. Fortunately, there was some bad news: "Agar has been surrounded for three days. The rebels have taken several notables hostage there."

But Agar was a small town to the extreme north, a little over six hundred miles from the capital. Nobody could take it seriously. He personally knew very well who was at fault: a little war chief who wanted a position in the government. Castaneda would arrange that very quickly. All in all, this bit of bad news was a sham.

In the street, people gave him alms. Small change. Crackers and even a candle. They said to him, "You whose voice God likes to hear, pray for me and my family."

And an old lady: "Man of God, pray for this miserable country."

The traveling stallholders congregated around cars, which honked to make them move and then took off suddenly; the reckless drivers hurled coarse remarks in each other's faces. He felt safe, lost in this chaos. Who would pay attention to him? Leaning on his walking stick, his body almost folded in two, he limped like a real beggar. He even allowed himself to act crazy; he shouted at strangers who treated him a little harshly for having crossed their paths. He yelled at one of them, "Get out, you nasty fellow, with a hard heart like the basalt from Tindou—may Our Lord make you burn in the flames of hell!" But he knew that he shouldn't be talking so much. With all the speeches he'd delivered over the years, someone could recognize his voice. Some people were too clever.

Leaning on a little iron city wall, he watched the crowd head toward the east of the city where the big market was. Once there, many were going to wonder what they went there for. They'd return to where they came from because it was so good to be part of the crowd. Others were lying in wait for a dirty trick and everyone was trying to get their bearings again after the war. Independence Avenue was in a bizarre configuration, almost in staggered rows. He could only see people from behind. A compact mass of caps, straw hats, headscarves, boubous, and shirts in every color. It was hard to say whether the crowd was pacing up and down the street. It was more like it was hit by a train or even forcefully sucked up by Maren's entrails.

The traces of fighting were still visible everywhere. The lights at the intersections didn't work anymore: they were covered in rust, and their electric wires, no longer functioning, were hanging out of their deep black dug-out eyes. Really young beggars, less numerous than in the past, had made those lights their meeting point. What became of the others? Many got killed and some were probably hesitant to disarm themselves. The UN was giving $723 to those who agreed to be demobilized. There was a whole campaign for that, with big blue posters everywhere.

For a few minutes, on Dostom Avenue, he had the opportunity to watch a very distracting scene that showed him to what extent times had changed. Three workers in gray suits and red caps were trying to stick a giant color portrait of President Mwanke onto the Satellite's bullet-riddled walls. In it, Mwanke stood in his office in front of a library, a medal around his neck, his right hand on the Constitution, staring at nothing. The photographer had explained to him what to do so that in the image he had the look of a visionary in his eyes. But even in the photo, President Mwanke seemed to be apologizing: "Please, don't pay attention to me, I am not here, someone is there before your eyes but there is no one." Mwanke didn't want any issues, after what happened between Castaneda and Nikiema. The latter thought, impressed, good old Pierre! You're really too much, my man. Nikiema smiled. Mwanke reminded him of his father: the king of Nimba too was colored, sparkling, and pathetic like a Christmas toy. And for the first time in his life, a bizarre question suddenly came to his mind: So who is Castaneda's father? I basically never knew anything about that man. . . . Even when I went over there, he didn't talk to me about his father.

As the minutes passed, the crowd around him grew more and more dense. It seemed to Nikiema that no one dared to pass in front of the photo without stopping, especially because of the quasi-historical moment of this display. As a result, the workers felt more important. That day in their life was out of the ordinary: they weren't putting up an advertisement for some bubbly drink or some pomade. The presidential poster was so huge—about eight feet by six and a half feet—that they needed a ladder on each side to hold each of its edges in place against the wall. A third worker, perched halfway up on one of the ladders, was holding the poster level at its middle. It wasn't an easy task and the spectators were under the impression that they were at the circus, admiring acrobats jumping on a bed of nails suspended in the air. When the image was finally in place, sustained applause burst out from everywhere. The crowd saluted the technical exploits of the workers. President Mwanke, looking so pleased with himself, was already of no interest to anyone. In any case, everyone knew that he was a useless moron. On top of it, right near Nikiema, someone insulted the president in a low voice and he thought with bitter satisfaction, turns out people aren't as stupid as we politicians thought.

He distanced himself. As he continued holding his hand out to the passersby, he was careful not to be seen several times in the same place. It would even have been dangerous for him to stay somewhere for too long.

The walls downtown were covered with other posters, white ones. Under UNICEF's logo, they showed lifeless bodies and lame children. Written in thick black letters was, "Don't cripple the future of our nation. Never again in this beautiful country."

The city was again red and white. It almost disappeared under the dense smoke of mopeds and public buses but also under the dust that rose from the rutted streets.

He must have overdone things somewhat, because he started to feel tired. Almost out of breath, he let himself fall onto a bench in the corridor of a vacant shopping complex, near the fish market. In fact, it was a succession of stores, stalls, and workshops. One was sure to find almost anything here. Glasses or shoe repairmen, tailors, import-export boutiques, and dispensaries. At the end of the hallway, in front of a *wax* and *lagos* store, a young man in a black hat offered books displayed right on the ground.

Below the market was a huge garage for mopeds. There were dozens of them, most of them blue. Inside the garage were carcasses of cars, green-and-white taxis, mopeds. Pools of motor oil and dirty water in several places.

A tall man, about forty, skinny and already graying, came out of a container with Italian writing on it: "Via Mentana 85 Perugia." The way he swept the place with his squinting eyes, you had an inkling that he was the master of the place. He undoubtedly sensed the presence of a foreign body in his territory.

He hobbled around, and each time he moved between his engines, his body was slightly curved forward and bent to the left. When he straightened up, his whole body tightened up at once and he stayed in that position for a few seconds, as if he were looking to detect someone in the distance. Was it because of his state of mind as a hunted fugitive? At first glance, the garage owner made a strong impression on Nikiema. That happened to him often in his life, seeing someone for the first time and knowing he would never be able to forget him. Just like that, truly for no reason. No reason he knew of, anyway. It could be anyone, for example a person disappearing at the corner of a street.

This garage owner, he guessed, was among those beings for whom life was a serious affair. He must have managed well during the war. If he had to kill, he had definitely done so without the least regret. And he profited from it too, to run his little blue-moped business.

He reminded Nikiema of Mumbi Awele. Like her, that man definitely knew the art of surviving the madness of men. The stranger also brought him back, without his knowing how, to his own triviality. At a time when his name alone had wreaked terror in the country, he had sometimes come across beings with a quasi-untenable force inside of them. Their eyes met then, and without them even giving each other challenging looks, the man lowered his head. Just like that. He was wearing a white undergarment covered with large grease stains. His biceps were knobby and skinny and his khaki pants were a little too wide for him. His red eyes took N'Zo Nikiema to some depths unknown to him. Were his eyes reddened by alcohol, drugs, or sleeplessness? He couldn't say. One thing was sure: he had stolen most of the mopeds that he was repairing and selling.

Nikiema repeated mentally what he could have said to Mumbi about it in his letters: *When I am dead and you've finished reading these words, go take a tour around the mechanic's place. His garage is practically on top of the building said to be owned by the Tapestry Makers. You pass in front of a dingy building pompously baptized the Business Center, you go down another 100 to 130 feet, and on your left you'll see a forest of blue mopeds. Try to talk to that man. Perhaps you will discover the secret of his power.*

"I want one of those," he said, indicating the blue mopeds.

Instead of answering, the garage owner turned around, stared at him for a minute, and signaled to one of his apprentices to take care of him. He went back to his work as if Nikiema had never been there. The kid approached him, looking distrustful. He had ashen black skin. His Cabral hat covered his temples despite the heat and he was wearing an immaculate red knitted shirt. What struck Nikiema the most was the single white ring in his right ear. Despite his effeminate look, the child reminded him of a young feline ready to pounce.

Under this blazing sun, in a den of iniquity with its odors of oil and gasoline, its metallic sounds, its little drug addicts, and its grumpy and cynical proletarians, he had the impression that he had failed. Nikiema especially realized that when it came down to it, he didn't know anything about the city of Maren. A real dump, it must be said.

The kid in charge of taking care of him was rather overwhelmed by his task. He got tied up in his lies. "Japanese mopeds. Oh! The Yamahas, Pops! The Peugeots aren't bad either. And then the South Koreans are rather up-and-coming. Did you know that, Pops?"

It was his first real contact with a human being in several months and he couldn't bear being taken for an imbecile. Walking away, he said, "It's OK, son, I'll come back tomorrow."

After he'd gotten away by about ten feet, the apprentice ran over to him and, pointing to his boss, said, "The old man's asking you to come back."

"What old man?"

"The boss. He wants to talk to you."

It seemed like an order and he smiled to himself as he did what he was told. In reality, he had no desire to leave. This lame garage owner fascinated him. He wanted to know more about him.

"Forgive him," said the man, coming toward him. "He's still a child."

"I don't blame him," Nikiema protested, a little annoyed.

"Oh! Sometimes he offends visitors and makes me lose clients. He's picked up some bad habits."

Nikiema looked the kid over more closely and wondered how many people's throats he had slit during the war. The younger the fighters, the crueler they were. That's what people said. Each time people ended up killing each other on a massive scale, experts came to Maren and questioned everybody. Later, they put their big words into reports and books. Thanks to them, we knew everything about those Lil Boys.

"The war?" Nikiema said, turning back toward the garage owner.

"Yes, he was in the Black Scorpion Group."

"The Black Scorpion?"

The garage owner couldn't believe it. "You never heard of Captain Kunandete? So you weren't here during the uprisings?"

He had the curious sensation that a police agent was asking him the question in one of the little dark rooms of the Satellite. He gestured vaguely. "I must have heard about the Black Scorpions, but I don't remember the name."

"It's true," the garage owner said, "they were all crazy and they had all sorts of bizarre names. Kunandete was one of the current president's men; he's come a long way since. Chief of the general staff. Not bad, eh?"

"Ah, yes . . . ," Nikiema said cautiously.

"You see that house over there?" the mechanic continued.

"The white one there, next to the bread stall?"

"Yes. Those youths raped the women there during the day and at night they ate them."

"No, that can't be true!" he said, truly horrified, backing away to get a closer look at the kid. So he did that too? At that age?

"What do you mean it can't be true? Yes, it's true," the garage owner said. Suddenly he seemed angry. Nikiema didn't believe, though, that he had said something hurtful.

"My name is Siriman Konté," the mechanic thundered as he hit his chest, "and no one on this earth has ever dared call me a liar."

"I'm not," said Nikiema. He was seized with panic at the idea of a crowd forming around them. This man scared him. Besides, he couldn't allow himself to be too talkative.

"These kids did this and every day they started over, again and again I tell you, till the war ended. When they raped a woman, she knew it was the very last time she would deal with a man. Well, a man . . . so to speak, eh. Babies, yes. I tell you, some of these women had buttocks like an elephant and all these kids, climbing all over their bodies like pesky little insects. I tell you, it was that house near the stall . . ."

The mechanic trailed off as if he himself couldn't believe the story he was telling.

Nikiema had not stopped nodding his head in astonishment. In his palace, he had known nothing about this. That's what this was—a war. When you're in an air-conditioned office, the officer draws some lines and generally describes some pretty movements. It's somewhat light and all really cute when the generals talk about war. "Here's the bolt, we have to blow it up." It seems stupid to say or even just to think: There are still people in this place who haven't done anything to us. Is it necessary to kill them? And to learn after breaking through enemy lines that—though certainly necessary—there were thousands of corpses rotting under the sun in the direction of Muatja? It's a meeting like any other in the palace, with mild-mannered officers, soft-spoken with sad eyes. Coffee. Tea. Cookies. Juice. It would be unheard of to talk about the Lil Boys in the house in the lower city. Eating young women! And he was there now to talk nonsense about Yamaha and Tenere motorcycles.

It was time to leave. He shouldn't have been hanging around this area.

"I want a moped," he said to the man.

"That's a line I like to hear. You have your papers?"

"My papers?"

The guy was immediately annoyed. "You have them or not? These are the new laws."

"But nobody has identity papers anymore."

The mechanic relented and whispered ambiguously, "I know. But they are still looking for the Elder."

"The Elder?"

"Yes, the tyrant."

"He must be far away by now," noted Nikiema coolly.

The man made an irritated gesture as if to say that it was none of his business. To sort of say, "These politicians are all the same, corrupt, liars, all motherfuckers. I'm just into my business."

"We can arrange something, regarding your papers," he said, digging in his ear with his left index finger.

Nikiema knew what that meant—he would have to pay more. Without thinking, he replied, "That'll work for me."

There was a furtive glow in the garage owner's eyes and there were slight signs of his whole body stiffening. He said abruptly, "Which brand do you want anyway?"

The question meant, Are you really a beggar? Nikiema's heart started pounding in his chest. "The cheapest and the best," he joked.

The mechanic smiled. Nikiema had the strength to return the smile and say breezily, in a conspiratorial tone, "You believe everything they say? It's not prudent to stay here. I'm sure everything will start up again. Our war is not over."

"No, it's not over," Siriman Konté said slowly, without taking his eyes off him.

Something was obviously nagging at him and Nikiema had no trouble knowing what it was. If the man had put a hand on his chest, he would have seen how fast his heart was beating and Nikiema would have been dead meat. But his breathing was normal and his body was not trembling. Nikiema had never suspected that he would have such sangfroid in the face of danger.

"How much does cheap mean to you?"

"Name your price."

"It costs me a lot of money to refurbish all these engines."

"I'm charitable, my friend."

Siriman offered him a ridiculously high price. Nikiema smiled. "You don't know the proverb, my brother? If you cannot give alms to a beggar, at least don't insult him. Let him try his luck elsewhere."

"It's not that," he said.

"What . . . the proverb?"

"You twisted it a bit. The damned proverb," Siriman said in a low voice. "But that's not what I'm talking about." Nikiema looked at him without saying anything. The mechanic added calmly, "If you don't want trouble, you should pay up." Having said this, he pulled out a ten-thousand-franc bill from the pocket of his pants. Nikiema had put his photos on the bills and they had not been changed yet. There was no more doubt. The man held the bill. He looked at Nikiema and then at the bill and said in mocking tone and with exceptional cruelty, "You'll give me a lot of these, Solar Giant of Mount Nimba."

Nikiema barely recovered from the mean allusion to one of his many titles as the tyrant in power. His mouth became very dry. He had the sudden urge to feel ice water run down his throat.

"How much?"

The man approached him without limping and said to him in a whisper, "There's no counting between friends."

I'm dead meat, Nikiema thought. Here I am like a rat.

The other mechanics guessed that something was going on between their boss and the beggar. They observed them sneakily without interrupting their work.

The mechanic said, "You can trust me. I have a sense of honor."

They entered the container and Nikiema handed over his money and the small pieces of diamonds that he had hidden in his private parts. "Is this good?" he asked ruefully. He was ready to lower himself to any degree to persuade this man.

The other one still looked like he was of two minds. He said dryly, "It will do." After a pause, he added, "Be careful. I recognized you by your voice when you came in and were talking to the little boy. And really, it's not very smart—you guys put your photos everywhere, on banknotes, in offices, everywhere. If it works out for you, try not to be too chatty. Nobody listens to your lousy speeches and yet you don't stop talking."

"Things aren't going to work out for me anyway."

"Of course not," the mechanic blurted out scornfully. "The new one'll be there a long time."

"Oh yeah? Mwanke?" Nikiema replied sharply.

The mechanic smiled. Nikiema appeared to be amused.

"Are you interested? Seems so, eh! A breed apart, aren't you, you politicians. You want to kill him, is that right? Like I said, the new guy's smart. No speeches, no fights, nothing. Cola nuts. Whiskey. Porn films and young girls. That's Mwanke. Long live the president, come what fucking mess may."

N'Zo Nikiema wanted to tell him that it was Castaneda who controlled the country, but he feigned surprise. "How is that possible? Can it really be true about the president, this Mwanke?"

Unfortunately the mechanic didn't like his ideas being questioned. "You still want to call me a liar?" he roared.

"Oh no!" exclaimed Nikiema, completely distraught. "I'm going to leave."

"Dirty intellectuals," the mechanic fumed. "Go, get in line. You've sold us to your white masters." He let Nikiema leave and stayed seated in his container, no doubt to count and secure his fortune.

Trying to push the pedals on his moped to turn it on, Nikiema felt his body stir with a violent tremor; sweat covered his face and blinded him. He was prey to a terror he had never experienced before.

The young mechanics laughed at him. They very quickly realized that he had never ridden a moped. One of them came to his rescue.

For the first two kilometers Nikiema was so focused on his actions that he forgot his situation. He thought hard: Don't fall off this machine. My God, definitely don't fall. He imagined, horrified, falling backward. Passersby would immediately surround him. It would end in a lynching. What an idea to put his photo on the banknotes! Instead of continuing straight on July 21 Boulevard, he turned into the roundabout called La Chaumière, the name of a nearby nightclub. Very skillfully, he resumed in the direction of Siriman's garage. If Siriman had called the authorities about him, then they would be looking in the wrong direction. He was headed for Independence Avenue, which was a one-way street. He went as fast as he could, already reassured. He thought for a moment about trying to get to the border. Would that be a good decision? It was now known that he was still in the country, and there would be checkpoints installed everywhere. He was still too shaken to be able to think. He returned to the small house in Jinkoré—his haven of peace after his perilous outing—to lock himself up. He already missed the house. He parked the moped against the barrier that separated the garden from the road. He needed to sneak in very quickly. The door had been ajar throughout the day. He had left it that way on purpose, to give the impression to the rare passerby that the place was uninhabited.

As soon as he drew the curtains in the living room, he recoiled violently from the smell of his own excrement piling up in the toilet. He also knew that the provisions in the basement were rotting. Looking around him, he realized that he was alone in his refuge for the first time. Just a few hours had been enough for the cockroaches, earthworms, large black and green flies, and even caterpillars to take over. He stood in the middle of the living room for a few minutes. He hesitated. Maybe he still had time to get away. He could take a weapon, if he found one, and risk it all. Fire into the crowd. He dreamt of glorious fireworks at a checkpoint. Noble N'Zo Nikiema. Died gallantly with weapons in his hands. The main thing was to not die like a dog under the shouts of a hostile public. He could leave again. Didn't matter where for. Just leave. He went in and closed the door behind him. It wasn't madness. Rather, it was the desire to resign himself to his fate, which he would live out with almost sensual delight.

—⁓—

The day after his return, he heard the sound of voices close to the cottage saying his name. He strained his ears but wasn't able to hear what they were saying. Maybe a military patrol.

On the radio, Siriman Konté, the mechanic, was telling the story of how they met, in his own way. No doubt, the man could lie with unbelievable poise.

At each flash of information, the same lines: "The noose is tightening. Controls.... Tyrant at bay.... Description..."

Listeners called in to make fun of him:

The Giant of Mount Nimba disguised as a beggar.... Ha! Ha!

Riding the blue moped of some random worker!

This man has definitely robbed our brave people right till the end....

Not even able to ride a bike, and he wants to lead the country!

God is with you, beloved President Mwanke! May all your enemies die in dishonor!

A philosopher got involved. Bloody legacy. The dark years. Time for mourning. In his humble opinion, there should be a public trial. Amused, Nikiema muttered, "I doubt Castaneda agrees with you, my boy."

He turned on the TV. The interior minister—he didn't know him, he was new—said, "The fugitive knows he's surrounded and we think he will turn himself in in the next few hours." There were some blunders, however, and the citizens started to worry. A medical delegate was shot down near a parking area by nervous police. "It's a scandal!" screamed a defender of human rights interviewed by telephone. The minister anxiously clarified, "We are ruled by the law," and then added, "We have opened an investigation. Our security forces are not above the law of the republic." The rest was easy to imagine. On the streets, passersby stared at each other, discreet and cautious. Following the minister, the TV had dancers on in flamboyant outfits. They writhed to the rhythm of techno music. N'Zo Nikiema saw his own death come toward him with a firm step. He fell asleep peacefully.

—⁓—

Even if he had started screaming, they would not have heard him. They made a lot of noise above his head in the living room.

He heard snatches of conversation.

" . . . "

"You really think so?"

"Search properly."

"Now what?"

"Someone was here not too long ago, I tell you."

"Could be, yes. Only for . . ."

"Yes I do. But then . . . Come see this."

The two voices were lost for a moment.

Then: "We will warn the colonel."

"That's better. He'll know what to do."

"Very true, my boys. We are too junior."

The sound of their boots on the floor tapered off after a few seconds. The small house was silent again. Maybe their boss would come back later on to inspect the premises. He did hear them say they would warn the colonel. N'Zo Nikiema was sure they were talking about the legendary Asante Kroma. He conjured up an image of the colonel with his striped hat and felt a little nostalgic. I've never been able to really get to know the guy, he thought. Taciturn and patient but also oddly effective.

Nikiema, however, was not the least bit concerned. Nobody would ever discover his underground hideout. From the small sliver of light, he guessed that the city was flooded with light. At midmorning, the sun above Jinkoré had a bright orange glow. Unfortunately at the end of the afternoon, Maren was plunged into darkness. The city had learned to live without electricity. It had started a few days before with the usual cuts. Then there were very short interruptions—a flash of light sometimes—but more frequent. This touched a raw

202

nerve with the population. Between power outages, radio stations broadcast reassuring messages. Twisted technical explanations. Calls for vigilance. Allusions to possible unrest stirred up by "the vengeful," that is to say, Nikiema and yours truly. *Peace has returned but you must not let your guard down. Peace is precious and fragile. The forces of evil have not disarmed. We all know that this man has a heart filled with hate.*

It then moved on to the question of a boom—extraordinary but logical—in the business of candles. By unanimous review, it turned out that never had so many been sold in the history of the country. The numbers were dizzying. Upon hearing this, Nikiema screamed angrily from the bottom of his hiding place, "Hunt down those who profit from these power outages!" In this case, it was the director-general of the National Electricity Company and a wealthy merchant named Marega. The latter had imported and managed to sell off millions of candles throughout the country. Collaborating with the two men was an engineer who was in charge of sabotaging the installations. A simple and lucrative combination.

For the fugitive, two weeks without electricity was a genuine personal disaster. It probably hastened his end. I came to this conclusion after I'd pieced together the last days of N'Zo Nikiema's life.

—∞—

Shortly before his death, N'Zo Nikiema behaved in a rather peculiar way. As his provisions began to decrease, he believed he could store them in his stomach. If I understood correctly, he sought to establish a reserve of fat, the way animals do when they go into hibernation.

This may seem foolish to you, but I could not otherwise account for his sudden gluttony.

He had always had a soft spot for apricot or berry yogurt. He had literally stuffed himself, as evidenced by the numerous empty cartons I found not only in the basement but also in the living room. Pastas were not of any use to him because they had to be boiled on an electric stove. Luckily, he stayed away from the *kilischi* and the dried fish which has to be left to gently melt on your tongue. Furthermore, he found that his body needed salt. But shortly after he arrived in Jinkoré, Nikiema had exhausted the cans of sardines and corned beef. Small act, big effects: this imprudence could be fatal. Canned foods, it seems to me, would have allowed him to better cope with the power outages.

As for water, he fortunately had enough to see him through what might come: at least three hundred liter-and-a-half bottles of Marwa and Mont Nimba. There were still several unopened cases. Nevertheless, Nikiema was still monitoring how fast the little blocks of ice were melting in the fridge. He collected the cold liquid in a bowl and used it in part to wash his body, and drank the rest. The feeling of well-being was short-lived but it was better than nothing.

At the beginning of his imprisonment he thought he had, so to speak, managed to tame the darkness. He knew the bunker so well that he could move around with no fear of stumbling over the chairs or the TV. His brain had learned to convert the objects and animals around him into locatable movements. Eventually the cockroaches under his eyes were no longer the insects we all know—brown and somewhat mysterious things, always on alert with their quivering antennae—but rather a succession of dark and stealthy motions.

Only a mouse would persistently break this beautiful harmony. Very restless, it disturbed Nikiema's rest night and day. With dull anguish, he would feel it grazing between his feet and then it would disappear with a short, sharp cry. Maybe it wanted to play with Nikiema? But Nikiema, unfamiliar with the habits of animals, wasn't quite sure. Thus it was out of the question to let it live. I understand that it is terrible to have to kill an animal which only wants to be your friend. But for Nikiema, it was simply a big misunderstanding between the creatures of God: to doubt the mouse's intentions, whether peaceful or violent, would not be of much use to him. It had to die. Nikiema's inordinate mind began to blame Science. In a sudden fit of rage he thought, the only thing these people know how to do is to go to Mars and then brag about it on Earth. We cannot rely on them to know what the mouse wants. Does it want to play with me or poke my eyes out in my sleep? And besides, Nikiema had no evidence of whether he was dealing with only one mouse. As far as he could remember, these mustachioed, squealing, and gluttonous rodents ran rampant in packs.

He decided to take action without further delay. He cut a piece of Camembert cheese, placed it under his boots, and stayed on guard with his foot slightly lifted. He was starting to get discouraged until the mouse appeared down the hallway. He saw it scampering and doing small jumps to the side and it approached the bait little by little without appearing to do so. It stopped for a few seconds and N'Zo Nikiema could see clearly that it was trying to weigh the pros and cons. Barely breathing, with his eyes half-closed, he managed to stay completely still. The beast leapt, muzzle forward, onto the cheese, and it didn't have a chance. He crushed it in one stroke and well after it was dead, he continued to trample on it with hideous grunts and grimaces and kept his legs screwed to the floor. On that day, he realized with astonishment not only that he had the urge to kill but also that he felt the necessity, almost absolute in this particular situation, to inflict the worst possible suffering on the animal. He later must have become aware of an even deeper desire: to remove all traces of the mouse, to make a porridge out of its flesh and to leave the blood to be sucked in by the cement under his boots to ensure that it had never existed.

He was also pleased to see that his legs were still strong and his eyes in good condition.

This relief was short-lived. Indeed, pretty soon he felt cockroaches and ants stirring over his naked and sweaty body. He could not even see them anymore. They walked along his neck and on his chest and back. He hunted them with his hand and they went away and left him in peace for a moment. But as soon as he fell asleep, they returned to attack. N'Zo Nikiema realized gradually, with terror, that he was alone and helpless in a deeply hostile environment. All these insects seemed to him to be working willfully, in a *conscious and concerted way,* toward his death. They remained in the shadows, watching his every move and sniffing around. He didn't believe they were flying around him by accident as they went along their path. No, this was deliberate: they were simmering the poison at the ends of their antennae, infecting him, and watching the movements of his eyes to gauge the best moment to return for assault. He remembered what had happened to Abel Murigande's grandmother. It was a terrible story. She was asleep on a mat and a worm entered her ear. While it unhurriedly ate her brain, the old woman beat her head against the wall, shouting that her head itched and calling for the help of Fomba, the Ancestor of Ancestors. This atrocious death had an effect on young Abel Murigande and he had often recounted it to N'Zo Nikiema. The latter could not bear the thought of something like this happening to him. More than anything, he was scared of being eaten from the inside, like a biscuit nibbled by a caterpillar or a centipede. So he began to stuff his ears and nose with cotton and began wearing thick clothing despite the heat. The basement turned into a veritable furnace for him. He fanned himself with newspapers to cool his face. This did not prevent him from being bathed in his own sweat all day long.

Furthermore, because of mixing all sorts of foods together, his intestines wouldn't stop making noise. This didn't bother him. In fact, he found it more and more fun to triumphantly pass gas. After contracting his abdomen for a long time, he would let out the sound with great force into the basement and it would burst upon his ears like little trumpets of victory.

He heard footsteps on the floor again. Nikiema looked up at the ceiling. I'm sure it's the same soldiers who came yesterday with the colonel, he thought. He felt increasingly delighted to be listening to them without their knowledge. What could they possibly report back, these little slaves of Castaneda?

Funnily, he didn't hear any voices.

"Mumbi...," he then whispered. Yes, it was her. She had definitely returned. A great panic immediately seized him. Sure, he had repeatedly dreamed of seeing Mumbi Awele before he died, but he didn't want her to carry an image of him in such decay.

But I don't want to leave the slightest doubt in the reader's mind: N'Zo Nikiema was wrong that day. The unexpected visitor was not Mumbi Awele. It was me.

I remember it very well. Ndumbe—he was killed soon after—and one of my men had come to tell me, "Boss, we were in the small house in Jinkoré ..."

"And then ...?"

"We felt something was going on there ..."

For one reason or another, I was not in a good mood, and I didn't let them continue. "You're not being asked about your feelings, you hear me, yes or no? You've been asked to find someone called N'Zo Nikiema. OK? You think he's crazy enough to hang out near Siriman Konté's garage after what happened to him there? Look for him in the suburbs, work with your guys at the border!"

Ndumbe and his colleague were not sure of their discovery, to tell you the truth, and they did not insist. They also blamed each other for the blunder. But then, two days after that conversation, I said to myself, it would be good to make a round of Jinkoré ...

During this first visit, I took my time. It seemed to me that it was one of those Rastaman types of artists who owned the house. He would have to have been gone for quite some time already. A thick layer of dust had settled everywhere, on furniture, on the occasional utensil hanging on the walls of the kitchen or placed on the shelves. I tried in vain to figure out where the odor of excrement, which the house reeked of, was coming from. The living room made me think of a badly lit art gallery. There were little sculptures and paintings everywhere. One of the paintings, done in dull yellow tones, was called *The Little Butterfly Girl*. A little girl in a white dress was trying to catch butterflies with her net. In the studio, several other canvases—showing another girl—were incomplete. After a few hours of inspection, I decided to drop it. I hadn't seen anything interesting.

It was only two days later, when I thought I had forgotten about the small house, that an idea began to germinate in my head. The work had to have been done inside, without my knowledge, as often happens to supercops whose intuition we praise. Suddenly I was certain that N'Zo Nikiema had at least stayed in this place and that the unfinished paintings were those of the Artist. I whispered, "The dancer from the Congressional Palace . . ."

I returned to the small house in Jinkoré the next day. Perhaps the reader will remember: the moment I crossed the threshold, N'Zo Nikiema handed over his soul. And so it is from this scene that the story begins. You remember also that I found Nikiema laid out in the living room and not in the basement. This detail is important. It means that the fugitive was not in hiding anymore, somehow. After all, people were frequenting his refuge more and more. The decision to abandon the bunker may seem absurd but I believe it was deliberate. Why? God only knows. I was reduced to all kinds of hypotheses. Perhaps N'Zo Nikiema wasn't able to breathe anymore in the basement. Maybe he didn't want to end his life in this rotten atmosphere and have his corpse immediately attacked and devoured by hateful creatures. This was something I could understand: even I was terrified during my first visit to the basement. Nikiema had stored large quantities of food there. These contingency measures had fallen apart due to a simple failure of electricity. Rotten food and N'Zo Nikiema's feces overflowing from the toilet gave off a foul stench. I frightened off a swarm of flies by moving my flashlight around on the shelves. They dispersed in a big buzz. There was no doubt that reptiles and rodents infested the place. There were many issues that prevented N'Zo Nikiema from closing his eyes at night as well as during the day. I suppose that with the intensity of these vigils, he felt reality slip away from him, little by little. He must have then said, "Since this is the end, I'd rather not die like a sick old dog in this swamp." N'Zo Nikiema had been the president of this country. If you have lived for nearly thirty years in luxury and in the glow of power, there are things you simply cannot accept.

I also recall that N'Zo Nikiema did not want Mumbi Awele to see him in the state that he was in. It's easy enough to understand but there's no need to dwell on it.

It had taken him much longer than usual to return to the living room. He'd had to sit on the stairs two or three times to catch his breath. Once in the open air, he had been almost blinded by the light. After the long days spent underground, he still had a little trouble breathing. Yet he had found the strength to shut the entrance to the bunker.

He had then stood against the edge of the big table for a few minutes and looked around the apartment. The soldiers who had passed through the house five or six days earlier had not touched anything. But he found nothing about the person who had come all alone the day before. At first, Nikiema had thought it was Mumbi. But then he had changed his mind: "No, Mumbi's steps would have been sharper and more confident. The visitor didn't know what he wanted. He was going in circles. The place was unfamiliar." And then the first thing Mumbi would usually do when she arrived was put on some music. "The Girl from Ipanema." Or something by Tupac Shakur. She liked him a lot too.

That said, he had been eager for it all to be finished.

It took him at least two hours to freshen up. He filled an entire basin with Mount Nimba, congratulating himself yet again on at least having enough mineral water in the small house. When his body was clean and dry, he splashed himself with deodorant. While trying to choose clothes in the wardrobe, he realized that his eyes couldn't see very well and his hands shook with a slight tremor. He wore the *faso danfani* for the first time. He couldn't help thinking that it would also most certainly be the last time.

Standing at the kitchen sink, he began to unhurriedly run satin-wood toothpicks in all the corners of his mouth. This quickly became a game: he found the smallest deposits of food with his tongue and then got rid of them with vigorous rubbing. Every time he passed the toothpick, a salty liquid slowly amassed in his mouth: blood expelled from his gums. He spit in the sink and resumed the operation, pacing up and down the room. Sometimes he stopped to inspect the tip of the toothpick. The end was covered with traces of whitish patches and was often slightly red. He brought the toothpick to his nose, sniffed it, and then rinsed it with a little water before returning it to work in his mouth. There was no hurry. He could not be in one anyway. He continued to suck and spit out the blood, determined to purge every last drop from his gums. When the spittle became milky white, he considered himself finally satisfied. After brushing his teeth with toothpaste, an invigorating and enjoyably cooling sensation spread through his mouth.

Shaving was less easy. For some inexplicable reason, Mumbi had decided that no mirror could come into the small house. Thinking back on the whims of the artist, Nikiema told himself that he could not blame her. He didn't claim to judge. But he had to admit that, for all practical reasons, it was best to shave in front of a mirror. The operation loses much of its charm when it has to be done blindly. You cannot even afford to occasionally wink and make faces at your image. Every few minutes, he ran his left hand over his chin and cheeks. And each time, he felt frustrated by the few rebellious hairs poking the palm of his hand. He persisted, changing the blade twice till the skin of his face was soft and smooth.

Nikiema slipped a revolver under his pillow and sat on the living room couch to cut his nails. Just as he finished with the left thumb, he saw his childhood in Nimba before his eyes. It was crazy how the image of Mansare had haunted him for some time. The old man had told him, "Noble Prince N'Zo Nikiema, one day you will be our king, and when that happens, for the good of Nimba, do not forget what your ears are going to hear now: the stories I'm telling you now sometimes have an ending much later."

Then there was a long silence. The words returned to echo in Nikiema's heart—Mansare had added, ". . . Or too late. Don't ever forget that either, Noble Prince." Master of the Word, Mansare?

"You were much better than that," Nikiema murmured. "You were the Master of Word Games." This was, in any case, a peculiar epilogue to the story of the hummingbird. The magnificent Mansare, he was so serene and so sure of himself. . . . Next to such nobility, his father was—he had to admit—a sort of solemn clown. But his father, not Mansare, was the king of Nimba. So, was this the real problem of his people? The one who in the end made the decisions for everyone was often, like his father or Mwanke, a moron, a popcorn-and-whiskey amateur. And he—had he not been the docile face of the same foreigners, anxious to save his power under any circumstances and at any price? Words formed in his head: End. Dog. Repudiation. He said aloud, his heart filled with bitterness, "I repudiated you, Master. Mansare, my memory is a tomb of your wisdom. But it should have really been its orchard. Now here I am, lost forever." The fact that he had called out to Mansare in this way made his eyes burn. Was he going to cry now? It was up to him. It was indeed one of those moments when, overwhelmed by an overly strong and almost unbearable emotion, he could still claim to have one-thousandth of a second to willingly decide whether he was going to burst into tears or hold them back. N'Zo Nikiema stood firm.

Old Mansare had a good technique for cutting fingernails: he skipped a finger each time and then returned to it. Nikiema was to learn later that this was how one carried out funeral preparations in Nimba. Through this technique, Mansare was trying to mystify death, to make death believe that young prince N'Zo Nikiema was no longer alive and that in killing him, death had a case of mistaken identity. A grave error, liable, unless under extenuating circumstances, for the death penalty. Good old Mansare! Funny too!

N'Zo Nikiema smiled at this final souvenir, stretched himself out on the divan, and hiked up the heavy woven *pagne* to his waist.

—◊—

"We won't be able to get it in—the door is too narrow."

211

This is perhaps the fourth time that we've tried to move the living room couch to the courtyard. Mumbi persists despite common sense: "Come on, Colonel, one last try."

This time, we go in gently, switching sides. Nothing we can do: a piece of tree trunk stuck in the wall is hindering the maneuver. It is actually a giant phallus carved out of wood and beautifully decorated with colorful beads and necklaces. I suppose Mumbi wears the same beads since they don't stop rattling around her waist as she leaves and enters the house. A visitor's eye cannot escape this phallus, which greets you, aggressive and ridiculous, at the entrance of the living room. But until now, I've avoided making even the slightest allusions. Because of modesty? Without a doubt. I should also say that these allegedly artistic provocations annoy me. If I'm saying this now, it is to correct my mistake. I recognize that I should not let myself be overwhelmed by personal feelings. A detail of this kind is invaluable. It's the little touches on the portrait that say the most about us, and, in this case, about the troubled personality of Mumbi Awele.

After the tussle with the couch, my body is bruised. "I'm no longer a young man," I say to Mumbi as I massage my shoulders and biceps.

"Well, we're going to have to dismantle the bed," she finally says. Apparently the idea is not particularly delightful to her. She also seems to doubt my goodwill. Anyway, she has often jokingly accused me of being a good-for-nothing.

Mumbi is wearing a pink T-shirt and faded jeans that are frayed around the thighs. The date of her exhibit is approaching and she has had to make herself look more Rasta—a childhood friend had suggested that to her, she told me. A red polka-dotted scarf protects her hair from water and dust. Since her return from the city two days ago, the small house has been turned upside down. Everything started, as it so often does, with empty chatter. She threw these ideas at me while I did the crossword in a very old issue of *Tomorrow's Times*.

"This place is rotten, Colonel."

Given the situation, there were not too many ways to interpret this little sentence. I was happy to nod vaguely in reply—and I must admit, a little embarrassed.

But Mumbi is focused on one thing. She got right to it yesterday and continues to clean with a lot of water. When she sees a little hole in the studio or the living room, she imagines thousands of insects swarming inside it and pours bleach and disinfectant on it. When a stain resists, she transforms it into a single-combat operation and doesn't stop rubbing until the surface is smooth and clean. This determination to destroy evil creatures makes me think, in spite of myself, about those moments of agony when, alone in the bunker, N'Zo Nikiema almost went insane.

"If I manage to sell a little during the show, I'm going to repaint these walls," she says, heading into the studio.

She comes back out almost immediately with a toolbox. While I look on the divan for which nails to pull out with the pliers, she begins taking all the small things out of the living room: poufs, wicker chairs, fan, etc. The ostrich eggs from Zimbabwe slip out of their bowls and she collects them as they slide off in all directions. She loves music and cannot keep herself from playing for a few seconds with the drums from Burundi and then with a small decorative *kora*.

She hands me a jar of varnish. "Start polishing everything that's made of wood while I put together something for us to eat." Seeing me hesitate, she says, "Really, you don't know how to do anything with your hands."

There is a sudden harshness in Mumbi's voice which clashes with our good mood of the last two days. I feel it's not addressed to me. In this precise moment, is my presence at his side the only thing she is aware of?

"It's true, I'm a dirty nerd," I say, laughing.

Her face stiffens. I remember some passages in N'Zo Nikiema's letters: Mumbi hates these jokes.

After a short demonstration with the varnish, she hands me the brush and asks if I want fried cassava or some *aloko* and fish kebabs.

"Both," I say playfully.

I know that gaiety shocks her but there's one thing I'm certain of: I am not going to worry about Mumbi Awele's moods. I don't want to be at her mercy.

Within a few hours, the courtyard is cluttered with furniture, old newspapers and catalogs, and kitchen utensils. We both find it hard to find a place to put our feet.

It makes me feel good to give Mumbi a helping hand. I enjoy these hours of relaxation because I can move around the yard without the fear of being recognized. It's not hard. This part of Jinkoré is not frequented much by people. The neighborhood will not really recover its facade from before the war. From time to time, workers pass by in front of the fence without paying any attention to us. In their eyes, we are a couple in the process of repossessing our home. I remain cautious nonetheless: I always keep my back to the street. You never know.

A mouse escapes from the stack of plates and rushes toward the gate. I try to catch it but it disappears in the grass.

I think about N'Zo Nikiema again. Basically, this is the day of his funeral. I don't know if I should say this, but yesterday when I was helping Mumbi sweep the room, I saw traces of flesh and bits of bone on the tiles—small splinters of transparent yellow, actually. They looked like broken glass. I picked them up carefully and put them in a handkerchief. They are still in my pocket and actually I don't know what to do with them.

Mumbi's hatred for N'Zo Nikiema makes me feel claustrophobic. I would like to leave. I know it's still risky but there's nothing more for me to do in the house.

This morning I told Mumbi, "I'm getting ready." I saw the slight frown in her eyebrows that showed she didn't really understand. "I'm going to leave," I said more precisely.

"Ah. . . . Sorry, I'm a little tired." After a short pause, she added, "Is it because I'm rearranging the house? It has nothing to do with you and you're not bothering me."

214

I've observed that as soon as we broach a serious subject, Mumbi reacts more slowly. She looks at me in a peculiar way and I feel she is very careful about what she says. Quite often, though, she is content to nod her head up and down and it is difficult to decode her actions.

"I know that I don't bother you. But I've already told you, it's absurd for a man my age to stay here just like that."

I wanted to philosophize about this idea of being "in waiting" but I held myself back at the last moment.

"There's no hurry, Colonel. They have almost forgotten you. In a few weeks, you can leave the country safely."

There was another silence. Always the same embarrassed silence. N'Zo Nikiema's shadow crept between us. Under our feet, there weren't just the abandoned human remains in the garbage. There was also a life and some dreams. There was, whether Mumbi Awele wanted it or not, a part of herself. I have difficulty believing that she and I will never speak about it.

We continue cleaning and polishing furniture in this somewhat heavy atmosphere. It's not possible, however, to bring it all back in before nightfall.

"We can leave the armchairs and ottomans outside until tomorrow morning," I say.

She agrees after a moment's reflection. "You're right. That'll allow them to breathe. It's also too late to assemble the bed piece by piece."

In the end, the most important thing for Mumbi is the decor inside. The house smells good with the scent of incense. Over the previous days, she did the laundry. We hung the *bogolan* curtains back on their rods and Mumbi came up with the idea to move everything around. Airier and more pleasant, the living room has a completely new look.

Mumbi has to leave. She says she has a meeting in the city to prepare for the exhibit. This surprises me.

"There has to be a meeting for that too?"

"There are a dozen of us exhibiting our work."

"Ah . . ."

I thought it was a solo show. I hold back from saying so. I believe she's not the best painter, but I don't want to offend her. After Mumbi leaves, I start watching *Panafrica*, a famous TV show about sustainable development. In my previous life, I never missed it. A young woman in glasses, black and frail, lost in a huge white boubou, is answering a reporter's questions. From what I understand, she's the minister of projects and capacity building. I catch some snatches of her sentences. She says in a halting shrill voice, ". . . To know how to put up these projects, it's a veritable science. I would even say it's an exact science. Some people like the convenience, the Africans are like that, but the donors know all our tricks. We can no longer deceive them. We've got to get to work and come up with good projects—you have to learn this like everything else in life. There are too many imposters who spoil the image of the continent. If we don't come up with good projects, no one will agree to help us." It is obvious that the minister in the white boubou is very pleased with herself. She knows all about the art of starving with an outstretched hand. She continues speaking for a long time about advocacy, capacity building, donor funds, and then donor funds again.

This gibberish means that the war is really over, I say to myself. There are words that do not lie. Castaneda's Lil Boys will no longer sever people's wrists. What will happen to us if people no longer have their two hands to receive alms from the big-hearted nations? Precisely, the woman says, "Let's not discourage the rich countries who want to help us—it would be really irresponsible." She adds, "Since the fall of the Berlin Wall, they must also think about their brothers in the former states destroyed by Communism, like Lithuania, Poland, and Belarus. And there is also Asia; a huge amount of money has gone to them since the tsunami. That tsunami was a real catastrophe for the African continent. We are not the only ones and the West has other things to do. Those people must live too. Their parents worked hard and now that they have the money to eat, it's not polite to disturb their meal with all our problems."

Listening to her, something surprising happens to me: I burst out laughing. Begging as an exact science? Is she sick or what? We should not let such stupid people speak. But my indignation almost amuses me. Maybe she's sincere but quite late. I've heard such things several times without finding them good or bad. Still, it's not like I'm going to start talking like those salon revolutionaries whose confessions describe in detail the Satellite cellars I had torn up.

I turn off all the lights around one in the morning while thinking about the details of my plan to leave the country. I cannot decide which would be the most secure border for me. I keep changing my mind and this means that maybe I am not ready.

In the middle of the night, I hear a noise inside the house. This could only be Mumbi. I half open my eyes to be sure. In my half sleep, I figure out that she is with a man and I hastily go back under my blanket. The guy, leaning on Mumbi, is staggering a little and stinks of alcohol. I can't rid my mind of the impression that she is a woman who leads a disreputable life, that bastard. In that moment, I really want Mumbi. A violent desire, furious but quickly suppressed. It is the first time I feel this way about her. You know, one of those dirty thoughts that always ends up entering your head from behind. It comes from a dark, distant, and improbable place and it lays siege upon your soul with its obscene grimaces and you have no way of knowing what it really wants.

I must confess: I also try to take advantage of this opportunity to discover things about Mumbi without her knowledge. Just having these thoughts makes me feel ashamed. I know that everyone won't agree with me, but according to me, Mumbi is a good woman. I want to remain loyal to her.

I think I go back to sleep after a few minutes. Around three or four o'clock in the morning, Mumbi wakes me up. This has never happened before. Just out of the shower, her body is wrapped in a cloth tied over her breasts. Her hair is wet, with large drops of water trickling down that she keeps wiping with the palm of her right hand.

I sit up on the edge of the bed. Fortunately, I have my pajamas on and I'm not too embarrassed by this situation.

"Colonel, I know you weren't sleeping," she says. Something in the tone of her voice indicates that this is an absolute obvious fact and that my answer means little.

"It's true, I heard you come in. But I went back to sleep."

"You saw me with someone, right?"

After hesitating briefly, I decide to be honest. "Yes I did." I want to add that I don't want to meddle in her life. The words don't come out of my mouth because I don't have enough time to let them form. It is horrifying for me to give her the impression that I am judging her.

"I want us to talk tonight," she says.

She stands up and holds out her hand. There is a moment of great confusion in my head. For a few seconds, I feel terrified. What does Mumbi want from me? She is half-naked and we are alone in this small house. I also don't know her very well. She shows all signs of having a split personality and I dread to discover, in spite of myself, her demonic side during the night. I don't want all these stories to continue mixing like circles in infinity that never touch. I say to myself, Why are things with us human beings never simple? I am afraid of her but I am also afraid of myself because I feel desire rising up within me, the kind of desire that can also be an urge for destruction.

I follow her into the studio. For fear of offending her, I have not dared to let go of her hand which burns within mine. On the wooden table in the middle of the room is a big calabash with a black-and-white motif. Mumbi lifts it and says, "Look."

I recognize Pierre Castaneda's head at once.

It has been sliced very cleanly at the base of the neck. Another skull has been placed across from it. Undoubtedly that of N'Zo Nikiema.

Mumbi speaks again: "The rest of the body is in the basement." She is silent for a second and then points at N'Zo Nikiema and Pierre Castaneda. "With these, I'll make an installation for Bastos II."

I remember that Kaveena had been kidnapped in this area a few years ago. It was not even the typical story of a little girl who strayed from her mother while playing in the park and wasn't found. At that time, Mumbi dreamed of becoming a dancer. She was coming home with Kaveena after a rehearsal at the Bastos II Youth Center. Near the intersection, a van had stopped at their height. A smiling, well-dressed man got out. He seemed to be looking for directions and Mumbi was about to help him when he quickly made her inhale the contents of a gas bottle. When she woke up after a few hours, it was night and Kaveena was no longer at her side. The few passersby later admitted that they had not noticed anything unusual that day at the Bastos II intersection.

That said, what does Mumbi mean by "installation"? I'm not familiar with artist jargon and don't know this word. I guess the meaning after watching Mumbi choose, in a way that appears arbitrary to me, the elements of her composition. Pebbles and shells. A small wastebasket. Spoons, etc. She then leaves me alone in the studio and goes to get dressed. Upon returning, she throws all these objects—including, it must be said, the inert skulls of N'Zo Nikiema and Pierre Castaneda—in a bag. She heads to the door, and a moment later I hear a car start in the silence of the night.

—∞—

It rained a lot last night. Almost all the roads to Maren are blocked. The inhabitants of the city are having difficulty making their way through puddles and fallen tree trunks. All morning, I've been seeing them hopping over yellowish puddles, umbrellas in hand. The sky is still overcast and the weather is mild. Without the potholed embankments and the windswept trash, it would be nice to walk randomly through the streets of the capital.

I park up by Mayo's fruit stall. Mayo is a young man with an oval face and a shady vibe. We know each other well. The stall was in the same place before the war, and upon my return to this area after Pierre Castaneda's death—almost two years ago—he came knock-

219

ing at my door. He also offered a helping hand to the workers hired by the new authorities to do up my home.

After serving two young girls from the local high school, Mayo approaches my door. "Hello, Father," he says. Depending on the day, he calls me "Father" or "Uncle" or "Boss." It's true, he could be my son.

"I have no more fruit at home, Mayo."

He offers me *solo* papayas. I love them. Small and somewhat ugly at first glance, they have a bright red flesh that melts delicately in the mouth. I also stock up on bananas, green mandarins, and *màdd*. I love that, too. A fruit that is tender and acidic at the same time. Its orange color has always fascinated me. The mere possibility of making iced *màdd* in my own home means that I am again entitled to the simple pleasures of life.

After paying, I'm about to start driving my little brown 205. But Mayo keeps his eyes fixed on me. I sense that he wants to tell me something and I encourage him. "Work is going well, Mayo?"

At the end of the day, it is nothing important. He recites a list of government offices. I hear a few awful words: "Land registry." "Primary approval." "Registration number." Mayo wants me to help him open a shop. He wants to sell something other than imported mangoes and apples and he has spotted a good location at the La Chaumière roundabout, etc.

"I'll see what I can do."

It should be fine. I love to help. These solicitations are unfortunately becoming more and more frequent and I'll definitely have to put a stop to them soon. My neighbors in this Lamsaar-Pilote neighborhood have a hard time admitting that I'm a lonely old fruit-and-crosswords amateur. For them, I remain the enigmatic and formidable Colonel Asante Kroma. This is largely the fault of the newspapers. After the fall of Castaneda's regime, they invented all kinds of fables on my account. To hear them and their truth, it would seem that the only one to overthrow Castaneda was I, your humble servant.

They found his famous striped hat next to Castaneda's skull.

It was Castaneda's fault. How dare he take on the powerful Colonel Asante Kroma! A fatal mistake . . .

The colonel with his clandestine networks, he's really too powerful. The white guy met his match. Huh!

To come on African soil and pretend to govern this country with a strong tradition of defiance and honor! What arrogance!

Only a coward like Mwanke could accept being his lackey. That's why he bolted like a rabbit the first chance he got.

Seems like the colonel is waiting for the great N'Zo Nikiema to return. Together, they will take the country in their own hands!

Phew! Not too soon, brother! So much for the corrupt ones!

It was really unjust to Nikiema! We've got to prepare a really big welcome!

It's amazing how quickly people forget. If Nikiema were to return, it would be enough for him to give a good speech to reclaim his throne at the palace. They also claim that I am trying to form some sort of secret government of a republican type. Heads will roll, there will be blood, etc.

And the colonel is really smart! He wants to play the part of a peaceful little retiree. We are not fooled, my brother! Hey! Hey!

It doesn't matter. When you are well informed and hear this nonsense, you can easily become cynical or dismissive. But I let them say it because it protects me. Mwanke's successor has sent me emissaries several times. Each time, it goes something like this: "Colonel, the white guy has ruined everything. Now he's dead and it's time to straighten out the country. We can't stay on the sidelines. The nation needs you."

"No, thank you."

They don't believe me, of course. As I talk to them, they are hoping to read between the lines and figure out my secret plans.

The only return that interests me is that of Mberi and our two children. These people will eventually realize this.

I read the newspapers every morning and I like to dwell on—and this is new—the culture pages. I look for Mumbi Awele's name. She has a normal career as a lesser-known artist.

Mumbi and I will never see each other again. And it wouldn't make any sense anyway.

—⁂—

I owe the reader the story of my last night with Mumbi in Jinkoré. You'll have to forgive me some inaccuracies since two years have passed. Besides, told from my perspective, the story is not quite the same. Far away from the small house in Jinkoré, my heart beats much more slowly. I'm not a fugitive exposed to a thousand dangers. The languor of my new life changes everything. It changes my mind. My look. Everything. As I write these lines, I don't have the smell of death all around me. No blood pours out of my words and their rustling is not the same. Yes, it makes a big difference.

I was certainly shocked to discover a part of Castaneda's body in Mumbi's studio. But I haven't thought about it much since. Should I take the risk of shocking some of you? Truth be told, the memory of this scene has not disturbed my sleep even once. It has not even turned into fleeting images for me, either. Funnily, Castaneda's thick face seemed more elongated than it had in his lifetime. He had turned blue or green, I don't know anymore. In a sense, Nikiema didn't exist anymore. The cracked teeth and the two dark holes for eyes were not enough to make a skull. I remember being especially struck by the geometric patterns—diamonds, circles, triangles, etc., all black-and-white—which decorated Mumbi Awele's calabash. She had placed a small garbage bin, multicolored pebbles, and seashells on a mat. I remember Mumbi unleashing the words with icy contempt: *With these, I'll make an installation for Bastos II.* This I cannot forget. In a way, N'Zo Nikiema and Pierre Castaneda did not count. They were each a simple detail in the composition, which was no doubt part of Mumbi Awele's vast design.

Mumbi stood in the back, her arms crossed. She looked at me while looking at her work.

When she left for town after stuffing everything into a bag, I took a little walk in Jinkoré. Maybe I needed to clear out all the emotions from this night at all costs. Or simply savor, without further ado, my newfound freedom? I made my way, without any fear, between ruined buildings, between concrete mixers, bags of cement, and ladders. A site watchman shone his flashlight at me and looked at me suspiciously. I said hello and he growled in response before leaning back against the wall. Bats rustled in the foliage of a mango tree and I got some dew on my face.

On the way back, I got a little lost. Luckily, I soon recognized the tall grass around the small house. Mumbi returned after an hour. We were going to go sit on the floor near the living room poufs when she said, "Let's go into the courtyard."

I thought that this was a better idea too. It must have been five in the morning. I looked up at the horizon. The sky was dark, but toward the south one could see the faint white lights dancing next to Blériot Avenue. It was as if the moon were playing with the clouds over there. In fact, this light was coming from the presidential palace and its grounds. This wealthy neighborhood is the only place in Maren where the public lights still function in the early hours of the morning.

Afraid of catching a cold, Mumbi had gone back to the room to get a gray turtleneck sweater. It took only two minutes of her absence for me to decide that I was not going to ask too many questions. Throughout my life, I've interrogated strangers, and often in a rude way, as one knows. And after coming in contact with Mumbi Awele, I realized I didn't even know how to listen anymore.

First she spoke about old N'Fumbang. "This morning, I'm a happy woman. I feel like my father will be reborn. I had stopped living on the day of Kaveena's death. After what I've just done, I feel worthy of him."

223

The old man had often said to her, "You must not forgive, Mumbi. We must avenge our little Kaveena." It was an obsession for him.

"When he felt his end approaching, he had doubts. He said to himself, no, these people are too powerful; Mumbi will not be able to face them alone. He also called them a serpent with two heads. He often tested me: 'Mumbi, is it not better to forget Kaveena? God will punish her killers.' He spoke this way, but the idea that the killers would not pay for their crime made him furious: 'Our girl has suffered so much. They narrated the story of the murder a thousand times in the newspapers, and each time it was harder for us.'"

Mumbi broke off momentarily, then added in a deep, absolutely unique and unforgettable voice, "My father was a man."

She then told me that she would often talk to him at Kisito Cemetery. "I'll be back there Thursday. I'll tell him how Kaveena's murderers ended up."

I think I understood then that Mumbi had done all this for Kaveena as much as she had for her own father.

I said to her, "And me, Mumbi? You know very well which side I'm on and what I've done in my life. You could have gotten rid of me but you did not. You don't even hate me."

Mumbi was expecting this—or at least she had thought about this at some point—and she replied in a voice that was both quiet and tense, "What do you want me to say? I'm not the mother of all the girls in this country. I wanted to avenge my own. I wanted to avenge Kaveena. Just her. If I had acted for a cause, I would have ended up not even knowing who to strike with all this gossip. I would have said, 'I will give the flesh and blood of my daughter so that tomorrow things are better in this country.' All these big words, you know. And over time, my pain would have subsided. But it would have been a lie. I didn't give Kaveena to anyone. One afternoon, we walked by the Bastos II intersection and strangers tore her away from me. They then took her to the Gindal Forest to be raped and cut into small pieces. So for me, Colonel, tomorrow or the day after tomorrow or even later in the life of this nation, I'll tell you what I think: it's not my problem. You understand that, Colonel?"

This was, without a doubt, the last time Mumbi would have to talk about Kaveena. She knew that and maybe it allowed the hate and the rage she had repressed over the years to come to the surface.

She lit a Dunhill, took a long drag, and threw the matchstick on the ground. Together we watched the small flame smolder on the wet sand in the courtyard. I took advantage of this pause to ask if she had, at least once, envisioned the worst.

"I don't understand," she said.

"It could have ended badly."

"Ah . . . of course! But you know, Colonel, he always told me the story of the little bird . . ."

"The hummingbird . . ."

"Mansare's beautiful old fable."

"Yes. The forest is on fire and the hummingbird fights against the fire all alone and then says to the other animals, 'At least I am doing what I can.'"

"That's right, Colonel. This fable was my nourishment. Each one must do what they can. I had to at least try for my daughter Kaveena. This Mansare, he was sublime. My father and he would have gotten along very well, I think."

We continued this way for several long minutes. She apologized to me for lying about the video. "I could never have watched it. I didn't trust you, that's all."

Mumbi burned through cigarette after cigarette. Her smoking these Dunhills began to bother me but I didn't say anything. And without really thinking, I said, "I don't want us to part on a misunderstanding, Mumbi. You hated N'Zo Nikiema. I didn't. Often, I even thought that you were unfair to him."

She shrugged, then said with a little smile that revealed some compassion for my naïveté, "I know. I saw you take the letter, notes, and everything you could in the house, tear them up, and throw them into the fire. Well, tell yourself this, Colonel: almost everything you've seen or read in Jinkoré is false. Even from the other world, this man continued to lie to us."

She looked up at me and I saw that she was expecting a response. I remained silent because I didn't know what to say.

A little before six o'clock, we heard screams. At first they seemed to be isolated and almost like an echo, but after a few minutes they seemed to rise over all the houses in Maren, creating a great clamor. You would have thought that some brave people were trying to track down a criminal. Mumbi and I knew that this was not the case. We secretly kept listening to these distant cries for quite a while. Their meaning couldn't escape us. In the Bastos II district, Mumbi's installation had been discovered. Rumors began to rise in a matter of minutes. Several groups of young men, probably from the neighboring construction sites, ran past the house. The rapid honking of cars began to drown out the other sounds of the city.

This excitement was predictable. Pierre Castaneda wasn't a nobody. In fact, there was a wave of panic when the circumstances of his death were discovered. I remember fearing real trouble at the time and maybe even a new civil war. No such thing happened. Castaneda's head, a little ravaged by the stray dogs, was repatriated to Haute-Savoie with a rather strange ceremony. The rest of his body was just written off. And that was all. I still cannot explain why the old strongman of this country was so quickly forgotten.

These politicians should be more modest.

Of course, instantly—and for several months—there was a devil of a racket. What's surprising about this? More than the murder itself, it was the staging, at once refined and barbaric, which scared and confused our citizens. People lamented, "Oh no! The secrecy, this cruel treasure hunt, it's the opposite of our traditional African criminals." The snobs sneered, "Hell, modernity! This thing, it's our real entrance ticket to the next century!" A woman from the university spoke about some sort of an aesthetic of nothingness. I think it

226

sounds good in a way. That is, if the Castaneda case had been widely discussed. The smallest detail deserves special attention. But I think these different stories, although often contradictory and fanciful, eventually combine into one, coherent and credible.

Thus, there are dozens of well-known versions of the discovery of Pierre Castaneda's skull. Listening to the authors, I have often wondered if they're reporting on the same facts. The bias and the bad faith of those within us is manifest. Others don't end up being caught up in their lies. At first I found it amusing. Today, with the serenity of the two years that provided me with hindsight, I see in these derivations a necessary evil. I know what I owe to these precious false testimonies. None of their excesses seem to me, if I may say so, too much. Thanks to them, I can tell you what exactly happened that morning in that precise place in our capital.

Well, here it is.

It is six o'clock in the morning. The city of Maren is still asleep. A young artisan baker—let's call him B. N.—is returning home after a night of work. On approaching the Bastos II roundabout, he sees some stray dogs circling an object. Initially it doesn't catch B. N.'s attention. He knows these abandoned animals well. Dirty, aggressive but fearful, they are always looking for a meager pittance around the garbage. The residents of Bastos II, who do not know what attracts these mangy beasts to the neighborhood, often complain about their chorus of barking at night. In fact, at some meetings, outraged citizens have banged their fists on the table, shouting, "Enough is enough, Mr. Mayor!"

But the mayor is incompetent and corrupt. The slanderers say that they are all alike, these government people who don't govern. Besides, he doesn't live in the neighborhood. So when the outraged citizens scream and bang their fists on the tables, he is laughing quietly. Sometimes he asks the policemen to exterminate the mangy dogs of Bastos II. In the middle of the night, the brave parents hear shots and it warms their heart. Love of animals is OK but we still need our rest. Except that the stray dogs always return to Bastos II, even more of them, hungry and repulsive as ever.

For the young baker who is used to passing by this intersection every morning, these animals are, so to speak, part of the landscape. Over the years, a sort of ritual has been established between them and him. When they hear the spitting of his old moped, they stand as one to greet B. N. While circling the roundabout, he senses their anxious and perplexed glances at him. He even thinks that they are his guardian angels. If he's in a teasing mood, he makes a little gesture of friendship or shouts out at them before disappearing into the nearby corner.

But this morning is not like the others. They seem too nervous and quarrelsome to him. Young B. N. has never heard such growling. He makes a half circle with his Piaggio. As for what he sees in that precise second, B. N. has not stopped recounting the detailed story since. Radios and foreign TV channels have handed him the microphone several times. In fact, he has always said the same thing: "At dawn, I saw stray dogs fight over a human skull covered in blood that they would roll over to the side and then corner once again with their drooling jaws." Often harassed by suspicious reporters, he has also claimed—in a tone far less assured—that he had glimpsed a second skull, a dried-up one, which seemed to have been forgotten on an old mat.

This is what remains today from the gossip we heard everywhere about this, if you will, foundational episode.

The inhabitants of Bastos II later declared that they were awakened by a long howl which seemed absolutely inhuman to them. Almost seized with dementia at that very moment, B. N. had gone around their neighborhood shouting that the end of the world was coming and calling all the gods to help him. He ran from one house to another: "Beware of them! Hey! Hey! These are not stray dogs but consumers of human flesh! I saw them! Hey! Hey! God is my witness about everything I've seen!"

Within a few minutes, thousands of people came out of their homes. Most of them were in pajamas but some had *pagnes* around their waists. They were all carrying clubs and flashlights. Some even waved their flashlights and the look in their eyes was a reminiscent of very ancient times. No one recognized their boss from Cogemin right away. And no one ever knew that N'Zo Nikiema and Pierre Castaneda had been reunited, in the dust and despite themselves, the dynamic duo of their glory years.

Subsequently, much was said about the calabash with black-and-white geometric patterns found on the scene. I don't feel like dwelling on it. I'll also let the reader speculate endlessly on the garbage bin and the little pebbles and shells mauled by the stray dogs of Bastos II and trampled on by the crowd.

After all, it was a work of art, an "installation," in the words of Mumbi herself. Everyone is free to interpret it the way they want.

—᙮᙮—

Sometime before noon, we tried to rest a little. Maybe Mumbi managed to sleep. I could not. At five o'clock, we were both up. There wasn't much in the kitchen and we made ourselves a salad and a sandwich with butter and cheese. It was a rather frugal farewell lunch. There wasn't too much effusiveness either when it was time for my departure.

I then helped Mumbi bring the furniture back in from the yard. The only thing left was to close the entrance to the basement. I knew she would do it methodically, without haste. She was determined to have no trace of Pierre Castaneda's and N'Zo Nikiema's passage on earth. For her, it was normal enough: Kaveena didn't have a tomb, her killers shouldn't have one either.

Toward dusk, I left the small house. I didn't know where to go and I didn't want to think about it. Either way, it didn't matter. With the madness in Maren, not a single inhabitant was thinking about closing their eyes on this historic night. Across the country, millions of people took to the streets chanting, "Freedom! Freedom!"

229

From Jinkoré, I walked straight ahead and let myself be carried by the movements of the crowd. I think I have never seen such a mess in my entire life. Young folks were slaughtering chickens and throwing them up in the air, urging their friends to grill them. A bespectacled man with gray hair, typical of a lifetime member of the party, passed by me shouting that the workers at Cogemin had launched an indefinite strike. After he disappeared, someone else confirmed the news. He even added that groups of armed patriots were headed toward Ndunga to confront all foreign intervention. Dancers on stilts were playing trumpets, women clapped their hands as they sang old tunes, and thousands of children were literally running around. A truck slowly cut through the crowd. Standing on a platform, its occupants waved small flags, and one of them, drenched in sweat, bawled into a megaphone, "Martyr Abel Murigande, do you hear us? Martyr Prieto da Souza, do you hear us?" The crowd roared in chorus: "Long live Abel Murigande! Long live Prieto da Souza!" This guy was a clever type, a real pro. I tried to guess who he was driving for. The simple reflex of a cop. When the populace screamed in joy this way, it was because people had paid a price. We usually never see them. They sit in their living rooms and they wait. When the party is over, they make a clean sweep and start all over.

I also saw hilarious onlookers force a dignitary from Mwanke's regime to dance topless. The man—I prefer not to say his name—complied, shaking with fear. It was clear that he would have done anything to save his life. Our eyes met and I was sure that he was shocked to recognize me. He was finally allowed to go. Pranksters pretended to kick his behind and he left the scene amid the crowds roaring with laughter, like a theater clown.

Alone in her house, what was Mumbi Awele thinking about all this popular joy? Maybe she felt a baffled shame, just like me. There was something unhealthy about this crowd's joy, though it was certainly legitimate. But I'm not the best person to judge.

I didn't feel it had anything to do with me anymore.

I could not forget the small, lonely house. Mumbi Awele's last words continued to haunt me. They had managed to sow doubts in my mind. *Well, tell yourself this, Colonel: almost everything you've seen or read in Jinkoré is false. Even from the other world, this man continued to lie to us.* Anyone in my place would have been disturbed. I wanted to go over this whole story again from the start. I still needed to know which. I mean: which beginning? And maybe even, which story?

Tunis, An Nasr
September 2005

Ayo A. Coly is Associate Professor of Comparative Literature and African Studies at Dartmouth College, and author of *The Pull of Postcolonial Nationhood: Gender and Migration in Francophone African Literatures* (2010).

Boubacar Boris Diop is author of six novels including *Murambi, The Book of Bones* (IUP, 2006), *The Knight and His Shadow,* and several others. He is currently writing and teaching in Senegal.

Sara C. Hanaburgh is an independent scholar of African literature and cinema and translator of Angèle Rawiri's *Fureurs et cris de femmes* (*The Fury and Cries of Women*).

Bhakti Shringarpure is Assistant Professor of English at the University of Connecticut. She is also cofounder and editor in chief of *Warscapes* magazine, which publishes art and literature about contemporary conflicts.